CHARMING YOUNG MAN

Charming Young Man

Eliot Schrefer

 KATHERINE TEGEN BOOKS
An Imprint of HarperCollins Publishers

Katherine Tegen Books is an imprint of HarperCollins Publishers.

Charming Young Man

www.epicreads.com

Library of Congress Control Number: 2023933515

ISBN 978-0-06-298239-1

Typography by David Curtis

23 24 25 26 27 LBC 5 4 3 2 1

First Edition

For Julie Hudson,
who once said that another future will always begin.

Prologue
1880

A BOY'S MOTHER STEPS INTO A CONCERT HALL, AND THE boy follows. The auditorium is so nearly empty that their footsteps echo. The boy looks small before wood-paneled walls under a ceiling of indigo paint dusted with silver stars. A few rays of sunlight survive the journey through thick leaded glass to light up his pale face, his soft, blond hair.

On the stage is a grand piano, currently under the command of a boy with jet-black hair and straight posture. His cowlick wiggles while his fingers sprint up and down the keys. Seeing the glossy wool of the performer's dress pants, the boy grips his own rough jacket, sewn from the scraps of his father's funeral suit.

"I can't play that fast," the blond boy whispers to his mother. Her son is right, so her only answer is to squeeze his shoulder.

The current auditioner finishes with a flourish, holding his hands in the air like it is only their dramatic stillness that keeps the final chord reverberating. Finally, with a humble smile (or really the kind of pride that looks like humility), he squints at the five professors in the front row, scribbling in their notebooks. "Thank you, Reynaldo," says one professor. "The list will be posted on Monday."

"Monday?" the blond boy—whose name is Léon Delafosse—whispers to his mother. "Can we afford an extra night at the hotel?"

"Shh, don't worry about that now," she whispers back. "We'll find a way, we always do."

One professor removes his hat and scratches a hand through his gnarled, silver hair. He pivots as best he can, wincing as his neck creaks. "Are you Reynaldo's family?" he calls out.

"No," says Madame Delafosse while her son shrinks into himself, his shoulders folding so far forward they could almost meet over his heart. "This is your next auditioner, Léon Delafosse."

"How old are you, boy?" the professor calls out.

"Six," Léon murmurs.

"But—" his mother prompts, pressing her hand against his back.

Léon unfolds his shoulders. "But I will be seven by the time the conservatory year starts."

The professor shares a skeptical look with his colleagues, then gestures to the stage. "Each one is younger than the last today. We'll be auditioning babies in a moment. Come on up, then. Don't waste our time."

Madame Delafosse lowers herself onto a seat midway back in the hall while Léon shuffles his way to the stage, climbing the wooden steps and alighting on the piano bench. He can't help himself; he runs a hand along the polished mahogany of the instrument. He's never played at a piano nearly as fine as this one.

One of the professors smiles kindly. "Normally students start at a smaller school and come to us a few years later. You're very brave to be here today. Just remember, no matter what happens, you can always return to audition for us again."

"Thank you," Léon says. His voice comes out so quiet, he suspects he's the only one who can hear it. "My mother is a piano teacher. She taught me. She thinks I'm ready."

His mother shifts in her seat. Madame Delafosse would prefer not to be anyone's focus.

"Your feet barely reach the pedals!" says another professor. "Are you sure that you're almost seven?"

"Yes," Léon whispers. "I'm sure."

"And you are familiar with the audition requirements?"

"Yes, madame."

"Begin when you're ready."

"Very good, madame. I'll start with the Bach you requested, and I have chosen the Schubert for the second piece, if you please."

"As I said, begin when you're ready."

Like his mother instructed him to, he plays the Bach with modern French pianism, wrists as high as possible, as if he is balancing a glass of water on each. It suits Bach, Léon thinks, for the music to feel like it might turn comic at any moment, like he's racing around trying to prevent something from spilling.

When he finishes, there is no applause. There are only the professors, scribbling in their books. One has closed hers, her pencil rolling on the floor. Léon doesn't know if that is a good sign or a bad sign. He suspects it is a bad one.

He cracks his knuckles. It's a habit his mother has been trying to break.

She doesn't notice, though, because one of the professors has worked his way back to kneel beside her. "Madame. Welcome to Paris. Do you . . . have the means to pay for the Conservatory? It is not cheap, and students do not become eligible for patronage until they are seventeen."

"My husband left us enough for now," Madame Delafosse says. "By the time that money runs out, I'm sure we'll have found another way to pay for Léon's training."

The professor glances at the stage, where Léon is busily wiping his sweaty palms on his pant legs. The boy almost begins the Schubert, but then remembers himself and waits for permission to start. He's far more worried about doing the wrong thing than hitting the wrong note. "I do hope you and he will find a way to pay for his training, madame. My name is Antoine François Marmontel. I will do my best to make sure Léon is the toast of the season once he is ready for a patron."

"He hasn't finished his audition yet," Madame Delafosse says.

"No, he hasn't," Professor Marmontel says. His eyes fill with delight. "I'll get back to my seat."

As Marmontel returns to his post, he reassumes his professorial scowl. "You may continue."

Relieved, Léon brings his fingers back to the piano keys. Auditioning has made him nervous, and playing the piano is the only cure he knows for nerves.

The Schubert Sonata in E-flat major does not call for

glasses of water balanced on his wrists. Instead, he returns to the country road he'd been on that very morning, cicadas loud in his ears. Allegro Moderato: He'd said goodbye to his sister and walked with his mother by the farmhouse where a red-haired boy lived. Félix, Léon's only friend, had gotten up as early as usual to walk the family horse, to limber her for the day of hard work ahead. Félix walked Clémentine in the dawn light through the weedy field to the road, waiting for Léon and his mother to arrive, then fell into step beside them. Andante molto: Félix said nothing—Félix and Léon usually said nothing together, that was something Léon loved about their friendship, that they could lie on their backs and twirl bits of grass and just be. Menuetto Allegretto: Félix and Clémentine walked with the Delafosses through fields of sunburnt barley to the train stop outside of town, a patch of dirt carved out of fields and forest. A goodbye. Allegro moderato: Léon and his mother boarded. Léon pressed his face to the window of the train car as it began to chug toward Paris, looking back at the gentle old mare, at his best friend, at a hummock of red hair over a splash of freckles, at Félix's wave, cheerful and maybe wistful. The last burst of notes in the Schubert was a return to that splash of freckles.

Professors could applaud sometimes. Léon didn't know about such things.

1.

1890

THE MAIL SLOT RANG OUT. HEAVY PAPER THUNKED TO the floor.

Léon's sister, Charlotte, was nearest, seated sideways on the armchair, feet kicked high while she darned stockings. She rolled off the chair to the floor, bounded to her feet, and retrieved the envelope. It was a familiar green blue. "It's here!" she said. "Léon, it's here! The announcement thing! From the conservatory!"

She'd already broken the wax seal before Léon fell through the dressing curtain, only half into his shirt. He rolled across the floor to save the time of getting back up, all to get to the letter sooner. He wrapped his arms around his sister's legs. "That's mine!"

She waved the letter in the air so the halves of the seal knocked. "Then read it!"

"I'm trying to," Léon said, lunging for it, in the process losing his shirt entirely.

"You're so slow getting dressed that you're actually going backward," Charlotte said. "Here. I'll read it to you while you go find your cuff links."

Léon crawled through the apartment on his hands and

knees. "No one back home used cuff links, and of course they didn't. They're ridiculous. There's no way to keep my shirt closed and also fasten them. I just don't have enough hands. Three, and I could do it."

"They're designed for men with valets to help them, stupid," Charlotte said as she tugged the sharply creased paper from the envelope. "It's a way to *prove* that you have someone helping you dress. You have to pretend to be one of those men with valets if you want to even make it inside the doors of this salon tonight. Therefore, cuff links for Léon."

"I don't want to go to any salons," Léon grumbled. "I want to play piano. Why can't I just do that?"

Charlotte held up a hand to silence him. She'd heard this tack often enough to be bored by it—and was becoming absorbed in the letter.

"What does it say?!"

Charlotte took on her version of a posh Parisian accent, instead of their native country vowels. "Paris Conservatory, it says that at the top. That's what comes first. 'Dear sirs and madams. The official patron sorting is complete. There was an extraordinarily strong set of competitors this year. The following is a list of conservatory supporters and the candidates they have chosen, in order of the financial amounts assigned. Only the first, Reynaldo Hahn, was able to secure enough patronage to cover all of his conservatory expenses for next year, but the other offerings are still very generous.'"

"Reynaldo! Oh, that's great news for him. He could really use it," Léon exclaimed as he popped around the curtain.

"Everyone loves him so much. He could be terrible at piano and still get enough patronage. Lucky for him, he's also a good pianist."

Dink, dink, dink, as each of his shirt studs fell through and hit the worn wooden floor. "Shit." He went back to all fours. "You don't have to read the rest of the names. I can't qualify for a patron through the official channels yet. You have to be seventeen, and I just missed it. They expect your parents to pay for your school fees until then. Or, you know, an outside benefactor or something."

"Oh," Charlotte said, her voice going quiet. They both knew there was no hope of more financial help from their mother. She'd used up the last of the money left from their father's bequest to pay for this last semester. With their only income Madame Delafosse's piano lessons, there was no way they could keep taking on this room in Paris. There was no money for a dowry for Charlotte. There might not be enough for butter and jam.

Léon's breathing became labored as he crawled around the room, collecting the fasteners. "I think I'll need you to help me with these," he said. "But before that, skip to the page where they say who's won each prize. There's only one for piano, which is outrageous since there are so many of us competing. There's also one for oboe, and there are only two oboists in the whole school! How is *that* fair?"

"Okay," Charlotte said, papers rustling as she searched. "You won for piano three years ago, and it was a big fuss because you were just thirteen. Can you even win again?"

"Marmontel was going to argue to the other instructors that they should consider me. Since I entered so young and had more years to pay for than anyone else before I turned sixteen. I'm a weird case."

"That much is certainly true."

Léon lobbed a cuff link at his sister, pinging her neatly in the middle of her forehead. She rubbed the spot absently while she flipped through the pages. "Okay, here's piano. Um."

"Charlotte!"

"It's not you. They've put Hahn."

Léon went still. "He already got full patronage, and now he gets the prize money too?"

"Léon, I'm sorry."

Prizes are a social game as much as a musical one, Reynaldo had said, and he'd been right. Léon ripped the dressing curtain to one side. His pants were still on, but his shirt was down to one sleeve, the rest fluttering in the breeze from the window. Charlotte was right; he was not only failing to get properly dressed, he was going backward. "If I can't even dress myself, if I can't talk anyone up because I'll just turn red as a beet and run away before I can say a word, how can I expect anyone to pay for my education? How can I then earn enough to keep you and Maman and me out of the poorhouse? Okay, outside mysterious benefactor it is. Someone who doesn't mind that I'm a clod who's only worth a franc when he's sitting on a piano bench. An outside patron is my only hope. Which means that, Charlotte, I need you to be my valet."

"Those society snots will hear you play tonight, and it will all be over. Someone will snap you up," Charlotte said, taking her brother's sleeves in her hands, a cuff link pinched in her lips. "You'll be fending them off. And that way I won't have to become a lady of the night under the Pont Neuf."

"*Someone* has to snap me up because there's no other option now," Léon said. "Now, help me with these darn cuff links."

Léon hurried along the streets of the Latin Quarter, dodging omnibuses and donkey carts, doing his best to avoid horseshit. His best was not enough because horseshit was everywhere. Including up the sides of his shoes, now. He looked out for clocks at the intersections he passed, keeping track of how late he was. Pharmacies tended to have them, and train stations. Despite all the recent posters from the French railway, begging people to set their timepieces to the nearest station clock, every business had its own time. Depending on where he looked, he was twenty minutes past when he said he'd arrive or thirty. Either way: late. Definitely late.

Did being late matter? Maybe it was a good thing! Léon had never played at a salon before. He knew from Reynaldo that the Saussine home was a grand, fenced-in manor; Reynaldo had whistled when Léon told him that he'd be playing there. The Saussine "at-homes" on Thursday afternoons were among the most sought-after invitations for Paris's artistic set. Monsieur Saussine was also a fan of Fauré's compositions and had been going to a recital at the Paris Conservatory when he walked by the rehearsal room where Léon was receiving his lesson from Marmontel on Fauré's first nocturne. The invite had arrived the very next morning.

Léon had that handwritten invitation in his jacket pocket. In case . . . they asked for it to enter? That didn't sound likely. He didn't know why he'd brought it. He knew how precisely nothing worked in high society. Nothing. Except for the high society pianos. He could work them. He'd just have to get to that piano bench as soon as possible.

It didn't help that his bow tie had come undone the moment he'd stepped out of their building. He'd been trying to fix it while he sped through the streets of Paris. Over, under, fold, tuck, unfold. The bow tie was worse than the cuff links, truly the ultimate test of whether he had a valet. For a kid unable to afford even a mirror and with just his equally ignorant and only slightly older sister for help (his mother had been off giving piano lessons), it was impossible.

Which was worse: make himself more late or arrive with an undone bow tie? He didn't know that answer either. The tears that hadn't come when he found out that Reynaldo Hahn won the piano prize came now. As he always did when feeling overwhelmed, Léon returned to the one thing that was sure to calm him: music. He started playing études in his head as he craned his neck downward, trying to see his own bow tie as he more and more frantically yanked at the fraying silk, his nice leather shoes squishing into ever-higher piles of horseshit. *Léon and the red-haired farm boy walked along burnt fields of barley. The clop of Clémentine's feet was the pace of the music.* The silk of the tie rustled to the rhythm of the notes and the imagined walk. This summer, as he did whenever he was back at home in Vernon, he'd walked those same fields with Félix, wordlessly taking the route they always took, visiting the lowing cattle, the Toussaint chicken coops, finally lying beside each other in the tall grass. The yellow stalks had shielded them from the outside world. They'd stared at each other, sometimes speaking and sometimes not, Léon studying the sweat that darkened the shirt that lay over the muscles of Félix's chest and wondering why he did.

His foot squished into the carcass of a pigeon and Léon cursed, returning his mind to the Paris street. The man at the secondhand shop had tried to show Léon how to tie his bow, but—oh no, the knot had fallen out again. Léon began anew, music and the vision of Félix's freckles buzzing through his mind as he became aware of the Saussine guests pausing at the house entrance, staring at him. He'd arrived, and his tie was still undone. Over, under, fold, tuck. Why was that so hard?!

The bits he could see of the tie blurred with tears even as an expensive black suit appeared in the background, buttoned down a narrow torso, a pink boutonniere pinned to one breast. Léon released the ends of his bow tie and looked up.

Enormous brown eyes, long lashes, a mustache over a full

smile. A boy who was the age others might be called men, maybe a couple of years older than Léon. "That doesn't seem to be going well," he remarked.

"No," Léon said. "It is not."

"Can I help you with it?"

Léon never knew the rules for how humans were supposed to interact. He never had. Did someone accept help tying a bow tie on the streets of Paris from a handsome stranger with eyes like a deer's?

As if sensing the doubts going through Léon's mind, the boy whispered, "It's better to be late than untidy. Here, let's duck around the corner." The young man passed around the Saussines' wrought-iron fence and stood in front of a picture framer's shop. Léon tailed after.

"They're infernal, cursed inventions," he said as Léon stopped in front of him. He paused, examining the worn fabric of Léon's bow tie. His fingers slipped between the layers of silk, where the seam had come undone. "May I?"

Léon nodded, watching as the young man took delicate fingers to fabric. To Léon's fabric. The nails on his silk were buffed and manicured. "It's a very foolish corner we've backed ourselves into, isn't it?" he said, eyes focused on Léon's throat.

Léon gulped, his Adam's apple hard against the collar.

"We're dressed by professionals every day, and so when a tie comes undone while we're out, we're at a loss. Our primitive ancestors would be so embarrassed." The young man examined his handiwork. "There. I wish there were a puddle, so I could show you your reflection. Or that I had a glass mirror, but only the Saussines themselves can afford to walk around carrying those. Here, this stud in the middle is only halfway in. May I?"

Without waiting for Léon's permission, the young man slipped his hand beneath the halves of Léon's shirt, the backs of his fingers cool against the smooth flesh of Léon's belly. "There."

"Thank you," Léon said. "Thank you very much. Now, I have to get inside."

"I'm attending the at-home, too. I'll walk with you," the young man said, sneaking glances at Léon as he matched his hurried steps toward the entrance. "Are you a relation of the Saussines? I don't think I've had the pleasure."

"I'm Léon. Léon Delafosse," he said.

"I haven't heard of you either, but I'm sure the fault is all mine. I'm very happy that it's being corrected now."

A man with a tall hat was at the gate, checking faces as guests passed. He waved the young man through, but he stopped Léon. After scanning a list of names, he looked up sadly, taking in the frayed silk of Léon's tie, his flimsy collar, dented and yellow. "I'm afraid you're not on here."

"I must be," Léon said, his face flushing.

"He's arriving with me," the young man said immediately, taking Léon's elbow.

The man at the gate peered at them suspiciously. But Léon's new acquaintance pushed past him and into the flood of arrivals. "Look how beautiful they all are," the young man said. "Like birds in a garden. Women get to wear all these *colors*. Look, yellow limes and grassy yellows and liquid-y dark chocolate. We men are stuck with black, black, black. Isn't that just too tiresome?"

"You do have that nice pink boutonniere," Léon managed to say. "That's something. Do you know Madame Saussine? I have to find her. She was expecting me to arrive an hour ago."

"Right to the top, a very good strategy," the young man said with a long-lashed wink. "I'd like to find her too. Let's go on a hunt, shall we?"

He returned his hand to the crook of Léon's elbow and steered him through the garden and into the house. "Look up," he said to Léon.

Léon did and was dazzled by a white globe with none of the warmth of gaslight. "What is that?"

"Electricity," the young man breathed in awe. "It will make it to my write-up, for sure. I'm covering the day's salon for *Le Mensuel*."

"How wonderful," Léon said, only because that was clearly what he was meant to say. Capturing a lightning bolt in a glass globe sounded like a reckless sort of magic. And he'd never heard of *Le Mensuel*.

"You're young to be here on your own," the young man said, serving himself tea from a samovar. "What are you, fourteen? I was with my parents last time, but now I'm here as a writer, so this is business."

"I'm sixteen. And it is for me too. Business," Léon said absently, eyes scanning the room.

"Are you seeing who's here?" the young man said. "I know, it's a veritable who's who. And this is just the people who are arriving in the first hour, who clearly can't be that important when you really think about it."

"No, I'm—ah, I see the piano." Léon made his way through the guests to the next room, where a beautiful wooden instrument stood before rows of chairs, like a furniture pastor presiding over a furniture mass. Léon found all pianos beautiful, even homely, cracked street-musician instruments warped by rain. The Saussines' piano was something else entirely, though: its varnished wood was swirled through with the colors of a cup of tea whose milk has been poured in but not yet stirred. Léon stood before the keys, running his fingers along them. Not pressing loud enough to make a note but just enjoying their glassy smoothness. This piano would be ecstasy to play.

The young man was back, this time with another young man beside him, taller and less handsome. "Lucien, this is the new friend I was telling you about. Lucien, this is Léon Delafosse. I tied his tie! I fastened his fastener!"

The words had some meaning in them that Léon didn't catch, something that made Lucien laugh. "Did you? Hello, Léon. Do you play? You're looking at that piano like you play."

"I do play," Léon said, looking out at the rows and rows

of chairs, at the grand portraits of grim-faced society giants that hung along the room's papered walls. "I'm here *to* play today, actually."

The first young man's wide eyes grew even wider. "You're the Fauré interpreter from the invitation! The student who's rumored to be France's next great pianist! Our Mozart!"

Léon blushed. "The invitation said that?"

Lucien laughed. "It said he *may* be France's next great pianist, Marcel. Grammar is what keeps the world in order. And don't cause this poor creature so much pressure."

A rustle of gown, and a woman made her way into the room. This had to be Madame Saussine; no one could have fit through the home's front door with that much fabric bustling at their hips. "Léon Delafosse, is that you?" she cried, with a clap that made no sound.

Léon hastened his way around the piano, his hands taking a prayer position, like he was in the dilapidated chapel back home in Vernon, waiting for a wafer and a taste of wine. "Madame Saussine, please accept my apologies for being late."

"It's no bother," she said gaily. "Everything ought to run late at a salon, if it's to be any good. I'm just glad you're here. I had someone posted at the carriage entrance to look out for you, but you must have arrived on foot. You didn't leave your carriage at a public garage, did you? I'm sorry not to be clearer. Where's your mother? I thought she'd come with you."

Léon took off his hat and worried it between his hands. "No, we, um, haven't rented a carriage or a horse for the season." He didn't want to explain about his mother: she was making a few francs by teaching back home in Vernon and wouldn't arrive until late that night; anyway, neither she nor Charlotte had anything suitable to wear to a place like this; Léon's secondhand suit had used up enough of their savings as it was.

No one quite knew what to say next, not even the boy named Marcel, who until now had had something to say about everything. Léon returned his hat to his head. *Society men must wear their hat if any window shows the street outside,* Reynaldo had explained. He had been kind enough to give Léon a rundown. There were so many rules.

Madame Saussine's voice lost some of its vigor as she finally took in Léon's youth, his clothes, his downcast eyes, his hands nervously tapping the piano. "Is this your first time playing at a salon, Léon?"

"No. Well, yes, but I know how it all works. At least I think I do."

"You'll find the Saussines will take very good care of you," she said gently. "Please start playing whenever you like. Small, tinkly music. You know the sort. Guests will wander in, and once enough of them are here, I will introduce you, and everyone will be seated. Then you will play the Fauré nocturne that my husband heard you playing the other day. You will not play the Fauré before that moment, please. I assume you have enough in your repertoire to fill the time until then?"

"Yes, of course," Léon said. He had enough in his repertoire to play until Wednesday. Before he'd realized it, he'd taken the itchy hat off again and pressed his fingers in hard enough to dent it.

How adorable, Marcel mouthed to his friend Lucien, who giggled.

Madame Saussine placed a hand on Léon's shoulder. "Thank you for sharing your talent with us."

"Thank you for having me," Léon said huskily. "This is so important to me. I wanted to speak to you about, after . . . about . . ." His voice dropped. ". . . patronage."

Madame Saussine laughed and looked away, and Léon sensed a warning in it: *Do not say aloud what is important to you.* If it wasn't too late, if he hadn't already ruined his chances, he would make sure to remember that. He blushed and retreated around the piano, as if it might physically protect him. His fingers located the ivory keys, and in them he found some strength.

Madame Saussine inclined her head to Léon, Marcel, and Lucien. "Gentlemen."

Lucien and the boy named Marcel gave slight bows, which Léon copied.

Marcel leaned heavily on the piano, like it was the counter in a café. "Léon, listen, I want to—"

"We'll leave you to get ready," Lucien interrupted, laying a hand on his friend's wrist. "Won't we, Marcel?"

Marcel fluttered his arms in the direction of the nearest chairs, looking bossily around the nearly empty room.

"These are reserved for Marcel Proust and Lucien Daudet, okay, everyone?"

Léon smiled, and the young men left, whispering and looking over their shoulders. Marcel must have been telling Lucien about how he'd fastened Léon's shirt stud, as he was pantomiming the process from start to finish, Lucien making delighted gasps all the while.

Then Léon was alone with the piano. The keys were a land he knew, their spacings regular no matter where he went. They would be the same distance apart here as on a discarded keyboard in an alley or in the thatched-roof cottage of his childhood. *A walk with Félix along a field of barley.* He knew the rules of society if the society was a piano. He knew those rules so well that they weren't rules at all.

He sat on the bench. His breathing became even. He played one note and then another. It was music.

At first the room was quiet, and Léon was playing only for himself. Then the air filled with conversation, the wooden floors vibrating as chair legs scuffed parquet. The conversations quietened.

Léon didn't look up. As he played, he almost missed the hubbub, because when people were chattering, it was easy to imagine that no one was listening, that it was just him and the music. The left hand was Félix, providing the rhythm and the calm; the right was Léon, dancing around it, showier and a bit silly but perhaps just as important. Both were needed to move the heart.

He was playing the pieces he and his teacher had decided on, in the order they'd planned, which meant it was now time for the Fauré. Léon looked up to see if he could get Madame Saussine's approval before he began, and when he did, he saw all the faces, all those lights of society, men and women, beautifully powdered and manicured, with their attention trained on him. It was enough to make him want to stop entirely, to flee to the room he shared with his mother and sister, to play the paper keyboard that he set out on his dresser, instead of this fine tea-with-milk instrument.

Fauré it would be. The nocturne.

He almost started playing but caught himself just in time when Madame Saussine cleared her throat. He pulled back his hands as if stung, watched her stand beside the piano and welcome her guests and announce the piece, her fingers tenting gracefully on the piano lid.

"May I play now?" Léon whispered after the applause lessened.

The applause turned to laughter. "Yes," Madama Saussine said. "You may play now."

The nocturne was only two minutes long. Whenever he played it, Léon imagined he was taking a long walk through a winter-dark wood with his left hand, glowing moths casting moonlight spells about the slow walker on the right hand. It was both flurrying and methodical, flighty and assured, fantastical and real. Léon channeled his summers home in Vernon, the times he spent in the hammock, dreaming up at the evening fireflies, keeping to himself while his mother washed the salad lettuce, whipping it overhead in a dishtowel to dry it, while Charlotte stomped along the creaking wood floors, searching for things to squabble about. The Fauré belonged in Vernon far more than it did in this sitting room in Paris.

He finished. No one clapped. Léon winced.

Then everyone applauded all at once. Léon kept his gaze on the brass piano pedals but could see the hands of Marcel Proust clapping frantically at the edge of his sight, his noise lost in the crowd's roar.

Madame Saussine was beside Léon, the frill of her dress absorbing him, his own legs disappearing into it. She held her hands up daintily and patted the applause down. "I think we all know we have witnessed something very special here tonight. I am a little faint to think about it, and that's not just my new whalebone corset."

The guests laughed, and Madame Saussine continued. "To think that after tonight, we have all played even a small part in this angel's rise. I know a great many of you will want to exchange a few words with the young Léon Delafosse. I hope you can stay for a while and talk to him." She turned beneficently to him, a fairy godmother.

He stared back.

"Léon?" she prompted.

"Yes. Of course. I . . . would be happy to meet everyone."

The crowds massed. He removed himself from the

protection of the piano, shook the hands of many men, held the lace-covered fingers of many women. The men kept their hats on, so Léon did too, even though its scratchy headband became the only thing he could think about. Always nearby were Marcel and Lucien, chatting with the crowd while they waited for their turn to admire Léon, Marcel taking occasional notes in a leatherbound book he'd return to his jacket pocket only to extract it again moments later.

Somehow everyone managed to be utterly interesting and to say nothing at the same time. How did they manage it? Léon stammered his way through the same few responses: no, he hadn't been nervous about the playing, just about his tie; yes, Marmontel was still teaching; the conservatory students were supportive to one another, mostly; his mother was a piano teacher so music had always been in the house, he really had her to thank; no, she wasn't there tonight. As he made his way through his answers, he hoped he wasn't letting them all down by not being fascinating or even interesting. He'd clearly excited them through his playing, but now they could all see he was a bore. Hopefully no one would say so to his face.

Reynaldo Hahn was never boring.

As Léon became tired by all the small talk, the reading of expression after expression, his answers grew shorter and shorter, and the crowd dwindled. Léon found himself unexpectedly alone beside the piano. Madame Saussine was nowhere to be found. Marcel and Lucien were gone. He really had to pee.

Even more alarming, the sun was low in the sky, backlighting the spires of Notre Dame in orange. His mother would be worried to find after her return from Vernon that Léon hadn't come home yet. Tomorrow morning the iceman would be coming for his payment. That money could only come from the honorarium Léon was earning today for appearing at the salon.

He had to find Madame Saussine, he had to get his ten francs, and then he had to get home. Maybe he might find someplace to pee, too.

The party's conversations had moved on from his performance, which meant Léon was able to make his way through the house without being stopped every few feet. It was large and complicated, with three floors and many sharp turns that always seemed to land Léon in rooms he'd recently left. Eventually, after using a toilet room that had silver wallpaper and running water (he really hoped he'd gotten the process right and not sent his pee straight to the kitchen!), he came across Marcel and Lucien sitting in the smoking room. When they glimpsed him through the yellowed panes, they tapped on the glass.

Léon slid open the door and took the only remaining spot, on the edge of an embroidered couch. The air was thick with smoke. Marcel offered him a thin cigar with a gold band, and Léon refused. He did wish he could keep that gold band, though. "Do you know where I can find Madame Saussine?" he whispered. "I need to get my francs."

Marcel shook his cigar case. "Please. I insist."

"No, thank you." Léon felt very tired. Every extra moment he spent in the Saussine home was another moment that he was letting everyone even further down with his awkwardness, dispelling even more of the magic of his performance. Putting further on the horizon his chances of securing patronage, of earning enough money for his mother to finally take a day off and for Charlotte to be marriable. His voice dropped lower. "I really just need my ten francs, and then I need to get home. My mother and sister will be worried about me. Can you help me find Madame Saussine?"

"Lucien, you'll be okay on your own?" Marcel asked his friend.

Lucien smirked in response, like some unpleasant truth had just been confirmed.

Outside the fumoir, Marcel let out a long set of coughs; he must have been holding them in. "I shouldn't be in there anyway. I can't even smoke! That's the irony. That's Marcel Proust in a nutshell, an asthmatic pretending to smoke. I don't know how anyone puts up with me at all." He pulled out a brown glass bottle, upended some liquid onto a handkerchief, and pressed it to his nose and mouth.

"Are you all right?" Léon asked.

"Camphor," Marcel explained briskly after taking a deep trial breath. "It's all very exciting. 'Very exciting,' how cliché, let me never say those words again. I'm too tiresome to live." He smoothed his mustache. His large, expressive eyes searched Léon's face. "This is all a bit much for you today, isn't it? I'll tell you what, I'm going to set you on this chair here. You can think of, I don't know, your favorite études? Then I'll find Madame Saussine, and I'll come back with your—what was it, ten francs, you said?—your ten francs and then you'll be able to go home and forget all about the whole loathsome lot of us. I'll loan you my groom and carriage. I'll be clinging on here until the Saussines kick me out, so the carriage will be back well before I leave. Don't even start to protest. I know you didn't arrive in a carriage, but it will look good for you to leave in one. Salon rules, I simply insist."

Léon gratefully lowered himself onto a narrow chair. It creaked and swayed. Marcel crouched before him and placed a hand on each of Léon's knees. It felt shockingly intimate, like when the back of Marcel's fingers had run along Léon's belly. The smell of camphor wafted over him, underlaid by secondhand cigar. "Thank you for helping me," Léon whispered.

"We're both weird outsider fairy creatures, you and me, aren't we?" Marcel said, his voice reducing to a dramatic whisper. Then he disappeared into the shadows of the hallway, as if by a spell.

Marcel soon returned, two five-franc coins clinking in a perfumed envelope. "Madame has had a bit of champagne, so don't be surprised if she delivers this money all over again tomorrow, forgetting this transaction even happened."

Léon accepted the envelope, placed it in his breast pocket. They would be able to pay the iceman tomorrow. He could go to the stationer and buy a new sheaf of letter paper to write Félix, blank sheet music to keep tinkering with his own compositions. "Thank you, Marcel. I'm glad I met you."

"You won't mind if I call on you, Léon?"

Léon shook his head. Marcel had been so kind; he would like to see him again. He could make sure Marcel didn't see his actual apartment. It would be nice to have a friend who wasn't a competitor. Someone who'd already treated him so caringly. Whose fingers had once touched the skin of his belly.

2.

THOUGH MARCEL'S DRIVER HAD RACED THE PROUST carriage through the streets, by the time Léon got home, his sister and mother were already asleep. He slipped in the apartment door, peeled off his shirt, rank with nerves, detached the dented collar and laid it over the mantel, and washed himself from the chipped enamel basin. There were soft snores from behind his mother's sleeping curtain, and an outstretched foot from behind his sister's. Otherwise the apartment was his own. Off came the insufferable cuff links, making quiet taps against the wood of the mantel.

Humming a tricky Beethoven passage, Léon waited for his eyes to adjust to the near dark before ripping off a corner of stale bread; he was using the reflected gaslight from the street so he wouldn't have to light a candle. He sat on his narrow bed behind its sleeping curtain, chewing and thinking. There had been delicious food at the salon, food the likes of which he'd never encountered, but he'd been too nervous to eat. He imagined that food now—rabbit chops, fresh tomato, jellied eggs—as he gnawed on the hunk of baguette, stale enough to cut his gums. As he lay back, still chewing, the weight of the bread heavy in his throat, he ran back over the evening, from start to finish, committing as many details as possible to memory. The joy of the performance, the embarrassment of all that talking. How did other musicians do it, find any words that could compare with a melody? All he'd ever wanted was to play piano. His goal had always been to have the Léon part of himself disappear into the music. That was the secret to good playing. *Losing* himself. But now these potential benefactors wanted to bring the Léon part of himself right back out. Why would they care about that? There was nothing worth knowing there.

It was only by leaving the events of the evening behind and thinking of music itself, a walk with a red-haired boy along a country road, the rustle of barley, that Léon was able to fall asleep.

When Léon woke in the morning, his mother was already melting the day's chocolate. Léon rubbed his face, got up, cut off another hunk of bread to dip into the drink, and pulled a chair up to the kitchen table.

"Yesterday?" his mother prompted as she knocked a cube of chocolate around a saucepan of milk, waiting for its edges to soften while the gas flame whispered below.

"I played Grieg, then Massenet, and finished with the Fauré. I tucked my own composition in the middle. No one realized, or at least no one asked me about it."

"So it went well?"

Léon shrugged. "The playing went very well. I'll never be a society gentleman, though, will I?" He didn't want to upset his mother, so he just left it at that. *Society is people in a room playing a game that no one has told me the rules to. I don't even understand why they want to play.*

"Your performing is the important thing," Léon's mother said resolutely. "It always has been. Ever since you were little."

"I hope so," Léon said. He didn't believe her. He suspected she didn't either.

"Did they remember to pay you?" Léon's mother asked.

"Oh, right!" Léon said. He bounded to his feet, fetched the pants he had worn the night before, patted through the pockets. Finally he found two coins and placed them on the table.

"Ten francs!" his mother said, picking them up and biting them, one and then the other.

"Madame Saussine wouldn't have given me counterfeit money," Léon said.

"I know, love, it's an old habit," his mother replied.

"Rent, grocery debt, iceman, milkman," Charlotte called from behind her sleeping curtain. "That's the order."

"Poor milkman," Léon said.

Charlotte staggered through the curtain, plucking her nightdress from her sweaty body. "It's his fault for being so good-natured. Iceman comes before him. Top floor apartment, tiny circular windows. We need ice. Also, I want to officially register the opinion that I think we should move back home, where it's cooler."

"And give up on my one chance to keep us all out of poverty? Yes, the Vernon poorhouse would be very damp and cool," Léon said. "And it's not like you have an ulterior motive here, not when moving back home would mean you could also see your dear André."

"There will be absolutely no seeing of André, so enough of that," their mother said. "Come, the hot chocolate is ready."

Charlotte lumbered to the table, standing beside Léon. She kissed the top of his head. "I'm glad that salon thing went well, Little Brother."

"That remains to be seen," Léon said, watching his mother tip their saucepan and pour hot chocolate into three teacups. Léon always took the cracked one with the duck on it. It was his favorite.

"Especially delicious this morning, Maman," Charlotte said after a long drink.

"I brought it back from Vernon for your sake. We'll keep trying different options for melting chocolate here. The Paris ones all taste a little spicy, I think."

"When this is done, I could write to André and have *him* send us some chocolate. Personally," Charlotte said, practically singing. She'd been caught walking alone through the woods with André, the baker's son. His father had made it clear that André would never be allowed to marry someone as poor as Charlotte Delafosse, which is why she'd been brought along with Léon to Paris for the conservatory term—a chastity emergency.

"You and André will have to pine away your teenage years in romantic solitude and complain about your parents, like everyone else does," Madame Delafosse said.

Why were they still talking about Charlotte when he'd just played his first salon? Léon crushed his head into his crossed arms, nearly knocking over his teacup. "I was a disaster, Charlotte. How can you be talking about anything else?"

"You're not very good at talking to people, it's true. And if you don't talk to them, they think you don't like them. Maybe we can just pretend you can't talk at all, make you some mute specialty act," Charlotte said. "Who knows, it might give you mystique."

"Charlotte, hush," Madame Delafosse scolded.

"I'll consider it," Léon said. "Seriously. Anything is better than being myself, that's for sure."

"Wait, listen," Charlotte said, clutching Léon's arm.

"Listen to what?" Madame Delafosse asked, cutting the remaining hunk of bread into threes.

"Shh, Maman!" Charlotte said.

Sighing, Madame Delafosse obliged. They all held still as they listened to steps approaching up the stairs. It was the concierge. When a family was as addicted to its mail deliveries as the Delafosses were, the concierge's gait was well memorized.

"André, Aaaandré my love, have you written a sweet poem for meeeee?" Léon sang as Charlotte crouched before the door. Having a mail slot was a rarity in Paris, and it was Léon and Charlotte's favorite thing about the apartment.

"You know, your singing voice only becomes even remotely bearable when you're teasing me, it's the weirdest thing," Charlotte said.

The slot rattled, and a card passed through. It wasn't the white cotton stock that André wrote his love letters on. Nor was it the pale green-blue of the Paris Conservatory. No, this paper was a rich and shining yellow, like a pearly yolk.

"Léon, I think it's for you," Charlotte said.

"Is it?" Léon asked, crouching next to his sister. "Don't worry, I'm sure your daily André love note will arrive in the afternoon post."

He accepted the envelope, the paper firm and smooth under his fingers. His full name was written across in black ink, in flowing and expressive penmanship.

He moved to a corner of the room for privacy as he worked his fingers under the wax, pressed with an ornate *P*. The seal was so fresh that it didn't break, parting wetly and dripping strands of wax on the paper.

Cher Léon,

Let this friendship grow. Would you consider visiting me at my family's Tuesday at-home? We Prousts are very annoying, every last one of us, there is no hiding that fact, but you and I can escape away somewhere and laugh about them together and in so doing perhaps annoy them, ourselves.

I pray that you accept my most sincere salutations,
Marcel Proust

"Who is Marcel Proust?" Charlotte asked.

"Someone I met last night. At the salon," Léon said.

"A possible patron?" their mother asked.

"I don't think so," Léon said, rereading the note. *Let this friendship grow.* "He's a working writer, so his family probably doesn't have that kind of money. Well, they have more than us, I'm sure, but that describes most people."

"If he's a writer, they're not a very good choice anyway. The Saussines would be a far more respectable association than an artistic family."

Neither Léon nor Charlotte knew what to say to that. Charlotte proceeded to whip the yellow card from Léon's hands and walk around the house, performing various dramatic renditions of Marcel's words.

Léon stared into his cooling chocolate. "Are you going to go?" his mother asked quietly, stroking the back of his hand.

Léon shook his head. "It's an invite out of pity. He doesn't *really* want me to come to his family's at-home. Especially if I'm not even invited to play."

"Hmm," his mother said as Charlotte continued her orations. "This invite might not be for the reasons you want, but I'm sure it isn't out of pity. To have made it here this morning, this card can only have been couriered over instead of mailed. No one sends a courier for anything out of pity."

Léon jumped to his feet and headed to the window, covering everything but his eye with the curtain in case anyone was looking up from the street. He saw no sign of Marcel or a waiting footman.

The mail slot pinged again.

It was a pale lavender envelope this time, soon followed

by a plain white cotton one. Léon's mother snatched them both up. "*Here's* the actual post," Charlotte said. "It's raining mail, and the clock's not even struck nine yet. This is so exciting!"

A slip of a note inside the lavender envelope, and something that clinked. Two more five-franc coins rolled into Madame Delafosse's palm. She held the note out in the other, adjusting to just the right distance that she could make out the text (years of squinting at students' sheet music had wrecked her vision). "'Dear Léon, Thank you for your luminous presence last night, and for your patience. This amount is hardly equal to the service of an angel, but we hope you will allow this pittance nonetheless. We pray that you accept our most sincere salutations, M. and Mme. Saussine.'"

Charlotte stopped in her tracks, plucked the new card from her mother's hand. "I'm confused. Didn't you get paid last night?"

Léon stacked all four five-franc coins on the table, rested his chin on the surface to peer at them on eye level. "Twenty francs," he breathed. "That's a lot of money."

"Wait, did she *forget* that she paid you last night?" Charlotte pressed. "Maman, does this make any sense to you?"

"Only some," Madame Delafosse admitted. She lifted two of the coins and placed them in her apron pocket. "These will go to our debts. We'll keep the other two on the table, for the next time someone comes collecting."

Léon blinked at her. "You don't think I should return the money? It's a mistake."

"No. Not with no other way to pay your fees or for this apartment. This money is nothing to any of them. I suspect she intended all along to pay you double but didn't want to embarrass you."

"Well, twenty francs means a lot to us," Léon said. It wasn't like he wanted to go out and buy a fancy suit or a five-course dinner or anything. But one of them could afford to get sick or break a shoe now. Léon returned his head to the tabletop. His bones felt leaden. To be worthy of how much his mother had sacrificed, and their entire bequest from his father. To be the wagon to which mother and sister both were hitched. It felt heavy. There was no better word for it.

Charlotte seemed to read his thoughts. She pushed the plain white envelope across the table.

So it wasn't from André, but from someone else. Without raising his head, Léon ripped it open and laid the page out flat, reading the few words inside at a queer angle.

Dear Léon,

How are you? I am fine here.

Since I don't go to school anymore, I spend more time at the farm. I go outside at dawn and come home in evening, because inside I just fight with Mother and avoid Father. I eat my lunch with the ducks by the pond. They have five little ones this year. There were six, but one was eaten by a fox I think.

I also don't go to mass anymore. I don't miss that. I do miss you and look forward to next summer when you will be here again. Do you remember the puzzle that we made years ago when we sneaked into the carpenter's shed? I have been putting the pieces together each morning as a way to say hello to you.

Your friend,
Félix

Léon smiled despite himself. Some of that weight in his bones lifted. He started writing his response in his head. *Félix, you won't imagine how wonderful everything is going here.* It wasn't quite true, not really true at all, actually, but Félix would never have the opportunity to live in Paris and attend a salon with rabbit chops, and it would be mean to complain to him. "You should be grateful, only grateful, Léon," he grumbled to himself.

Or he thought he'd said it to himself. Léon hadn't realized he'd spoken out loud until his sister pulled him to his feet and linked her arm through his. "I'd like a walk out, and you look like you could use a day at the piano to settle your soul."

"I'm booked through with Paris students and need your help with lessons today, Charlotte," Madame Delafosse said.

"Yes, and the first student is at eleven. I can read the appointment book as well as you. I'll be back long before then," Charlotte said gaily. She tipped her head toward her brother's, so their foreheads touched. "And you and I can pass by that shop selling those new bicycle things. I want to try to ride one, but rules say members of the weaker sex must have a chaperone present."

"Absolutely not," Madame Delafosse said. "You know those vibrating seats are a route directly to sin."

"Maman. Surely you don't believe that nonsense," Charlotte said.

"Perhaps not," Madame Delafosse admitted. "But I wouldn't want anyone to see you riding one. Bicycles are for suffragists and no-goods."

"I promise you I won't come back a suffragist. Will I, Léon? You wouldn't let me become a suffragist, not my sturdy brother."

Léon laughed. "Your 'sturdy brother,' that's a good one."

"I don't know, you'll have to watch me very carefully," Charlotte said. "A bicycle is a dangerous step. I'll be headlining the Moulin Rouge next."

"You will not ride a bicycle, Charlotte," Madame Delafosse said. "Promise me this."

"Maman," Charlotte said, letting the word land with no further explanation. "Come on, Léon, get dressed."

3.

OF COURSE THE FIRST THING THEY DID WAS STOP AT THE tinkerer's shop. The bicycle's wheels were so skinny, and yet it stayed upright when it was moving and fell only when it was still! Charlotte clattered one of the contraptions up and down the block, hollering all the way. Léon stood by and watched, confused and excited and embarrassed. Did suffragists holler? They probably did. The siblings returned the bike, promised to buy one eventually, and continued on their way to the conservatory.

Léon bid goodbye to Charlotte and went inside. His favorite rehearsal room was free, the one with the unusually bright piano that sent all the notes Léon produced crashing one into the next. Not good for a performance, but it was useful for rehearsing, since the odd acoustics made each piece sound new again.

He played right through lunch and only noticed he was hungry when he grew lightheaded on the piano bench, when the keys began to bend and puddle under his fingers. He stood, rolling his wrists.

Léon wandered through the medieval building, up and down curving stairwells that had once housed the warrior scholars of the Dark Ages, students defending civilization with books and swords. Léon liked running his hands over the stones of the walls, imagining those young men, their strong bodies and quills and fierce determination. Soon he found what he was looking for, food left over, this time from a woodwind sectional. He often scavenged after hours from the conservatory's surpluses, if he was lucky bringing home a bundle of slightly stale sandwiches for the whole family's dinner. This time it was rolls, ham, and cornichons. There was no more butter left beyond what remained on the knife, but the ham and bread would fill his stomach just fine.

Fortified, he headed back to the rehearsal room, wrote a list of all the good things happening to him to send to Félix, and played until the conservatory's closing bell sounded. Eviction from paradise. Léon shut the piano lid reluctantly and gave its surface a loving stroke. He'd finished by working on his own compositions. Even though he knew they were moody and unsubtle and involved far too much key bashing, he thought they might have some promise. Humming his latest melody, he slung his satchel across his torso and headed to the entrance.

Charlotte had said she would swing by to walk home with him, but she wasn't waiting outside. Who was there was Reynaldo Hahn, smoking and laughing with two friends. Dancers, by the looks of them—though they weren't in costumes or anything, while they talked, they flexed their calves to lift up on their tiptoes and adjusted their arms into various intriguing positions.

The two dancer boys broke off their conversation as Léon

approached, watching him admiringly. When he saw who had caught their attention, Reynaldo slung his arm across Léon's shoulders and forcibly stopped him from slipping past. "Léon Delafosse, have you met Henri and Benoît?"

Léon shook his head shyly. These boys were too beautiful for him to look at.

"This is the one that other boy was searching for?" asked Henri or Benoît, Léon hadn't been able to catch which one was which.

"The very one," Reynaldo said, his grin showing off his deep dimples.

"What do you mean?" Léon asked. "Someone's looking for me?"

"A young man with deep soulful eyes. One of those sad people who appear happy. We told him Léon Delafosse only ever came out after the closing bell—oh, there he is now! See if you can nab some of his camphor cigarettes from him for us, would you? I've never tried one."

"Hello, Marcel, look who we found for you!" said Henri or maybe Benoît, waving frantically.

Marcel had been walking along the edge of the pavement, concentrating on the rotting fruit rinds and occasional dead rat with upmost concentration, as if each one had the power to unlock a secret of the universe. He looked up and saw Léon, and his rain-cloud expression broke into midday sun. Marcel crossed over to them, taking the first few steps fast and then controlling himself so he was more casual on the final approach. He was indeed smoking one of his camphor cigarettes, the paper old and yellow and glowing at the lit end. Léon had heard of them but never been near one. It smelled like an exotic shrub was burning.

"Monsieur Proust," Reynaldo said flirtatiously, bowing low over bent knee. "We found your Léon for you."

Both Léon and Marcel blushed at that.

Reynaldo, Henri, and Benoît stared at them expectantly, as if they'd paid for front row seats and were now waiting for the promised drama to unfold.

Marcel began and restarted a few different words in response, clearly unsure how to answer. Léon was no better.

Reynaldo Hahn laughed. He placed a hand on Marcel's arm. "This is adorable." He placed his other hand on Léon's. "And you're adorable. That's all you two need. We'll leave you to it. Have fun."

"I wish *I* had sweet, droopy young men waiting for me after rehearsal," said Henri or Benoît as the three stepped back.

"Is that a camphor cigarette, by the way?" Reynaldo asked.

Marcel opened his cigarette case and offered it to the boys. They each pulled out one, placed it between their lips, and drew close enough to Marcel's mouth that their cigarettes lit. Boy mouths neared, and then boy mouths withdrew. Léon was mesmerized. Arms draped casually around one another's shoulders, Reynaldo and the dancers receded.

It was just Léon and Marcel now. "That was nice of you," Léon whispered.

"I can be nice," Marcel said. The outgoing boy at the

party had been replaced by someone else, someone quieter and dearer.

Léon shuffled his hands through his pockets.

"If you're looking for those ten francs, don't be silly," Marcel said with a wink. "Those were from Madame Saussine. I warned you she might forget and pay you twice."

"Are you sure?" Léon asked. "Because I'm starting to think you might have paid me yourself."

"Pish tosh," Marcel said. "Come on, we'll get dinner, and you can treat us from your extra ten francs. Might as well put them to use."

"I would, but my sister is picking me up."

"Oh," Marcel said, disappointment clear on his face. "She could come with us, if she wanted?"

"Come where?" said a voice behind Léon. Charlotte arrived as if on cue, out of breath and hair unkempt.

"Hello, you must be the sister Delafosse," Marcel said, after giving Léon a chance to speak and being met by silence.

She nodded. "Yes, I'm Charlotte. And you are?"

"Marcel Proust. I met Léon at the Saussine salon last night."

"And you sent that beautiful yellow card this morning!" Charlotte exclaimed. "I love your paper. Where did you get it?"

"Thank you. And don't remind me how quickly I sent that card, it's so embarrassing," Marcel said. "That was terribly eager of me. The paper is from Zurich, actually, I can give you the name of my stationer."

"Don't be silly, it was sweet. We're just country folk, and eager is a virtue for us. Wasn't it sweet, Léon?"

"Yes, it was sweet," he managed to say. Léon was a soup of feelings. The card *had* been sweet. And he *did* want to go somewhere with Marcel instead of going home. It was exciting . . . and the fact that he was excited made him feel weirdly ashamed. There was something both gentle and immoral about Marcel Proust. There was nothing *strong* about him, and the beauty of that felt like dark magic. Léon was sure his mother would loathe him, for starters. But his mother loathed anyone unconventional, which meant that she would loathe anyone who Charlotte and Léon liked, so he might just have to get used to it.

"And now I've shown up outside the conservatory, even more eager," Marcel said. "I really did have business in the neighborhood, I swear it. I was at *Le Mensuel*, turning in my write-up of the Saussine soirée. You have a very prominent mention, Léon, right in the first paragraph. I thought I would stop by the conservatory on the way home to see if you were here, that's all."

Charlotte looked between them, clearly waiting for Léon to say something. Anything.

"Well, here I am!" Léon chirped. He cringed and bit his lip.

Marcel's expression got even softer and dearer, like he'd come across an orphaned puppy.

"I have a special invitation tonight," Marcel said. "To the house of the Count Robert de Montesquiou. A small gathering, which makes this invitation all the more precious. I'd hoped you might come with me."

Not another occasion for Léon to trip over his words and embarrass himself. No thank you. "We have to get home, our mother will be waiting for us," Léon said.

"Are you kidding? She'll be fine! I'll tell her," Charlotte said. "Tell us more about this party. Sounds like a gas."

Marcel licked his fingertip and ran it along his mustache. "I thought of you, Léon, the moment I heard about it. Robert's parties are very selective, and I know this is the time of year when the conservatory students are trying to find their patrons, and some of the guests will have seen you once already at the Saussines' home, and now this can be your second round, a real introduction, and well, they could actually get to know you, and you might find a patron. Someone to care for you. So there we have it. Marcel has revealed the truth. What he's hoping for you. Even though we've only just met."

Charlotte's eyes widened. "How kind! That sounds wonderful!"

It did sound wonderful. And kind. And terrifying. "I'm sure I'm not wearing the right clothes," Léon said.

"You look splendid," Marcel said. "Your rustic dress adds to your appeal. It's simply perfect."

"My insufferable brother manages to look beautiful even though he has the worst taste in clothing and pays no attention to his appearance," Charlotte said. "Just look at that skin. He does nothing for it. Whereas I could buy every liniment available and still look like I'd spent the night sleeping on a tennis racket."

Léon flushed again, cast his gaze down at the ground. "I really should practice. Maybe another time."

"You have to go!" Charlotte exclaimed. "Marcel, Léon would love to go. I accept on his behalf."

Marcel laughed. "I like you already, Charlotte Delafosse."

"Yes, I do have my own charms, despite my woeful complexion," she said. "You should see me ride a bicycle."

"Wonderful," Marcel said, visibly working through the rapid shifts in Charlotte's conversation. "It's settled, then."

"I'll let Maman know not to expect you," Charlotte said, giving Léon a hug. "I'll get her on a winning spree in cards so she doesn't even think to worry." She sighed. "I'm so jealous. I'll want to hear everything."

"Robert's home is on the other side of the Seine, near my house," Marcel said. "I have plenty of extra rooms, if you think that might be . . . and we're the same size, so I can even offer Léon a change of clothes in the morning."

"Which means he will finally wear something fashionable to boot!" Charlotte said, clapping. "At least until you make him return the clothes. This is shaping up perfectly. Little Brother, this is the night your whole life changes. I can feel it. There's something like a fairy tale in the air. I can hear the narration in my head. You simply must go."

Léon looked between his sister and Marcel, fear bittering his throat. It mixed with excitement—a deep excitement that was more complicated and primal than he could think of a reason for. Was it sexual? He shook the immoral thought from his mind before God could notice it.

The night your whole life changes. For better or for worse, that felt likely to be true.

This was not the only home of the Count Robert de Montesquiou-Fézensac; he just made do with it when he was in the city. That was how Marcel put it, but it seemed to Léon that there wasn't much "making do" about it. They stood on the curb across the street, gawking at four stories of beautiful stonework, oil lamps lighting up ruddy merriment, patterned glass separating inside joy from outside gloom.

The arriving carriages were clogging the entrance, so to save time Marcel had had his driver drop them off on the corner. They approached on foot, just like they had at the Saussines. This time, it felt like they were equals. It also felt like they were interlopers. Thrilling.

Rain dripped from the brims of their black hats as they watched the entrance, waiting for the right time to insert themselves. A painted carriage door opened, and the most beautiful woman Léon had ever seen emerged. Her waist must have been cinched hard to be so narrow, but she floated painlessly, in a cloud of silk. She looked at Léon and Marcel briefly, her face full of light. But the light was not meant for them; her eyes moved on and Léon was back in darkness.

"Who was that?" he whispered.

"The Comtesse Greffulhe," Marcel replied. "The most prized invite to any party. This will be an occasion for the ages!" His face turned suddenly panicked as he patted his jacket pockets and tilted his head—which made the rain that had collected on his hat run right down the back of his coat. Léon lunged, placing his hands under the brim so that the water collected in his hands. For a moment there was only the oily lamplight, the cold water from the sky, the warmth of Marcel's nape beneath Léon's clammy fingers.

His hands were on Marcel's neck. Skin, muscle, blood.

Marcel relaxed as he pulled a small leather book from his pocket, and a length of writing charcoal. "I thought I forgot this. I'll need my notes for my next write-up, especially with the countess here!" Then he seemed to notice his soaked back, saw Léon's hands hovering in the air, ran his fingers over his own neck, the wisps of soft, dark hair, and burst out laughing. His laughter was so earnest and so full that Léon started laughing too.

"Shall we go in?" Marcel finally asked.

"Would they even let us in looking like this?" Léon asked, lifting his soaked arms. The fabric of his coat wasn't waxed. He was fully drenched.

"If it were just me, then no. But you are a golden passport. Look at you!"

Léon flushed and allowed himself to be led to the carriage entrance. They passed alongside the countess's rain-beaded carriage, then lined themselves up behind her, like a fairy queen's groomsman. Near someone so dazzling, they entered unseen.

The front hall was lacquered in a brilliant red that set

the gaslight dancing. After scraping their soles on the metal bar beside the door, then buffing them on the wheel of hard bristle beside (it wouldn't do to track street filth through the count's home), Marcel and Léon stepped in.

With a rustle of silk, the countess vanished upstairs. Marcel placed a finger against his lips, then moved his hand to the banister.

"Wait, Marcel," Léon said. "Have you actually been invited to this party?"

"How bourgeois. Does anyone need to be invited anywhere when the world is so large?" Marcel asked back.

Was that question an answer? Léon decided it was not. He squished his toes in his soaked leather shoes.

"I don't think I should go up there," Léon said.

Marcel placed a hand on either of Léon's shoulders. "Of course you should. We're both getting something out of this. I'm getting my piece for *Le Mensuel*, and you just might find a way to keep playing piano. We have a secret mission. What could be more exciting than being two handsome boys on a secret mission on a Sunday evening?"

"But we're not supposed to be here."

Marcel laughed. "Believe me, as long as we laugh at everything we hear like it's the wittiest thing we've ever encountered, then no one will mind." As he leaned closer, the scent of camphor wafted from him in almost visible waves. "Besides, you don't know anyone here. So we might get kicked out—what will you have lost?" He gave a mournful sigh. "Me, however. My family almost has a name, so I have some cost to bear. Maybe I'll just have to come spend my days at the conservatory if this is the night high society closes its doors to Marcel Proust once and for all."

"That won't happen. You know what you're doing."

"See, you've said it yourself. I know what I'm doing! That's proof that you should follow me."

Marcel started up the staircase, the old wood creaking even though his steps were softened by plush black carpet. From above came the sound of wine bottles popping, of liquid pouring into glasses, of hushed conversation and bright notes of laughter. "I'm going up," Marcel said over his shoulder. "If you want, you can leave. But I'm not missing this."

With that, he disappeared upstairs. Léon was suddenly alone, and the easiest way to fix that feeling was to follow. So that's what he did.

Marcel was waiting for him just as Léon turned the corner. He snaked an arm through the crook of Léon's elbow. "Oh good, you've made the right choice. Our mission begins. This is like out of a Dumas novel!"

They'd passed through the red room and the black room; this room above was the color of cream. Cream floors, cream ceiling, cream couch, and cream rug. Even the hunting scene on the walls had been painted in hues that never strayed beyond white or yellow or tan.

A footman had just set down a tray of champagne and left the room. Marcel plucked one flute and then another, handing the second over. Léon sipped his first champagne ever. A tiny starburst.

The Comtesse de Greffulhe was only one room ahead; some of her gray ruffle still trailed behind in the cream room. Marcel headed toward it.

It was all Léon could do not to gasp out loud, like the peasant he was. The colors shifted to purples in this next room, a space big enough to hold a ball—or a pianist's concert. There was no furniture on the floor, but purple chairs had been bolted to the wall all the way up to the ceiling. No one could sit in them, unless they could fly first, but sitting in them was clearly not the point.

Guests clotted the corners of the room: men in dark coats, women in jewel tones, none of them as striking as the silk countess.

Even she couldn't compare to the room's star inhabitant.

A tortoise was lumbering through. It was larger than any Léon had ever seen, the size of a prize pig back in the Vernon market. Its long neck was cracked with age. Each of its steps was a great and shuddering effort.

The creature had been encrusted with gems. A half dozen rubies studded its back, glued onto the shell. They caught the lamplight, facets purpling in the reflection.

"So beautiful," Marcel said.

"So sad," said Léon.

"Both beautiful and sad, perhaps," said the countess, who was standing near them. She angled her head prettily when she spoke.

For a moment, the two boys were dumbstruck to be

addressed by a goddess. Then, "Yes, very much so," said Marcel, nodding madly.

"What is its name?" Léon ventured.

The countess laughed. "Its name? I'm not sure it has one. Maybe you will name it, Monsieur . . ."

"Delafosse. Léon . . . Delafosse," he stammered.

"Now, Léon, is 'Delafosse' your name or the name of the tortoise?"

"It's my name," Léon breathed. "My family's name."

The countess held her hands to her chest. "Robert will love meeting this little creature."

It was funny, to be called a little creature by someone so beautiful. Léon felt strangely powerful. He would gladly spend his life as her magical familiar, grooming her hair with his fairy hands before she went to bed each night. Beauty was strange that way. *His* beauty might be strange that way. He hadn't known he had it. He hadn't known that boys could have it—and he was still unsure whether they should.

The countess tilted her head, causing ribbons in her hair to fall about her shoulders in a glittering spray. "I know how my cousin operates, you two. Let him greet his invited guests, let him start the party, and then return to this room once he's had his drinks." She tossed out a jewel-like laugh. "You have not been invited here, that is quite obvious. Marcel, you're using this beautiful thing as your ticket back on the Montesquiou invite list. I'm onto you, but your secret is safe with me. Now, go hide away. Shoo!"

Marcel kept his wide stare constant for a moment, clearly debating whether to continue his bluff. Then he stirred into action, placing his and Léon's flutes on the table and plucking up two full ones. He handed one to Léon, linked his arm back through his, then steered them to the far side of the room.

They were in a narrow dark closet—no, it wasn't a closet, there were circular stairs at the far end. Servant stairs? Marcel clanged his way up, missing a tread and stumbling but somehow keeping most of his champagne in the flute.

Up and up they went. Rooms passed on either side: a quiet study, dim bedrooms, one with a maid pausing from beating pillows to watch them pass. At the very top of the circular stair, Marcel gave his drink to Léon to hold while he worked a heavy bolt. Neither of them had thought to grab an oil lamp on their way up, so they fumbled in the dark, metal scraping on metal, until Marcel heaved and the door pitched open, revealing stars.

Carved out of the tin roof of the Montesquiou manor was a shallow balcony, nestled between dormer windows. Around them were the hushed streets of the wealthy neighborhood, the bustle of Montmartre beyond. To the side, Léon could see the new Eiffel Tower cutting a triangle out of the moonlit clouds.

"Ugh, don't even look in that direction," Marcel said. "It's such a monstrosity."

"Yes, it's an embarrassment," Léon said, because that is what everyone was supposed to say about the tower. He considered what *he* thought, for the first time. "I like it."

Marcel looked at him for a long moment and then burst out laughing.

"Hmm," Léon said as he picked up his champagne again. He took another sip. It was like mineral water only more rotten, more sweet, more complicated. "I like this too," he said, clinking his flute against Marcel's. The night air, the stars and moonlit clouds, their secret location at an uninvited party—it was all coming together to make him courageous.

Marcel lay back on the tin roof, slick with the evening's rain. He rested the base of his flute on his narrow chest, pinched the stem between thumb and forefinger. Never taking his eyes from the clouds seeping past the moon above, his other hand waved in the open space beside him. It was an invitation. A peculiar invitation—a Marcel sort of invitation.

Léon lay beside him. The metal was cool and wet against his back. There, beside him once again, was this warm human being. No, not just that. A warm *boy*. Unlike any boy Léon had met. He didn't swagger. Instead he . . . looked. He saw. He worried.

"Léon," Marcel whispered. He leaned onto his side, propping his head on a delicate hand that disappeared into his thick, brown waves of hair. "I know this is much faster than friendships usually progress, and I'm glad that you're willing to put up with my queer nature. I just don't believe in being small, in talking small. Do you? I believe that if you find someone who is a spirit brother, you know it right away. And I don't find them very often. I have found one in you."

Léon didn't know what to say to that. Marcel's intense

gaze, the words the likes of which no person had ever said to him. It was making him feel tangled and swelling emotions. They were familiar, actually, but he'd only felt them before when playing music.

"I'm sorry if I've made you uncomfortable. You don't have to say anything back."

Léon was at a loss for words—again. He wished that they could not talk for a while. That they could just lie on this tin before the lights of Paris, like he might have done in a field with Félix. He placed his flute of champagne to one side and took Marcel's hand. Its fine bones gave easily under Léon's fingers, unlike Félix's rough laboring hand.

Marcel drew in his breath, let it out with a shudder. He leaned forward. His lips, full and red beneath his thin mustache, parted under the moonlight. Léon smelled champagne above the scent of rain vapor rising from the surrounding brick.

Marcel held steady near Léon's lips. "I'm sorry if this is just a little too decadence-of-the-big-city. I know that maybe, in Vernon, good Catholic boys didn't—"

Léon pressed his lips against Marcel's. The wet tin at his back, the sounds of the city beneath, even the beauty of the moonlit clouds, disappeared. Instead there was this feeling of emotion above language. This feeling like music.

4.

THEY FLOATED DOWN THE STAIRS, MARCEL LEADING
Léon into the noise of the party below. Léon ran a fingertip
over his mouth as they descended. Marcel's lips had been
on his moments before. This sensitive boy's lips. There was
a feeling, a good feeling, a goodness. Not so evil and unnatural, no matter what Father Moulin back in Vernon would
have claimed.

He reached out to touch Marcel's back, to feel the blades of
his shoulders beneath his jacket. He stumbled. Champagne.
"Marcel, let's leave this house. Let's go somewhere else."

But Marcel had already opened the door. Light streamed
into the hallway as Marcel and then Léon returned to the
party.

Somehow the countess had found her way up onto one
of the chairs bolted to the wall, her ankles flailing prettily
at the height of everyone's shoulders. Her fists were full of
flowers, upended from one of the room's careful arrange-
ments, and she laughed gaily as she strewed them out among
the party guests.

One young man caught an especially large blossom, then
went around stealing flowers from everyone else. He took
an exaggerated sniff of their perfume and then performed

an elaborate bow. When he turned, Léon realized he wasn't seeing a young man at all but a middle-aged woman in silk trousers. Judging from the crowd's applause, this woman in men's clothing was someone everyone but Léon knew.

Marcel took advantage of the distraction to loop his fingers around Léon's wrist and tug him to a corner of the room, where they were less noticeable. "The Bernhardt," Marcel said reverentially once they were hidden behind a wall of men in evening suits.

When Léon shrugged, Marcel's eyes widened in shock. "Sarah Bernhardt? She runs the Théâtre de la Renaissance. Her Cleopatra is all anyone is talking about this season. They say she'll play Hamlet next year. Can you imagine? Can you just?"

Sarah approached the countess seated on the wall, kneeled before her, placed a flower between her own teeth, and opened her arms. The countess laughed ever more, kicking her delicate feet in the air. Then the woman in men's clothing reached forward and—in a move whose intimacy made Léon suck in his breath—reached her arms around the countess's hips and lifted her off the chair.

Light as it was, the countess's body still caught Sarah off balance. She gasped and then the tulle of the countess's dress fully engulfed her. Sarah started shouting something, the words lost in the fabric. The guests in the room hollered as Sarah turned in a circle, the countess laughing and kicking her legs.

Léon looked about in wonder. "Everyone here is drunk!"

"Yes!" Marcel said. "Completely and fully." He handed Léon a fresh flute. "We should catch up."

Léon didn't think they had much catching up to do. He looked at the sparkling wine in his hand and then resolved not to drink any more of it. His head already had a lightness to it, and he didn't want to lose track of himself entirely. Marcel had no such qualms, though, taking a gulp before joining the crowd's cheering.

Léon cast his gaze about the room, keeping his head low and his eyes half-lidded. Could he see and not be seen? That sounded best.

The men's shoes were crafted from leather so thin it revealed the shapes of the toes beneath, and were anointed with delicate buckles of gold and silver. The women wore the sorts of stockings that Léon's mother would stop to admire in shop windows, gasping at the prices and muttering that surely no person could actually afford them. Everyone here, woman and man alike, fell into such splendid poses. All the same, it seemed like it must be exhausting to spend an entire evening finding new splendid poses. How could anyone relax?

It was beautiful, that was for sure. The gaslight, the brilliant reflections from jewelry and mirrors, the blur of colors and faces, all put Léon into a happy calm. His gaze wandered, memorizing details to tell Charlotte later. Finally he came to Marcel, and he let his attention rest there for a long while. The neatly trimmed sides of his hair, tapering to an elegant neck. Delicate, short-lobed ears that Léon realized he wanted to nibble all the way around, like the rind of an orange.

Marcel was so absorbed in the party that Léon could study him without worrying about being caught. Those were the lips he'd kissed just now. They were right *here*, in the company of others, moving slightly as Marcel silently narrated what he was seeing. Here was the brow, so smooth and unconcerned, though his eyes were darting about so much that he was probably worrying about ten things at once. Here was the neck, slender and vulnerable within a still-damp collar. Léon had cupped his hands around that neck just an hour ago, when he'd caught the rain from Marcel's hat.

Léon had desired other boys before, classmates in the conservatory or Félix back home. He'd imagined what it might be like to press their lips or bodies together, but he'd been sure they would push him away, that the world would stop and tell him how wrong it was. And yet, just now, on the roof, two boys had kissed. And here they were back in the party, and no one was angry. The world was continuing.

No one was paying a lick of attention to them, here in their corner of the ballroom. Léon plucked his courage and slipped his hand beneath Marcel's waistcoat, rested it over the soft, heavy cotton shirt at the small of his back, warm with the heat from his body. Marcel leaned against the papered wall, pinning Léon's hand tight against him. The muscles of Marcel's back shifted as he moved his weight from one leg to the other.

It felt shocking and daring and all-at-once, like the moment of diving into the quarry pond during summers back home. Léon took a long drink of champagne. Apparently he'd be drinking more after all.

Marcel continued scanning the crowd, and Léon could sense him already working on his write-up. His delicate lips twitched. Looking at those lips, Léon became aware of eyes on the far side, staring at them, taking in everything that Léon had thought was happening in private. His heart surged with fear.

This young man was tall, taller than Marcel and much taller than Léon, long stretches of purple satin running up the sides of his black pants to match a taut purple jacket. Gold rings glittered along his fingers; his brows were sharp arches over a long line of nose. He carried a cane with a turquoise handle, though his upright dancer posture said he had no need of it; he was tapping the cane's tip rhythmically against his elegant shoe.

The meaning of his smile was unmistakable. It had a journey to it, went to a frightening place and then returned home to safety: *I see you. Worry—no, don't worry. I see you.*

With a great cry, the countess and Sarah Bernhardt collapsed, setting the room roaring with laughter. Marcel sprang forward to get a better view, leaving Léon with his hand in midair. Suddenly alone, he cupped his hand before placing it in his pocket, as if he might hold on to Marcel's warmth.

The tall boy was still staring at him, only his smile was bigger now. Mocking him? Léon squared his shoulders against the wall, cast his focus to the floor. When he dared look again, the boy was still peering through him, green eyes twinkling, a winter sea at dawn.

"Robert!" called the countess. "Where is my cousin? I've fallen, oh my brave knight, help me!"

The tall boy kept his eyes locked on Léon for a moment more, then his expressive eyebrows drooped. He sighed, winking at Léon. "I must go be a savior. But you should know that I am a reluctant savior who would much rather stay here." Robert thrust his shoulders back, sprang his long body away from the wall, and waded into the throng, hands outspread. "I'm coming, my darling, I'm coming!"

The crowd applauded and formed a circle about the trio. Robert wrested Sarah to her feet. She orated as he did: "Unhand me, knave! How dare you get in the way of my wicked plans?"

Like it was a stage battle, she did a balletic flip along Robert's chest, landing on her feet on the far side of the countess.

"I'd always predicted it would be *you* who one day rescued *me* from the ravenous Miss Bernhardt, Cousin," Robert said to the mass of gray tulle on the floor.

"You make a far more convincing maiden than you do a rescuer, it's true," the countess said from the ground. "Now help me up. This season's fabric is especially heavy."

Robert went to lift her, and she clasped her lace-gloved

hand around his wrist. When he pulled, she rose into the air . . . until Robert's reedy body buckled and he tumbled down on top of her. She screeched as he rolled to one side, disappearing into her frills.

"I'll save you!" Sarah Bernhardt announced before diving back in, disappearing up to her neck in fabric.

Finally the three of them came to rest and got themselves to their feet, to the room's diminishing applause. "I will never again play the hero," Robert said, pressing his hair flat against his head.

"Nor shall you play the maiden—to your perpetual dismay," Sarah said.

The room laughed, and the bright volleys of conversation continued. Léon watched it all from against the far wall, looking for Marcel. But he was nowhere to be found. Maybe he was up on the roof again?

Léon picked his way through the party, faintly aware that Robert's attention had returned to him. He climbed the creaking metal stairs to the upper floors, lifting a gas lamp from a hallway console table to accompany him. His mind returned to the kiss under the dark sky, the touch of Marcel's hand against his back, those long lashes covering soulful eyes.

No one else was on the roof.

He was surprised by the feeling of relief that followed. Léon extinguished his lamp and sat where he was. Marcel would come find him eventually, but he would enjoy the quiet until then. Now that the champagne was really settling in, he decided this was where he would rather spend his time, not in that room with its fast talk. Up here, he didn't have to face that voice inside telling him he had too little to offer.

All the same, a thought got louder and louder: *Come back, Marcel.* It was insistent, that thought. For the first time for as long as he could remember, something was louder in Léon's mind than the call to the piano.

But Marcel didn't return. Léon tried to get his mind back on the moon and the night sky and the distant Eiffel Tower, even to start playing through an étude in his mind, but he couldn't manage to find peace. The wine was making his head enter loops he couldn't get out of—and it had started raining again.

He decided he would go home. It was late to be alone on the streets of Paris, and he didn't really know the way, but he wasn't going to crouch on the roof like a burglar, waiting to be discovered. Even if that meant he might have to leave without saying goodbye to Marcel.

Léon picked himself up and got unsteadily to his feet. Rue de l'Université was very far down below. He gripped the railing as he reached for the door handle. It didn't budge.

Maybe he'd missed his grip in the rain. He pulled again. It was sealed tight.

Léon knocked on the door politely. Then, he pounded and kicked. It was made of such solid metal that it barely made a noise.

He slumped against the door and drew his wet shirt-sleeves around him. *Great work, Léon.* Either the door had locked behind him automatically or a servant had come by and secured it from the inside.

Whatever had happened, he'd be spending a while out here. At least the night was warm, even if it was also wet. He leaned against the railing and closed his eyes, a boy's lips in his mind; in the haze of the champagne, he wasn't sure whose.

5.

A RUSH OF SOUND. LÉON OPENED HIS EYES TO SEE A pigeon no more than a foot away, bobbing its head as it searched for food. Startled, Léon raised to his elbow. Equally startled, the pigeon took to the sky.

Dawn pinks were fading. Léon had slept through the night. He was still on Robert's roof.

He tugged at the door. Still locked.

Léon sank back down. It could be hours—oh God, it could be *days*—until someone came out here.

Léon plucked his handkerchief from his inside pocket and slid it under the door, so that it might be visible on the far side. At least someone walking by to clean might realize someone was outside.

Then he settled in to wait. His head pounding—this must be what a hangover was—Léon sat near the edge of the roof, so he could track who was coming and going four stories below. He could call out to someone passing by. If it were Marcel, he definitely would. Anyone else might be a little too embarrassing.

But the house door below never opened.

Instead, it was the door right beside him.

As it creaked open, Léon leaped to his feet. It wasn't Marcel at the opening. It was Robert.

Dressed in a purple silk dressing robe and shearling slippers, he stepped out without checking first for any unexpected pianists on his roof. He stepped on Léon's foot, yelped, and flung his cigar clean into the sky. Both shocked beyond words, he and Léon watched it flip end over end before disappearing into the street below.

Then Robert shrieked. Léon shrieked too, just a little quieter.

"Good god, what are you?" Robert asked, then drew his robe tight around his body, sashing it tight along his narrow waist, as if to cut himself in two. "Oh. It's you!"

Léon got to his feet, his head now pounding twice as hard. "I'm so sorry. I really am. Marcel showed me up here, then I lost him and came back up and the door locked behind me and, well . . ." He cast his hands out.

"Well, what? You turned into a pigeon?"

"No, I . . . well yes, I guess basically I did."

Robert peered over the edge. "My poor cigar." He turned to Léon, cocking a hand on his hip. "It was a Cuban. So. Would you like to remain a pigeon, or would you like to join me for breakfast?"

Léon couldn't remember when he'd last eaten. "Breakfast, yes. I mean, some breakfast would be lovely. Thank you for offering me breakfast."

Robert looked about to say something, then turned on

his heel and strode down the metal stairs, waving in Léon's direction. "Come. There will be spiced chocolate! Maybe. If Céleste remembered to buy some."

"Thank you," Léon called after Robert, though the count had disappeared so completely into the dark that he probably hadn't heard him.

Léon took a long look around the roof of Count Robert de Montesquiou, said a mental goodbye to the pigeon, then returned his soggy shoes to his feet and started down the stairs. The shoes squeaked as he went, so Léon gave the soles a little rub on the first carpet he came to. He'd already snuck into Robert's house and drunk his wine and spent the night on his roof—all he needed to do now was track dirty water through his house, too.

"You'll see a room to the right with the door open," Robert called up. "Change out of your damp clothes and into a robe and meet me at the bottom. I'll have Céleste make up a second setting for breakfast."

There was indeed a door ajar to the right. Léon tented five fingers on the wood and eased it open. Behind was a surprisingly plain room, its walls the color of fresh milk. A trio of robes hung on the door of a closet, burgundy and black and angel-feather white. He chose the burgundy.

It ran over his fingers like liquid, the satin difficult to catch and hold. The moment the robe was off the hanger, it had slipped through his fingers and puddled on the carpet.

Léon lifted it back up, bunching the satin in his fist to keep hold of it. Stepping behind the closet door to stay out of view of anyone entering the room, he shucked off his shoes and socks, and then—after double checking that he was still alone—peeled off his wet jacket, pants, and shirt. Finally he stripped off his underwear and, entirely naked, felt the trapped moisture of the night rising from his skin. He gave himself a wipe with the driest part of his discarded shirt, then slipped on the robe. It was so much warmer than his clammy flesh—it felt like he'd slipped into a warm bath. Like he'd been rescued.

He paused to look in Robert's full-length mirror, then ran his fingers through his hair and pulled the two halves of the robe closed. The satin was so soft, it made all the small, fine, invisible hairs on his skin rise, was gloss on his belly and back and nipples. Cinching the robe tight, he padded out in bare feet. Then, thinking better of it, he selected the plainest slippers he could find in Robert's closet, a dusky wine-colored pair with some symbol from a foreign language stitched in black. His feet swam in the slippers, clapping the soles against the floor, but he figured it was better than arriving to breakfast in his bare feet.

Léon padded down the stairs until he came to a room facing the street, heavy with dark wooden furniture, lace doilies, and oil paintings nearly black with age. Robert lay on a low couch beneath the window, heels drawn up under him, staring out the paned glass at the activity below. He hadn't yet noticed Léon, so Léon kicked the slippers off. Robert's feet were bare. "Thank you," Léon said. "I hope this was the robe you meant."

Robert glanced his way and nodded before returning his gaze to the street below. "It suits you. I wore it once. I'm not sure it was washed since, sorry about that. Come join me on this couch. There's something I want to show you."

The satin rippled over Léon's bare skin as he tiptoed over. He sat opposite Robert on the couch, the frame creaking and their toes nearly touching, the musty scent of the antique upholstery rising around him. He could feel individual springs under his thighs.

Whereas Marcel gave off that spicy, burning fragrance of camphor, Robert's scent was softer and deeper, lacquer and flowers and swans on a pond. He pointed down to the street below. "There's a flower vendor who sets up at the end of the block. She's at least a hundred and twenty if she's a year. Always with that dingy hat on her head, with the grimy lace carnations about to fall off it. She sets up at dawn, but I've never seen her sell a flower before noon. I sit here and write my poems, watching her. She isn't frustrated, she isn't bored, she just stands there, waiting for someone to buy a flower. Look at how perfectly still she is. Oh, breakfast is here. Thank you, Céleste!"

Léon looked to the doorway to see a maid with a silver tray. On it were fresh rolls, a dish of butter, a pot of jam, a silver coffeepot with delicate china cups and saucers. "Remember that your monthly tea with your father in Roissy was rescheduled for today," the maid said. She had strong arms, tightly wound hair, a steady gaze. She used the formal "vous" for Robert.

"Yes, of course," Robert said. He tilted his head at Léon conspiratorially. "I mustn't miss tea with Father, not if I want my allowance. It's like going to Latin mass. I just keep my gaze blank and let my mind wander and then praise His marvels at the end. I make some vague claims about giving up poetry and marrying a suitable woman and becoming a stockbroker like Papa someday as we say goodbye."

"If there is nothing else, sir?" Céleste asked, patting her apron.

"You've thought of everything, as ever," Robert said, looking over the silver tray like it was a buffet cart. "There can be nothing else when you've been so very thorough."

Once Céleste had left, Robert swung his legs around, tugged the table and tray close, and poured a dark brown steaming liquid. "Milk, sugar?"

"I don't know. Is that coffee?"

Robert looked about to say something biting, then managed to contort his face into a lopsided grin instead. "Never had coffee. I see. We'll do milk and plenty of sugar, then. It's the best way to start. It's what children do."

He handed Léon a cup and saucer. Léon laid it on his knee, did his best to keep the saucer level on the slippery burgundy satin while he lifted the thin lip of the cup to his mouth and sipped. It tasted dark brown, just like it looked. But the sweetness was very nice. He'd only had sugar once or twice before; it was far too expensive for the Delafosses, who drank their morning chocolate bitter.

"You appear to have sneaked into my party last night," Robert prompted.

Léon considered trying to explain that he'd only realized that fact once he'd already arrived, but it all seemed a little unbelievable—and unkind to Marcel. "I did," he said. "I'm sorry."

Robert laughed. "I hope you had more fun than Marcel Proust did, at least."

"I was locked out on the roof all night and woken up by an angry pigeon, so I doubt it."

Robert's eyes narrowed. "Marcel had a fit of asthma and had to be driven home, so I wouldn't say he had a better time of it, not by any stretch."

"Oh no, that's terrible," Léon said. He bit his lip. It really was. He would go to Marcel as soon as possible to see if he was okay.

Robert smiled widely. "It is, it is. So, Léon Delafosse, I know you didn't intend to stay over, and I'm sure you would have retreated home to your piano as soon as you could *if* you'd been able to, but I'm glad you did. Stay over, that is. Even if you chose such an unusual location for your bed."

He crossed his legs narrowly at the thigh and set his chin on his hand. "I have this problem, you see. I spend a week planning a party, and it comes and it's rapturous, it's all I ever wanted, it makes all the papers . . . then everyone goes home and I don't hear from them. Not a card or a thoughtful present or anything. They're just waiting for the next time I throw a party, you see. I am always the inviter, never the invited."

Robert waved dismissively at a brass tray balanced on an ottoman. "Well, I receive *some* return invitations, of course I receive *some*, but I don't receive *many*. I wake up and each day is yawning and empty and I need that cigar on the roof to find my feet again. To say to myself, 'Robert, you were the only of your siblings to survive childhood, and you will live on your own and die on your own and that's just the sum of it.' The shock of that empty feeling almost makes the party not worth it. But then I go and host another and invite that feeling back again. The cycle repeats. I want to suffer, of course, but that's hardly original, is it? Suffering? Wanting to suffer?"

"I've never thought about it," Léon said.

Robert smiled. "But you *are* a Catholic, like me, so you must like suffering, at least a little. Anyway, this time I opened the door and you were there, the pianist from the Saussine salon. France's Mozart had gotten trapped in my home, like a nightingale."

Léon smiled shyly. "More a pigeon than a nightingale. I am certainly not like that. Not like any bird." His face scrunched up. What was he trying to say? Unable to resist his growling stomach, he put his coffee down, took a roll, broke it in two, and started eating it plain rather than risk buttering it the wrong way. "Were you at the Saussine salon?"

"No, I wasn't, but that was the sort of evening that

spreads. Everyone's heard *so* much about it that it's all turned boring. We have nothing left to pick apart, you see. I'm sure Madame Saussine is beside herself with joy."

"I do think I played well that night," Léon admitted.

"I took piano lessons like any good young man in society," Robert said. "But I'm afraid that, unlike you, I did not have a muse looking over my shoulder, except for my poetry of course—what are you looking at? What's wrong?"

"Nothing's wrong." Léon realized that his attention had been pulled to a corner of the room, where there was a pile of blue fur. "Is that . . . alive?"

"Oh, no, and when it was alive, it was not blue. It's a fox skin. Only it's cerulean now. And dead. I have a pink tiger skin upstairs, I'd be happy to show you. Anyway, Léon, I am an artist like you, I must admit, only my talents are not for music but for poetry! I am currently at work on a collection. Have you heard of Oscar Wilde, in London? I am France's Oscar Wilde, like you are its Mozart. It's not much, but I am aware that the poetic greats would also say that their poetry is not much. Coming to terms with not being much is what all wise men do. I suggest you do the same. Though not too vocally because no one is drawn to the unambitious either. I suppose I'm only bringing this up to you because I want you to be impressed because you've impressed me."

Léon struggled to think what to say. "And the tortoise . . . ?"

"Very much alive. That beast will outlive me, to the chagrin of my eventual children." He burst out laughing, covering his mouth. "Children, could you imagine the thought?

Issuing from me? Horrifying. I once spent a 'special night' with Sarah Bernhardt and vomited for twenty-four hours afterward. Now I'm officially celibate. No, Céleste is out in back, feeding la mademoiselle tortue, her own tortoise, breakfast as we speak. Hers is a trifle greener than ours. Come, try the jam with your bread, or did they not have jam in Vernon? Is this a first for you too?"

Léon felt a small flame of anger. "Of course they have jam in Vernon. I adore jam." Had he ever said "adore" before? He wasn't sure.

"Oh, good," Robert said, his voice controlled. "I do too. I'm glad you enjoy it."

Léon dolloped jam on his bread, then let his hand rest on his own thigh. "I'm sorry. For coming uninvited. For spending the night on your roof."

"It didn't importune me in the least. And I get to wake to a handsome young man in my house. No, I think I should thank *you* for the last few hours' turn of events. Although I am sorry about that cigar. It was the last of the Cubans."

Something struck Léon, something so horrible that he had to know the answer right away. "You didn't . . . *you* didn't lock me out on the roof, did you?"

Robert went into momentary shock, eyes wide, then he burst out laughing, only barely managing to put his cup and saucer down before the laughter took over, his long body rippling as he roared. "Oh, I wish I had! That would have been far more interesting a thing for me to do than I'm capable of. No, the most interesting thing I do is throw parties. I enjoy them more than I enjoy the guests that come, you see, so I'm not even an interesting friend. Sometimes I decorate my poems too, and I'm worried the art surpasses the words. Would Oscar Wilde worry about such things? Perhaps I can decorate some of your music, as a tribute to a new friend. I'd do the initial designs, at least. They're painted by La Gándara. See, there I go. I'm trying to impress you in my own scattered way."

"I'd like that," Léon said, his attention lost again in the pelt of the dead fox, dyed blue. "Thank you. Not the impressing, the decoration."

"Marcel and you . . . have had a long friendship?" Robert asked.

"No," Léon answered. "We just met." He wasn't sure if they'd started speaking some code, if a "long friendship" meant something in particular. If it did, he didn't know what.

Robert nodded, satisfied, like something momentous had been revealed. "Marcel manages to be in every necessary place at every necessary time. But that's the very thing that makes me suspect he might be unnecessary to any place and any time."

Léon wanted to say something witty and confusing back, but all that came to mind were earnest things.

"All that's just to say that Marcel is a bit of, well, he's a bit of a gossip," Robert said. "Gossips are great fun, but you don't want to lean on them for sustenance."

"Okay," Léon said slowly. "I'll remember that."

"In fact, Marcel hasn't been invited to my parties for a

long time. I think he knew just what he was doing, bringing you along. He knew how much I would like you and thought you'd be the thing that might get him back into my affection."

"Oh," Léon said. Had Marcel been using him? He didn't want to believe it, which didn't mean it wasn't true.

"Léon, can I ask you something, even if it's impertinent?"

Léon wrapped the robe tighter around him, untied and re-cinched the sash. No matter how he arranged himself, his calves were exposed, their downy, blond hair catching the morning sun. "Please."

"Have you secured a patron?"

Léon shook his head.

"Would you . . . like to have a patron? So you can devote yourself to your art?"

"Yes," Léon said. It was a relief to speak so plainly. "I've been at the conservatory longer than most, and it's . . . getting impossible to pay for it, to be honest. I don't qualify for official patrons through school until next year, but in the meantime I'm . . . I'm just trying to pay my tuition. And help my family."

Robert's face turned grave. "That is a serious matter. I'm sorry to hear it."

"Thank you," Léon said. "It's a little hard to bring up in casual party conversation. I'm sorry if I was preoccupied, if it made me not a fun guest last night."

"Are you kidding? This is the way my parties always go: everyone's so excited for their chance to speak that no one actually listens to anyone else. If I remember right, you didn't say a word at my party. If you're quiet, then *you're* the special one."

Léon smiled. "Ah. I might have been thinking about this society party thing all wrong."

"I won't tell you not to worry and to just be yourself instead," said Robert, "because that would be a horrid and bourgeois thing to say, but do stay at least *partway* yourself. Unless you're me, in which case being yourself is loathsome and you should be anything else you can think of, anything at all."

Léon laughed. Robert did not.

"And you are that," Robert said.

"Are what?"

"Special. It is quite evident."

Léon felt his face flush. Heat rose in waves from the burgundy silk at the base of his throat.

Robert de Montesquiou looked at him, a question in his eyes. Léon looked back. There was something in the angle of Robert's long body, the ache behind the wit, the insatiable hunger to be someone in the world, that was sweet.

Léon took a bite of his bread and jam. It was conserved from blueberries. Robert watched Léon chew and swallow. "I have to admit," Léon said, "this is much better than the jam in Vernon."

Robert gently flicked a crumb from the corner of Léon's mouth. "Of course it is. Everything is wonderful here. That jam is the same jam Queen Victoria eats."

Something about this conversation, always edging on inappropriate and unnatural topics, made Léon's skin feel extra alive. But now, twice in the space of a few hours, he was feeling stirred in a way he'd never felt around a girl. *Father Moulin, I have sinned. I have inappropriate desires.* Maybe it was just this satin fabric stirring him this time. He hoped.

A downstairs bell rang. Robert had been slowly inclining his head toward Léon's, but he paused in space. Male voices rose from the foyer, laughter and quick speech, followed by a few polite words from Céleste.

Then there were footfalls on the stairs, more boisterous laughter. Léon leaped to his feet, like he'd nearly been caught in something terrible. Robert stayed where he was, amusement on his face.

A trio of young men appeared at the entrance to the room, in beautiful suits and with waxed mustaches, their hair carefully parted and pomaded. "Robert, come and wander with us—oh, are we interrupting?" the one in front said.

"Not at all," Robert said, not bothering to get to his feet. "Gentlemen, this is my guest, Léon. He spent the night after my party. Perhaps he would care to join us on our stroll."

The men stared at Léon and Robert with gaping and admiring smiles. They were clearly coming up with their own explanations for the situation. Shame flooded Léon. Unnatural. Abomination. What would happen if word got back to the conservatory, to his mother? "I need to go," Léon said. "I'm sorry. I need to go practice."

"No, you should stay," one of the young men said laughingly.

"You and the Comte de Montesquiou are having too grand a time for us to interrupt."

But Léon was already out of the room, tripping up the stairs to the dressing room, kicking the door closed with the heel of his bare foot, tugging on his damp, cold clothes from the night before, whipping a hand through his mussed hair, and then barreling down the stairs, taking them two at a time to make it go all the quicker.

As he passed Robert's breakfast room, he let himself glance in. Robert looked at him, wounded and angry, and then pointedly returned his attention to his three guests, poking one in the ruffled frills on his chest to make some point that Léon didn't catch. The other young men ignored Léon.

He continued down to the hallway at the bottom, where Céleste was kneeling with a gleaming silver tray and brush, going after the bits of dirt the men had tracked into the house. She paused, finding something in Léon's expression.

"Leaving already?" she asked softly.

Léon nodded, tears in his eyes.

Céleste sighed in a way that made Léon think situations like this occurred often at Robert's home. She laid a hand on Léon's forearm. "Our Robert has a good heart. He might play at being mean sometimes, but he has a good heart. He likes you. I hope you come back."

"I really have to go," Léon said, brushing past her and out into the street. He was instantly anonymous amid the clatter of carriages on cobblestone, the clip of hard-soled feet along packed dirt, the shouts of newspaper criers and men at carts selling roasted almonds. No one paid any mind to the hastily dressed boy tumbling out of the Montesquiou household. No doubt many hastily dressed boys had previously tumbled out of the Montesquiou household.

He started along the street, toward home. He'd come so close to having a solution. To getting someone to sponsor him. To maybe be something more. But then that trio of boys had come in, with those looks in their eyes—those looks that said he was the count's plaything. If Léon accepted Robert as his patron, that's how everyone would look at him. No, he couldn't do it. What would his mother say? After sacrificing so much, working those long days for scraps of money that went straight to his tuition, so her two children could get married and start their lives right . . . only for him to become a sexual pervert?

All the same, that might not be something he could become. Not if it was something he already was. Despite his doing nothing to become it. The cruelty of it all felt crushing—all his thoughts said what he was doing was wrong, but the *feelings* were pure and real, and felt only like desire, the heart-opening sort of desire that could someday become love.

A window creaked open above him. Léon looked up to see Robert, still in his robe, leaning out. "Here, catch," he cried, hurling something small and heavy Léon's way.

It was a leather pouch. The tie loosened when it hit the street, and coins rolled out. The young men, out of view behind Robert, burst into laughter.

Léon did not pick the coins up. He glared at Robert. What was this supposed to be, a tip? Payment for services rendered, like he was some demimondaine? Léon might not have known all the subtleties of patronage, but he knew it didn't work like *this*. "How dare you?"

"Those are not for you, silly," Robert said. "If it were a present, I would have thrown you the blueberry jam. Though I suppose the crock would have shattered. I want you to please buy the flower woman's stock, so she can go home and put those tired old feet up."

Robert returned to the conversation inside, closing the window behind him. Léon was alone on the street. An urchin looked at the purse on the ground and then at Léon, as if to ask *are you going to take that?*

Léon picked up the coins and the purse. He'd been paid. But it wasn't for him. Robert was kind within his strange callousness. It was all so confusing.

Léon headed to the end of the block. He'd buy the old woman's stock of flowers, and then he'd drop the flowers off inside Robert's entrance for Céleste to arrange. Then he'd never see Robert again.

The old woman burst into tears, the dingy lace carnations on her hat trembling as she placed her hands over her heart. *Thank you.*

6.

A LESSON WITH MARMONTEL, FOCUSING ON PHRASING. Normally this was one of Léon's favorite subjects. But today the only way he could play was tensely, his notes all staccato, like he was avoiding a fight by saying as little as possible. There was a letter in Léon's pocket, handed to him by the front desk attendant as he'd walked in that morning. He'd read it and put it in his jacket pocket right away, in shame. Faked his way through his lesson.

As they finished up, Léon realized he could ask Marmontel what to do about the letter. But the bearded old man shared a dusty apartment with his wife and four cats, living off her inheritance, and so had never had to play high society. He might tell Léon to do the wrong thing about the letter, and then Léon would have to contradict his mentor.

No, he knew whom he should ask for advice, even though the idea of the conversation filled him with dread.

Marmontel's disappointment at Léon's phrasing showed only in the small sighs he gave as he packed his teaching books up in his leather case, little gusts of bad breath that Léon had come to associate with care and love and gentle disappointment.

Reynaldo wasn't scheduled to see Marmontel until an

hour later, so Léon knew where to find him. Sure enough, he was lounging in the stairwell that the students had made into their lounge. He was laid out flat, somehow picturesque even as he reclined on a dusty floor of broken stone tiles. His shiny, black hair, cresting in two waves along a sharp middle part, gleamed while he lectured an adoring semicircle of younger students.

Léon coughed. "Reynaldo, could I talk to you for a minute?"

Reynaldo propped himself up onto an elbow. "Shy Léon Delafosse speaks to me first! This is a big moment in my life. Scram, kids."

The younger students scattered as Reynaldo sat up, leaning his back against the wall. He was Venezuelan, only a year older than Léon but with a man's fullness to his face. He was handsome enough to fluster Léon, handsome enough to make him so impossible to attain that he didn't quite fire up any desire. Unlike Marcel, who was so amazingly . . . available.

Léon crouched beside him, then felt too awkward and let himself sit fully on the floor. "I could use some advice."

"The Beethoven cadenza again?" Reynaldo asked with a laugh. They both knew Léon didn't need any musical advice.

"I received this," Léon said as he withdrew the letter from his inside breast pocket. A wrinkle had been pressed into the paper by his own body heat.

Reynaldo unfolded the paper with his long, pale fingers, dusted with black hair on the backs. He read it aloud:

Cher Léon Delafosse,

I wish to let you know how ravished we were by your performance at our home last week. Even Brigitte, the little one's severe nanny, praised it based on what she heard from the upstairs rooms. A Brigitte compliment is hard to come by; our children have never managed it. Artistically speaking, we do hope that you find a name under which you would fit, a house with whom you could travel to St. Moritz or even America, finding higher and higher audiences for your performances and your compositions. Let us who live baser lives of financial concerns help you stay aloft. We wish you the best of luck in that search. If you ever care to join us at home for a dinner so we can get to know one another better, do let me know.

    Ferdinande de Saussine

Reynaldo looked up, clearly confused by Léon's worry. "They followed up. This is good news."

"It is? They didn't offer to be my patrons. They wished me luck finding one. That doesn't sound like good news."

Reynaldo squeezed Léon's shoulder. "They're not going to bow themselves down while you just stand there, giving them nothing. Even if you're the best pianist France has ever known, they're not going to make an offer that they don't already know you'll accept."

"Oh," Léon said. He thought for a moment. "How will they know I'll accept if they haven't offered yet?"

"The conservatory should really give a course just on how to navigate patronage for awkward country boys like you. It works a lot like Caracas society does, though, so I'm happy to provide my services. As long as you acknowledge me when you're accepting the Legion of Honor someday. Can I give you a course now?"

Léon nodded. "Yes, please do."

"Rule number one is the most important. Society is a little like playing a piano. You *can* try too hard. Above all, don't show effort. In conversation that means to be humble, be content to be wherever you are, compliment everything, and don't try to be funny if you're not funny. Don't tell them you really need a patron, even if that's the first thing on your mind. If you're ambitious, you're suspicious. Be yourself with me or with Marmontel, but don't be yourself there. That's not what gets rewarded."

Léon fished a scrap of sheet music out of his bag, began to pencil notes on the back. "Don't try too hard, got it."

Reynaldo laughed. "Taking notes on trying too hard is trying too hard."

Léon put his pencil down.

"I'm teasing," Reynaldo said. "Take everything a little more lightly, that's another note for you." His eyes narrowed shrewdly as he looked Léon up and down. "Whatever you have to do to get it, invest in a nice shirt from DiMauro's. Just one. You can wash it by hand and hang it in your apartment whenever it needs another wash. These rough muslin things you wear over and over are just not going to cut it chez Saussine."

"They're not muslin," Léon said. But he knew perfectly well what Reynaldo meant. Léon did the mental calculation. If his mother went back to teaching on Saturdays, and they held the milkman off again, he might just be able to manage a shirt from DiMauro. He trusted Reynaldo to know what it took. He'd linked up with the Racine house and suddenly was wearing imported shoes and talking about his plans to tour Germany. If he said Léon should get a particular shirt, Léon would find a way to get it.

Reynaldo took up Léon's scrap of sheet music and pencil and wrote a list on the back. "This is the most extreme option, but you're my most extreme case. Here are five phrases to memorize, that you can say when you're socializing at their home. That's part of this, Léon. You have to learn how to talk to people."

Léon looked over the list. *I believe that the Dreyfus Affair is less about the man than about the needs of national security. Have you heard of this new term, "homosexual"? They call this the Age of Invention, but that's really going too far.*

"They're interesting things to say, ways to get people engaged," Reynaldo explained. "If you memorize these, you won't just do that 'mrm-hrm' thing you do while nodding your head."

"I understand," Léon said. He did do that "mrm-hrm" thing.

"The Saussines have invited you to dine in their home.

If you had charmed at the salon you played, yes, you might be fielding an official offer right now and figuring out what to do with your knighthood and hundreds of francs. But don't despair. It's not over yet, Léon. Just write to them, angle your way into a dinner, put yourself out there a little more, and be interesting. You don't have to be fascinating, just interesting. And wear that shirt from DiMauro's. Do all that, and you'll get to a debut recital at the Érard, and from there you are made. The recital is the key, and if that goes well, you are set for life. The rental costs a thousand francs, though, so find whatever person will get you that. Understand?"

Léon nodded. It would have been nicer to hear that he should just be himself and it would all work out, but that had evidently been too much to hope for.

As Léon was leaving, the front desk clerk flagged him down and handed him a weathered envelope. "You had a new one arrive in the late morning post. You are popular today, Delafosse."

Léon accepted the letter, pressed it to his chest as he stepped out of the gloom of the heavy stone conservatory and into the sunlight. He couldn't make himself look at who it was from. It was white cotton paper, so it probably wasn't from the Saussines. But what if it was? *Dear Léon, you are boring. Please send us Reynaldo Hahn instead.*

A horse carriage clopped by, nearly spraying Léon with offal. He opened the envelope. It wasn't from the Saussines.

The letters were rough and unpracticed, a handwriting he knew as well as his own.

Dear Léon,

How are you? I am fine here. Clémentine lost a shoe somewhere between that pond she likes to drink from and the barn, and I have looked for it but I cannot find it. My father is still drinking too much and becoming sick from it, and my mother is forgetting more things. She stacked her undergarments in the kitchen cupboard. I continue to go on walks with Cécile. I think she is very nice and does good impressions. I don't think you ever liked Cécile much did you?

I look forward to your letters, always. Father still thinks novels ruin the mind so your letters are my only thing to read except for the Bible. I guess I play cards with Maman too. We are too tired with the planting season to play more than one or two hands before it's time to go to bed.

When might you visit Vernon again?

Your friend,
Félix

Léon read it twice. It was all very Félix. He loved that horse so much.

He composed a letter in his mind as he walked home, then worried he'd forget it all before he got home and so stopped in the Jardin des Tuileries to write down his response on the backside of Félix's own letter.

Dear Félix,

I am sorry to hear about Clémentine's missing shoe. Though I do remember that pile of horseshoes you kept in advance, so I'm sure she is back to four shoes by now.

Everything is absolutely amazing here. I feel so lucky. It is better than I could have imagined. Marmontel continues to teach me piano techniques I won't bore you by trying to explain. I have started to make it in high society! Can you imagine? You would think I were an actual gentleman if you saw me going into these homes. They have to be about ten stories high, and everyone coming in and out looks like that picture of Marie Antoinette from the history book in school.

You might not recognize me if you saw me, Félix! It's just so wonderful here. Paris is everything they say.

Please say hello to Cécile for me. I'm sure she is lovely to walk and talk with.

Your friend,
Léon

Whistling happily, Léon folded the paper in two, giving it a nice sharp crease. He didn't have an envelope in his bag, so he would have to take it home first. But then he'd get it right off to Félix.

As he slotted the folded letter neatly into his music theory book, Léon felt a chill flood of something he realized was loneliness. He wanted Félix to be proud of him, and not to worry, but who could he be *honest* with? Charlotte and his mother were depending on him to keep them from poverty. Marmontel didn't have an interior life, as far as he could tell. Reynaldo was Reynaldo. Robert de Montesquiou might have become a friend, but that adventure had ended terribly. Could he be honest with Félix? Everything he was going through felt foreign to their life of woodland walks and feeding ducks. How could Félix understand?

Marcel, though. A young man interested in Léon for who he was. Maybe. *We're both weird outsider fairy creatures, you and me.*

Marcel, who'd collapsed at Robert's home. Léon knew the Proust address, from when Marcel had first invited him to his family's at-home. It was almost on his way home. If he rushed, Léon would have time to stop by before he headed home without needing to explain a thing to his mother and sister.

7.

LÉON KNEW ENOUGH ABOUT HOW SOCIETY FUNCTIONED to know he wasn't supposed to knock on a door unannounced. Even if Tuesday was the Proust at-home, he ought to have a card to leave, so he could wait outside while they decided whether to admit him. But Léon didn't have cards. So when a servant opened the front door, Léon handed a folded sheet of music paper of a composition he'd attempted, his name scrawled across the top.

"What am I to do with this?" asked the servant, a knife-faced woman with hair in a tight bun.

"What is it, Lisette?" said a voice behind. "Oh, hello there." A woman appeared, masses of dark hair, eyeglasses on a chain, soft and matronly clothes. "Who's this?"

Léon held his dark hat in his hands, peered nervously at the woman. "I'm Léon Delafosse. I'm a new friend of Marcel's. I wanted to see if he's okay?"

"Are you? He hasn't mentioned you."

"We were at a party together the other night. He had to go home early, on account . . ."

"Of his asthma, yes. Come in." She held open the door and beckoned Léon through.

"Thank you," he said as he stepped in. "I've been worried about him."

"Lisette just made up a tray with tea and madeleines," Madame Proust said. "You can take it up to him. I'd ask you not to stay too long, but Marcel is very good about keeping things short when he's not well. But I'll say it anyway: don't stay too long."

Léon soon had a painted tray in his hands and was heading up narrow stairs. He put the tray down on a console table and peeked in the open door. Marcel's bedroom was on the first floor, overlooking the street. It was dark, nearly black, the air musty and close. Léon rapped on the doorframe. Marcel, lying on his back with a silk mask over his eyes, slowly raised it and blinked at Léon. "Oh, hello," he said.

"Hello," Léon whispered. "I have today's tea with me."

Marcel chuckled. "You don't have to be so quiet. You're not at a funeral."

"Right, right, of course not," Léon said as he brought the tray to the foot of Marcel's bed and set it down on the mattress.

"It's nice of you to come," Marcel said. "I overexerted myself at the party, I guess. Maybe it was exhaustion, asthma, ennui at the utter meaninglessness of all human interaction, trying to impress you, I'm not sure. Sometimes I just need to lie in bed and read poetry by myself for a few days is what it comes down to."

"That sounds very nice, actually," Léon said, looking

around the room. It was so airless and quiet. Weren't people with breathing trouble supposed to go stay on mountaintops or at the seaside or something?

"How was the rest of the party?" Marcel asked.

"You won't believe me when I tell you," Léon said, perching at the edge of Marcel's bed. "I went upstairs to find you and got locked out on the roof all night."

Marcel stared at him, slowly processing the words. Then he burst into a laugh that trailed into a cough. "So that's where you were. I thought Robert might have locked you in a dungeon and wouldn't release you until you'd read all his questionable verse."

"No, no," Léon said, feeling his face flush. "Though I did eat breakfast with him. Then his friends came and they made me feel like a bug."

"I know those precise Monday-morning friends of his," Marcel said. "I can just imagine it. Robert is like them when he's with them, but he's not like them when he's not. Unlike them, who are *always* them." His nose wrinkled. "Does that make sense?"

"Yes, surprisingly," Léon said, holding the plate of madeleines out for Marcel. It was made of very thin china, and he worried that even the pressure of his thumb and fingers could break it.

"Nothing to eat for me today," Marcel said. "Though I will take some of that tea, with cream."

He watched Léon prepare the cup, a pleasant and abstracted smile on his face, like he was watching children play in a meadow far, far away. "I think Robert really likes you," he said.

"I don't know about that," Léon said. "It doesn't seem that way at all to me."

"I believe it wouldn't. That's your charm. But take my word for it. I write society pieces, which means recognizing all the ways we like and loathe one another is my life's work."

Léon remembered Robert's accusation that Marcel had used him to get back into his graces. If it were true, Léon's unawareness was why Marcel found him so useful. He pushed the thought out of his head because he hoped people were better than that. "I wondered if he might want to be my patron," Léon said, "but I'm not sure. Madame Saussine wrote, but I don't know what she meant either. I had to ask Reynaldo Hahn for help."

"Ah, the delightful Venezuelan I encountered outside the conservatory, with his dancer cherubs," Marcel said. "How could I forget that particular creature? Tell me what the Saussine letter said."

"I actually have it with me," Léon said, opening his leather bag. Many letters tumbled out. It had been an important few days for letters. He wasn't sure why he was carrying them all around, maybe he thought they'd sort themselves out while they tumbled around his bag. He picked out the Saussine note, tucking the letter from Félix out of view.

Marcel read the Saussine letter. "I'd say this means they will offer. But they want you to make it clear that you'll accept before they make it."

Léon took the letter back and peered at it, turning it upside-down and flipping it over, as though secret writing might appear. "That's just what Reynaldo said. How do you know that?"

"I don't want you to learn how. Then you wouldn't need me around to serve as your society translator."

"I accept," Léon said, watching Marcel close his eyes and breathe in the steam from his tea. *Please don't turn out to be using me,* Léon thought.

"You wouldn't be in a bad position if you allied yourself with the Saussines," Marcel said. "But promise me you won't accept a firm offer from them without considering Robert. I could speak to him for you. I'd be honored. He's like us, do you know what I mean? Only he's better than us, really, because he's also a count. Connections to Isabella Stewart Gardner in Boston, British royalty, all of it. Me, I'm only upper middle-class and have to work for my immortality, and you . . ." He let his eyes complete the sentence, taking on a pretend scandalized expression.

"Robert hasn't offered."

"I could make that happen, I think," Marcel said.

"You would do that for me?" Léon asked.

"Don't fall over yourself thanking me. It would do my wagon well to be hitched to yours. I could continue to stay in Robert's orbit, even though he's bored of me."

Ah, there it was, out in the open, as easily as that. Léon realized this might be a way forward. Marcel could be using him, a little, and he could be using Marcel, a little, and they could still like each other during all of it. There was something else, though, some other words Marcel had used, that he needed to know more about. Shame bittered his tongue, but he plucked up his courage and spoke anyway. "What did you mean before, 'like us'?"

"I think you know very well what I mean," Marcel said from his bed, eyes shining. He paused long enough to take a sip of tea and sigh in contentment. His voice lowered so it was almost inaudible. "There's a new word for us. The Germans and English use it: homosexual. It sounds so scientific, doesn't it? I don't know what they'll call normal, natural people now. 'Polysexual'? 'Heterosexual'? I'm sure they'll find a word."

Léon's heart raced. His skin turned cold and pricked with heat at the same time. How could anyone say such words out loud? He matched Marcel's whisper. "I've always heard it called 'unnatural' or 'perverted.'"

"Sure, that too," Marcel said. "But now it's a thing to be, not just an act to do. I kind of like it. And what's wrong with being unnatural, anyway? Animals don't read books, so that's unnatural, and no one's complaining about that."

"Plenty of people say reading is unhealthy," Léon said. "My friend's father won't even let him read novels."

Marcel's eyes danced. "A friend! And that look on your face as you said it! You haven't mentioned him before. Is this a special sort of friend?"

Léon flushed and shook his head. He'd known Félix for so long, since they were little children. And Félix was a good Catholic boy. He was taking those walks with Cécile Boicos. Maybe here in the city, boys kissed boys. In the countryside, that could never happen. The Devil would come right up in person to drag them down to Hell.

"I will continue to just call it 'the vice of the Greeks,' like my parents and their parents did, because I guess I'm old-fashioned, and judging by those beautiful statues, the Greeks seem like wonderful things to be." Marcel shrugged. "You see my point. We are a secret brotherhood. We'll still be in this brotherhood when we're married and have wives. We'll always find one another, boys like you and me."

"What makes you think I'm . . . like that?" Léon asked. Heat was rising from every inch of him.

"When a boy is so beautiful, the god of love doesn't let it go to waste. Every beautiful man has a bit of the Greek in him. Women don't admire male beauty enough, so it's reserved for other men."

It was a ridiculous theory, and unfair to women. Léon almost said so. But he was too afraid to say anything more. The truth was that Marcel was right—he was one of them, this new species of subhuman that people called homosexual. At the same time, he knew in his heart that he *couldn't* be. Those people were cast out from their families. They prowled the docks and died in gutters and spent their eternity in Hell. Better to live a lie married to a woman than to have that future . . .

Unless what Marcel said was true, that they could be in a secret brotherhood all their lives? But that would mean lying to everyone too. Most of all his wife. It all just felt so *wrong*. And yet it was also *him*. Society judged sins because they were things you *did* and could correct. This was something he *was*, that he had no control over. How unfair it all was.

"This seems new to you," Marcel said softly. "We don't have to say any more about it right now. But I'm ready to when you're ready."

"Thank you," Léon said.

"I knew very young and wrestled with it for a long time before I finally admitted it to myself. I wish I'd had someone speak to me the way that I'm speaking to you." He sat up, tucking his linen duvet tight around his narrow chest. "Enough soulful talk. Here's a fun thing: I'll be ready to face the world again soon, just in time to attend *Around the World in Eighty Days* and write it up for *Le Mensuel*. Maybe you'd come with me."

"I'd like that," Léon said. He'd heard about that show. It was the hardest ticket to get in Paris.

"Perhaps by then you'll be Robert's protégé, inviting *me* to *your* society party afterward."

Léon laughed. "That's not very likely."

"We'll know after today," Marcel said.

Léon laughed some more. Then Marcel's words sank in. "After today? What do you mean?"

"This is Tuesday, Robert's day for erranding and making calls. He had me leave your address with him at the party. That can really only mean he's on his way to your home today. He's probably there already."

Léon stood. "Are you being serious?"

Marcel nodded. "Quite."

Léon imagined the count arriving at his dingy home. It was his mother's day off from teaching, so she would be there. Would she and Robert . . . *talk*? The prospect was too horrifying even to contemplate. "I should go," he said.

"You probably should," Marcel said ruefully. "But I hope you do take me up on my offer. To talk more. To see each other more. To be whatever name we choose for what we are to each other."

Léon nodded, then turned and dashed down the stairs.

8.

LÉON SPED THROUGH THE STREETS, VISIONS IN HIS MIND of Robert and his mother sipping tea in silence. His mother's disapproving rage: *This is the sort of person you choose to spend your time with?!* She'd rethink everything she thought she knew about her son, would whirl on him when he opened the door. *Invert. Pederast. Pervert. How will you marry up and improve our chances when you're too busy corrupting yourself and insulting God?* It was enough to bring tears to his eyes.

He was at the Place de la Concorde when he spied Robert, circling the grand obelisk before heading, just as Marcel had predicted, toward Léon's home.

There was no driver, no footman, just pure unadulterated count on the streets of Paris. Léon's first impulse was to race forward, to catch Robert before he got any closer to his house. But his feet didn't obey. He didn't know what he'd possibly say.

The count was wearing a tweed suit and a cap in soft green plaid. It was a surprisingly subdued look for him. He looked like Étienne, the favored son of Vernon's most prosperous farm, a boy who'd never given Léon the time of day. Léon wondered: Had Robert dressed this way to appeal to his mother? As if to say *I am your superior, but I can exist in your world. Do not be afraid.*

A stream of boys ran their hoops along the Champs-Élysées, and Robert had to wait for a break in their game to cross. He smiled generously at them. One of the boys offered his stick, and suddenly Robert had tucked his cane under his armpit and was batting his hoop around the plaza, laughing. Once he'd returned the hoop and was back on his walk, Robert's shoulders drooped and his walk slowed. He picked at the lacquered bulb of his cane, then pressed his shoulders back and picked his pace back up.

Once he'd reached the Louvre palace, Robert paused outside a tabac, lit a cigarette, and perfected the angle of his cap in the window. He smiled, though the smile looked forced and empty. Léon almost took the moment to walk up to him. *Oh, Robert, I'm surprised to see you here! What are the chances?* But then Robert was in motion again and Léon started to follow. There was something exciting about watching Robert, with the count unaware, when previously he'd been the one with all the power. Léon was like a deer who'd taken up hunting.

Then they were on Léon's block. As Robert took out a slip of paper and double checked the address, Léon saw the outside of his home through the count's eyes. It was a perfectly respectable four-story, a few elegant blocks from the opera. Nothing overtly slummy about it. Three ancient women stared down at Robert from their various balconies as he approached. He did draw attention, a young man who clearly knew himself, with his towering elegance and that sharply tailored suit. Robert made a great show of inspecting the cured hams displayed in the charcuterie window until he slipped in the front door behind a delivery boy struggling with an overfull handcart.

Léon counted to ten and then followed.

If Léon was lucky, Robert might see the hall as charming and ramshackle, like something out of the latest Zola novel. Wood paneling painted to look like aged marble, sagging stairs circling a shaft of sunlight weighted with dust. The concierge was watching Robert ascend. Then she looked at Léon, standing at the front door of the building. *Is he here for you? What have you gotten yourself into?*

Robert was huffing by the time he reached the top landing. He rapped a smart melody on the Delafosse door. *Marriage of Figaro.*

The door cracked open. Léon's heart seized as he watched from the shadows below. At the other side appeared his mother. Her iron hair was pinned in peasant curls. "Hello," she said. "Can I help you?"

"Hello there. I was hoping to call on Monsieur Léon Delafosse. Is he at home?"

Léon pressed himself farther into the shadows. With each passing second, it was becoming too late to announce himself.

"No, he's not, I'm sorry. He's still at the conservatory." Léon couldn't see his mother's face too clearly, but he could imagine it shifting as she tried to figure out who this stranger was. Léon had described Robert after the party; she'd figure it out soon enough, if she hadn't already. "Though he should be home already. Would—" Her mouth shut. Manners called for her to invite him in now. But she was clearly embarrassed to. "Can I assume that you are the Count of Montesquiou?" she said.

"You can and have and are correct to. You must be Madame Delafosse."

She opened the door wider and performed a tragedy of a curtsy, knees shaking. "I am. Would you—" She sighed and cast her gaze to the ground. "Would you like to come in?"

"It would honor me," Robert said, and passed by her regally, like Cleopatra into a palace.

The door closed.

Oh God.

Léon was motionless, just him and the dust motes in the sunbeam from the building's skylights and the concierge staring at him, leaning on a mop propped in a bucket.

It soon became unbearable not to know what Robert and his mother were saying. He raced up the stairs, taking them two at a time, and stopped in front of his door. It had always been loose in its frame, which annoyed Charlotte to no end, but Léon was grateful for that now—there was enough of a gap that he could see and hear what was passing inside.

Léon's mother was apologizing for every object in the house, from the spotted curtains to the grimy soap dish. When she gave no sign of pausing, Robert interrupted her and asked if she might be able to spare a cup of tea and a crust of bread. As she busied herself by the gas stove,

Léon peered through the keyhole and had a terrific view of Robert as he leaned against the wall. Robert had only a kind smile on his face, no disgust.

Montesquiou took in the apartment like he was at the zoo. Léon saw it through his eyes: low but large enough not to be squalid; three beds behind three screens, like they were all traveling in the steerage hold of a ship. Sparse furnishings that maybe had too much of a piano theme. The tablecloth was trimmed with embroidered keys; the cupid on the mantel napped atop an ivory quarter note. It was tasteless . . . but so was having a jeweled tortoise, in its own way, right?

Robert moved out of view. "Oh!" he called. "I see that you received the little map of the Érard hall I had sent this morning. I'm so glad." By pressing his temple against the wall, Léon could just see what Robert was referring to. He was looking at an enormous seating chart tacked up into the crumbling plaster.

"Was that you?" Madame Delafosse called. "I wasn't sure. Well, I suspected, but I wasn't sure. Of course. Aren't you kind? Every student pianist dreams of unlocking the world with an Érard recital. Léon will be so excited to see you had this sent over."

He *was* excited. Robert knew just what he wanted most in the world—to share his music—and had proven it. Léon heard the floorboards creak under Robert's feet. With its worn rugs and age-softened boards, walking in the Delafosse apartment was like walking on forest moss.

Léon heard nothing more. Were they whispering? Saying awkward nothings to each other?

But there she was, his mother, huffing into view through the keyhole. She must have leaned against the wet sink and was oblivious to the stain soaking her shirt. She served Robert from their dented teapot, filched from a pile of household supplies left behind after a neighbor died.

"Léon told you about me?" Robert asked from out of view, somewhere over by the far wall.

"Yes," Madame Delafosse said evasively. "He was out all night and explained about your party. Maman never really learns anything specific about these things, you know."

Robert said nothing.

"I know he is so grateful to have met you," Madame Delafosse continued. "And the young Monsieur Proust as well. You don't know how many times—"

"Did he *explain* anything about our interactions?" Robert interrupted. "About my interest in him, about what my family might be able to offer him?"

Léon watched his mother's finger clock twelve hours around the lip of her teacup. "Was Léon expecting you today? I mean, is he late to an appointment with you?" she asked.

"No, no. I was strolling the neighborhood and thought I'd pop in. I imagined he'd be hard at work playing his piano and that I'd check on him, like Minerva on her Arachne."

Silence.

"I'm afraid I'm not familiar with them."

"One shouldn't expect you to be."

"Léon will be by very soon."

"I'm glad."

Silence again.

Léon wondered: Should he go in? Pretend to have just arrived home? He placed his hand on the doorknob, and was about to turn it when he heard his mother and Robert suddenly talking over each other.

Robert: "Do you not have a piano here?"

Madame Delafosse: "You are so handsome. Are you quite pursued by the ladies?"

The more dangerous question wins, so Robert was the first to answer. "I am pursued by very many, though more with laughter than with pursed lips. I prefer women friends to male friends, generally."

Madame Delafosse smiled tensely, which caused a crumb, that Léon had been watching dangle from the down on her lip for some time, to fall into the crevasse of her bodice. "My Léon is very lucky, then."

"He is lucky for his talent," Robert said. "Which of course he got from you. He is about to become an object of great desire in society. That is partly why I'm here."

"Could you explain what you mean?"

Robert laughed. "Why do you think I sent the Érard plan over? My goal is to have him play a sold-out concert there within the year."

Léon sucked in his breath. He removed his hand from the

doorknob. He didn't want to do anything to interfere with what might be about to happen.

Léon watched his mother's face closely. She looked delighted and then wounded. Was she . . . jealous? Was that a thing mothers could feel? For the first time, Léon couldn't quite read her. "He must finish his education," she said. "That is our first priority."

"Of course he will. But I hope you will consider a patron for him to help you do so. Not just for financial reasons. Tuition is one thing, of course. I know you know the benefits of the *de* that is part of my name. My family's nobility can make introductions that no piano teacher can."

"This is a very kind offer. Please, come sit beside me," Madame Delafosse said.

Now they were both out of view, on the couch. Léon slumped against the front door and listened. His mother and Robert talked about the weather, the Dreyfus Affair, the price of beer. They sounded almost like they were friends. Their voices got quiet and intimate enough that Léon could no longer make out the words.

The concierge, mopping the stairs and each landing, was finally approaching Léon's position. He got to his feet. All he needed was for Robert to overhear him trying to explain to the concierge why he was sitting outside his own door.

Tension drawing his stomach tight, Léon placed his key in the lock and turned it. He went inside, adopted a surprised look. "Oh, hello!" he exclaimed.

Robert flashed an earnest grin, or as earnest as he was capable of. "Léon! Your mother and I have been chatting."

Léon was no good at faking. He couldn't even meet Robert's gaze while he thought about how to respond.

Long seconds ticked by from the Delafosse's battered grandfather clock.

Léon watched Robert's expression go from excited to angry. He stood. "You're clearly not excited to see me. I'm sorry for the imposition. I've promised to visit my buyer to inspect a Chinese urn before the afternoon is through, and I'm late. Would you walk me out, Léon?"

Léon looked at his mother and then at Robert. He didn't want to say anything, so he could avoid screwing this good news up, but by not speaking he was screwing everything up all the same. "I've only got a few minutes at home before I have to go back out. I'm due to play accompaniment for the academy dance corps."

"Yes of course," Robert said briskly. "I'll see myself out."

"Léon," Madame Delafosse scolded, with a kind smile to Robert. "Don't be rude! See our visitor out."

Léon slowly began to knot his scarf.

But Robert turned sideways to pass Léon, his body only inches away, and then was hurrying out the door, whisking his cane through the air behind him. "Goodbye to you both, good day, goodbye."

Léon turned in the doorway, mouth opening and closing.

Robert was in the hallway, eyes sparking with anger or sadness or, most probably, a combination of both. He stumbled and gripped the railing, then rushed past the concierge. "What are *you* looking at, Quasimodo?"

Then he was at the bottom of Léon's building, hurling the front door open into brilliant light.

Léon returned to his senses and raced after him.

9.

LÉON WAS BREATHLESS FROM HIS RUN DOWN THE STAIRS. "I'm sorry! Robert, don't go. You caught me by surprise."

Robert came to a stop on the street outside the Delafosse building and slowly turned around. "That much was abundantly clear," he said stiffly. "I'm surprised by you, too."

Léon looked up and down the street, whipped a hand through his hair. "Will you let me walk with you to your appointment? Please?"

Robert burst into motion so suddenly that he lost his balance, jamming his cane into a paving stone. "I'd rather not. I clearly made a mistake coming here."

Léon shoved his hands into his pockets, scowling. This was starting to feel a little unfair. "I needed a second to think. You can't hold that against me."

"I don't want you to have to *think* before you have to do something as simple as see a guest out of your building, which any civilized person would know they ought to do."

"You can call me uncivilized, then," Léon said. He was angry when he said it, but once the ridiculous words were out, he began to smile.

"Uncivilized," Robert said, now with his own smile. He sighed and took on a wondering expression. "What good has civilization done for us, anyway, you might ask. And it's a good question. You ought to ask it." He began speeding down the street, twirling his cane so suddenly that he nearly knocked over a passing charwoman. "Are you coming?" he called behind him.

Léon scrambled to catch up. His shirt came free of his waistband, and he busied himself tucking it back in as he went. It struck him as funny, suddenly, that sometimes one wound up with one's hands in one's pants in public. "What's this about a Chinese urn?"

"I don't know, Léon, because I haven't seen it yet! Oh, nuisance."

"What?"

"I've managed to spear this old brioche with my cane." He waved it about in the air. The pastry was gray brown with street dirt.

"Let me help." Léon kneeled before Robert and, with his bare hands, tugged the brioche from the copper-shod tip of Robert's cane.

"Thank you," said Robert as they continued down the street.

"Why do you carry that, anyway?" Léon asked, wiping his hands on his pants. "You don't seem to need it."

"Because it's got lapis lazuli inlay, that's why. You might as well ask why I have a jeweled tortoise."

"Okay. Why do you have a jeweled tortoise?"

"That seals it, you officially *are* uncivilized." Robert began whistling a jaunty tune as they walked, hopping on unexpected beats of the song. He bought a green silk scarf from a stall and draped it on Léon's shoulder. Léon didn't know if it was a gift or if he was just carrying it.

They reached the Seine and crossed toward the Hotel de Ville. Léon toyed with the edges of the new scarf as they stopped at the highest point of the bridge, staring at the deliverymen sailing shoddy boats down the river, at piled-high crates of clothes, tiles, chickens. Prostitutes lingered along the stone steps leading up from the bridge, faces chalky white, shocks of red on their cheeks.

Was Robert going to tell Léon about the offer he'd made to his mother? Or was Léon being handled, like a bride whose dowry was still under negotiation? Reynaldo had warned him to beware whom he refused. There were many ways to go wrong, especially since Léon didn't know all the rules yet. But he could also go wrong by being too cautious, right?

Léon plucked up his courage. He'd had this feeling the summer before, at home in Vernon, when he'd been standing with Félix over the old quarry, the water far below, knowing he'd survive the fall but still having to fight his every instinct telling him not to jump. "I'm confused by you, Robert" is what he finally said.

Robert lowered his chin to his hand and stared into the water. Two ducks fought over a greasy piece of paper under the bridge. "Of course you're confused by me. I'm confused by me too."

"Oh," Léon said.

"The truth is that *you* confuse me," Robert said.

"I do? No. I'm simple," Léon said.

"No one is simple. You're more complex than you know."

Léon's breath sucked down out of his mouth, left it dry. Robert was right, of course. It was odd, but no one had ever called Léon complicated before. He suspected that no one *wanted* him to be complicated. Especially not his mother and sister. The complex reality of Léon—his attraction to other boys, his desire to be loved, not just to make pure music alone in a turret somewhere—was something that might break his family's heart. He ran his hands through his hair, gave it a little tug to feel the glint of pain.

Robert turned around so he could lean his elbows on the stone, hanging his head back to warm his long neck and jaw in the sunshine. "Nice is boring. It's a horrible waste. It means not owning your desires, not being frank about what you want. It sounds miserable, only nice people never admit that. They just stay quietly unhappy by swallowing down everything that might have made them interesting."

"Who's frank about what they want?" Léon asked. "No one manages that."

"I am," Robert said. "And it's a gift to the world."

Léon laughed. "You're right. You are unusually frank."

He stood next to Robert, almost touching. The sun warmed through his shirt, heated the triangle of his skin that was exposed at the collar. "This is nice," he said.

Robert snorted.

"Sorry. I take it back. Not nice. This moment is . . . authentic and wicked?"

"Mmm, much better."

Even the word *wicked* felt thrilling. Maybe Robert knew what he was talking about. "I embraced Marcel the other night," Léon ventured.

Robert rolled his eyes. "Don't tell me I'm sharing you with *Marcel Proust*. My lord."

Léon felt like his body itself was twinkling. There were people walking by, not that any of them could hear what they were saying amid the hubbub of Paris. He might have money to pay his tuition at the conservatory *and* have a romantic entanglement *and* have his future made. Life was suddenly larger than normal. He rode the wave of his excitement and gave Robert a crooked smile. "Who says you're sharing anything whatsoever about me?"

Robert went still, then turned so his side was against the bridge post, the better to stare into Léon's eyes. "Do you have something to ask me?"

Was Robert asking what Léon thought he was asking? After that fateful party, after wandering into this society where it might be okay to love men, to be odd and passionate and cheery and not manly and stoic, it was like some dam had broken and now his feelings were gushing, all the harder for how long they'd been held back. There was almost no chance that anyone Léon knew was nearby. Léon's eyes widened at the boldness of what he was about to ask. "May I kiss you?" he whispered.

Robert's eyes widened too, and his body went rigid. "That's not the question I meant."

"Oh," Léon said. "I'm sorry." He shut his eyes, mortified.

When he opened them, he saw Robert was now standing a few feet farther away, leaning on his cane. "Come on, let's keep moving. I really do have an appointment about a Chinese urn. And I thought you had somewhere you had to be."

It was like golden daylight had come into a long-closed room, roused Léon from bed to stand at a sunstruck window, and then he'd blinked and the curtain had pulled shut. Tears brimmed at his eyelids, whether from the shock and embarrassment or the cold air of early fall, he didn't know. He wiped at his cheeks, in case there were tears there.

"I'm supposed to be at the ballet rehearsal," Léon said as he fell into step beside Robert. He'd never been late for an accompaniment gig, but if he kept walking with Robert, he'd be late for this one. He wasn't sure if the instructors would still give him his franc. They certainly took every opportunity to yell at the dance corps whenever they missed a step or forgot to think about their hands.

Robert stepped into the street. "You should go to your job. I know you need money. Better to be late than to skip it entirely."

"Okay," Léon said. Once again Robert had found a way to flummox him.

"So, the question you meant to ask me is . . ." Robert prompted.

Finally, Léon cast his arms out in exasperation. "I don't know, what is it?"

Robert threw his own arms into the air, his cane slapping the side of a passing carriage, startling an old woman who'd been snoozing by the window. "You're hopeless. Okay, I'll give you your line, you flailing actor. 'Robert, mon cher Comte de Montesquiou-Fézensac, will you be my patron?'"

Léon stared. The card from the Saussines was still in his satchel. Proper, conventional. Robert was in front of him. He might not be just a patron but someone who would allow Léon to be a version of himself—the "homosexual" version, the real version—that he thought he'd spend his whole life hiding away.

All the same, Robert was unpredictable, cruel and then kind. What would he be promising himself to? Could he trust this man? "Really?" Léon asked, to buy a shred of time.

"You have to ask it," Robert said.

This was the moment. Robert would probably not give him another chance. And if Léon went home, his mother might talk him out of the choice, steer him toward the more conventional path of the Saussines. But Léon didn't want to be conventional. Léon wanted to be great. "Robert, Comte de Montesquiou-Fézensac, will you be my patron?"

Robert went down on one knee, took Léon's hand in his palms. Another passing carriage splashed dank water at his back. "Yes, Léon, a thousand times yes."

Was this a romantic scene, or were they performing a satire of a romantic scene? Léon didn't know and realized that maybe Robert didn't, either.

Robert got back up to his feet and sauntered into the street, waltzing around a donkey cart. Once he was on the far side, he flicked the mud from his shoes and called after Léon. "Perhaps someday we'll also explore that first question of yours!" Then he disappeared into the streets of the Marais.

10.

THE CARD CAME ONE WEEK LATER. IT WAS SHARP IN Léon's jacket pocket, corners poking into the tender skin of his belly. Its text was uncharacteristically spare, considering that it was coming from Robert. "The nineteenth is my birthday. I'm turning eighteen, though I don't count weekends. Would you have lunch with me?"

Léon had read it quickly, then stuffed it in the pocket of his jacket. Now it lived in there, its edges announcing themselves from time to time even while Léon tried to concentrate on other things. It was next to a card from Félix, whose paper was softer and whose text was just as spare: "I walk Clémentine more than I should, because otherwise I'll be home when Cécile calls. She calls too often, but my parents keep inviting her back. There is nothing else to tell you."

Léon and Marcel had a date to go to *Around the World in Eighty Days*. "This show is pablum, mainly for tourists and the bourgeoisie," Marcel said gloomily while they rushed along, hands clapped to their hats so they didn't blow off in the day's bluster. "I almost don't want my name attached to the review."

"Why wouldn't you?" Léon said. "I heard it has hot-air balloons, a working train with a steam whistle, eighty mechanical serpents—"

"And a cast and crew eighteen hundred people strong. I read the posters too. It's just . . . we can't exactly call it *art*, can we?"

So what? thought Léon.

They filed into their seats, right near the front. The house manager came by to greet Marcel by name, asking him if there was anything he needed, saying he hoped he enjoyed the show. "We shall see about *that*," Marcel said darkly as he pulled out his leatherbound journal.

Léon stared at the proscenium. Candle stars studded a wooden midnight sky. Along the edge was a white crust. Marcel explained it was quicklime, to be lit for some dramatic moment when it would cast the whole scene in limelight.

Marcel was busy taking notes, scrutinizing the bits of set that poked out from the curtain folds, giving little sighs or shakes of the head as he scratched in shorthand. It was adorable, how seriously he was taking his task. Léon couldn't resist tenting the program, laying it between them, and placing his hand over Marcel's.

Marcel looked at him, face impassive, then brought his attention back to the stage. Finally, he returned to Léon from whatever distant land his thoughts had brought him to, and a smile curled his lips. He squeezed Léon's hand back, under the shield of the program.

When the curtain dropped for intermission, Léon turned

to Marcel, his mouth wide-open. "Can you believe it?" he asked. "There was a steamer on the high seas, and it exploded! It was on *fire*!"

"Dear Léon," Marcel said gently. "It didn't really explode. It went down a trapdoor."

"I know," Léon said, withdrawing his hand.

"What did you think of the actress who played Aouda?" Marcel asked. "I found her quite convincing."

"Yes," Léon said. "She was quite convincing. Would you like to stretch our legs?"

"I'm going to take some notes. You go, please, enjoy yourself," Marcel said, not taking his gaze up from his pencil and notebook.

Léon slipped down the aisle and into the imposing lobby, painted to look like marble and lined with statues of nymphs and gods. He wandered up to the balcony, to get a view of the set from a new angle. Maybe there would be something he could tell Marcel, to help with his review. When he turned, he saw that much of the audience had returned to their seats, and their eyes were on him. He cast his eyes down shyly, but not before noticing how many of the men had been admiring him. It was almost always men, not women, who were drawn to him—it was like they sensed who he really was.

A little scared, a little excited, he worked his way back to the stairs. One man in particular, seated next to a wife drowning in the ruffles of her collar, took a long drink of Léon with his eyes. Marcel had spoken about meeting men like this in underground clubs, living secret lives entirely separate from their proper society personas. He'd invited Léon to go with him sometime, but Léon hadn't yet dared. *Is this my future?* Léon wondered. *To marry and then spend my life hiding lust and wonder?*

He offered the man a blank smile, then descended the theater's creaking, carpeted stairs. With each step, the sharp edges of the card in his breast pocket poked his ribs. Robert, wanting to spend his most important day with him. That was an honor, wasn't it? Léon should try to live up to it.

By the time he'd made it to his seat, he had a plan.

"This show is closed on Mondays, isn't it?" he asked Marcel.

"Mm-hmm, they all are," Marcel mumbled, lost in his notetaking.

Léon pulled out the card he'd received from Robert, held it out. "I received this. Robert would like to have lunch with me on his birthday. We saw his house, that jeweled tortoise, and each room a different color, and I saw, I saw a blue fur. Anyway, I think this show might actually be just his thing, don't you? All bright lights and adventure and so grand? I can ask around at the conservatory, if anyone knows someone who works for this show, and we could have a small table for lunch right here, set up in the middle of that wooden ocean, maybe they'd even light up the candles above us. That would be *something*, right? Lunch here for Robert's birthday? Quicklime instead of birthday candles?

I mean, even Robert and all his money and connections might not think to arrange that sort of thing for himself."

Marcel took a long time finishing whatever he was writing in his notebook, his face inscrutable. "Robert wants to see you on his birthday. How wonderful for you. He certainly hasn't started to include *me* in any of his functions again. A lunch here would be something, indeed. But Léon, Robert *throws* parties. He doesn't *attend* them. And I certainly don't think"—he stifled a sudden giggle—"that he'd want to spend his birthday surrounded by all this claptrap."

Léon sat back, stung. "Oh."

"It was a good idea, though," Marcel said, patting the back of Léon's hand. "You had no way of knowing how badly he'd take it. And I am glad that he's brought you so fully into his life, I really am. I have my own pathways into high society, it's not as far a climb for me as it is for you, I'm not jealous, really I'm not."

Léon nodded, hands tight in his lap.

"I know you want to be . . . pleasing to your new patron. But don't try too hard. You'll be like me to Robert soon enough, cool to the touch. If you have kept yourself more unavailable from the start, you'll be able to manage that transition more gracefully. Keep some of yourself back, always."

Léon remembered the feel of Marcel's hand grasping his under the program. Maybe what Marcel meant to say was *keep some of yourself back for me.*

Mercifully, the orchestra started up. Léon leaned back in his seat while the lights lowered, the sounds of Marcel's furious scribbling still audible even over the swell of violins and trumpets and drums. Claptrap.

Three hours of a rented carriage and rented groom, pressing and starching of a shirt bought from DiMauro's like Reynaldo had suggested, a gift of a tie pin from Pierre Tremblay, ate up every last franc Léon had earned from playing the Saussine home. Well, one version of that payment; the ten francs from Marcel had gone to iceman, rent, grocery tab, milkman.

Léon had gone the day before to select which carriage he wanted to rent, but when he arrived the morning of Robert's birthday, he learned that the carriage he'd selected had broken an axle. Instead, Léon was waved to the unreserved line, where a tired mare with half a tail chewed weeds before a sloping carriage. Its sides had been scraped in an accident, revealing bright streaks of raw pine. "Hello!" Léon called up to the driver.

A grunt and a toss of the head.

Léon got inside, gave the address of the Montesquiou home, and then settled in for the ride. He had no idea what time it was anymore, but it had been eleven when he passed the steeple clock, which meant he was still roughly on time. The carriage's wheels made a map of Paris's cobblestones on Léon's shuddering jaw, but he liked the sensation that he was part of the road. The window on the left wouldn't open, so he maneuvered to the right side of the carriage to crack the window and feel even more a part of the streets as he passed.

He'd taken plenty of omnibuses before, but it was his first time riding alone in a carriage, and it felt thrilling and decadent. More and more of his life was feeling like it was out of a novel. He settled back in the velvet seat, sighing in satisfaction, and wondered if the people he passed imagined where he was heading, what business this important young man had that was pressing him across town. Through the narrow window at the front, he watched the horse lift her woeful tail and drop a steaming pile of dung on the Rue de Rivoli.

Once the carriage had shuddered to a stop in front of Robert's home, Léon wasn't sure whether he was supposed to go in or wait outside. If only there were a guidebook he could consult. Unfortunately, he was just supposed to *know*. Then there was Robert, whistling as he emerged from his house in a strawberry waistcoat and chocolate pants with a mint-colored cane, the front door closing behind him, pressed gently shut by the white-gloved hands of servants.

Léon waved through the window, and Robert waved back primly, coughed. Then Léon realized that if he had his own groom, that groom would have descended to open the door for Robert. This rented driver was doing no such thing, so it was up to Léon. He swung open the door, hopped into the street, greeted Robert, then held out his hand to help him into the carriage.

For a moment, Robert was clearly aghast at the ripped fabric of the carriage's interior. Then he forced a sprightly expression. "Well, isn't this a gas!"

Léon flushed, then got in and knocked on the carriage window to set the driver into motion, like he'd seen so many do before.

He smiled shyly to Robert as the carriage lurched forward. "What do you get for the birthday of the man who has everything? I don't know the answer. But I maybe do! I thought, he eats in all the finest houses, so I should take him outside!"

"I'm quite unsure what you're trying to say right now," Robert replied. Then he saw the picnic basket at his feet. "Oh my."

When they arrived at the Jardin de Luxembourg, Léon saw, just as they'd planned, Charlotte guarding a patch of grass covered with a gingham picnic cloth. As the carriage came to a stop, Léon stepped out and opened the door. Gawkers paused to take in the count stepping down majestically, dressed like a tray of candy.

As planned, Charlotte disappeared into the crowd, leaving the cloth with its place settings. Picnic basket under his arm, Léon gestured Robert toward it.

They perched on the gingham. Robert was clearly unsure whether to sit directly on the fabric in his fine suit, and so he went only halfway, in a sort of awkward squat.

That tipped the whole situation over. Suddenly it all looked cheap and terrible to Léon: the family tablecloth with the olive oil stain in the center, that refused to ever come out; the chipped Delafosse tableware; the sandwiches from the boring corner place, sweating through their waxed paper. What had he been thinking?

Then he saw Robert's face. His eyes had the same twinkle they'd had when he'd stumbled over Léon asleep on his roof. The thrill of adventure.

Inch by inch, Robert lowered himself to the cloth, until his fine chocolate-colored trousers were right atop the Delafosse picnic gingham, which had been woven by their next-door neighbor back in Vernon.

"This is perfectly rustic," Robert declared after a long and complicated look around.

"Thank you?" Léon said.

"I should tell you that I have always hated my birthday," Robert continued, batting a bee away as he laid himself flat on the cloth. "I know most people reserve that feeling for when they're old, but a birthday . . . it feels like this event where other people are forced to do things for you, and then I find myself hating those supposedly nice things they're doing, and we've all got a little extra burst of tension in our lives now, don't we?"

"I've always liked birthdays," Léon said.

"Today I might like them as well," Robert said. "Because I'd expected nothing at all from you, and you've brought me out of the house when I might have gloomed around all afternoon and stared out of the top window like a tragic heroine from some gothic novel. So thank you. Even the weather is fine today."

Léon glanced up, squinting. It was Paris in early autumn. Not an inch of blue to the sky, though the gray was bright.

A pigeon, tilting its head to look at them through one eye and then the other, took a tentative step on the cloth. Léon waited for Robert to shoo it away, but instead he ripped away the heel of his sandwich baguette, crumbled it in his fingers, and scattered it in on the fabric. The pigeon ate a few crumbs and then, bobbing its head in Léon's direction, lost its courage and flew away.

Robert was a new man on the ride back to his house, talkative and energized. Léon started sweating, then he realized why: Robert had his eyes on Léon's at all moments. Now that he was aware of it, it became all Léon could think of. It made him cast his gaze down all the more, trying to shield himself from some of the intensity.

Through great force of will, Léon forced himself to look into Robert's eyes. There they were, greens and blues under a sharp, fine brow. Léon leaned in.

Robert startled, pressed a hand at Léon's collar to push him to the other side of the carriage. "No."

Léon felt himself flush. "I'm sorry."

"I'm not like that," Robert said. "You've mistaken me."

Shame surged up from Léon's belly, made his skin prickle and turned his chest and armpits slick. Hadn't Robert said precisely that they'd revisit this question of kissing? And now he was rejecting Léon for trying it. Suddenly Léon was very tired of shame. "I see. For—forgive me."

They traveled long minutes in silence, the carriage clattering this way and that, side to side and up and down. Léon breathed through the bad feelings that kept coming up. Robert was unfair and inconsistent. He'd lied to Léon. But maybe Léon deserved lies; maybe honesty wasn't for perverts like him. Maybe he should give this all up, find a girl to marry, become that man in the theater, looking hungrily while his wife read her program. Léon kept his eyes trained outside the window, so Robert wouldn't pick up on what he was feeling, so Léon wouldn't risk losing his patron.

"I'm just not meant for a life of the body in any way, you see," Robert finally said. "My body is disgusting. It brings everything filthy into my life. Only my thoughts are pure. Sometimes . . . I wish I could float away from my body and be just a mind instead."

Léon let himself look at Robert. He was unsure of what to say.

"And now we're at my house," Robert said, opening the carriage door and stepping out.

11.

LÉON HADN'T PLANNED PAST THE CARRIAGE RIDE WITH Robert.

How it had gone when he'd run the day over and over in his mind: he'd given Robert his tie pin in the carriage, they'd embraced goodbye, Robert had given Léon money to pay his fall tuition, then Léon had returned the carriage and walked to the conservatory, where he could work on writing out the tricky allegro passage of his first sonata. But now here he was, sitting on the edge of a patchy velvet seat, cold October air streaming in, no money in his pocket, Robert leaping over a dark gray puddle to his front step. Saussine opportunity long gone, and maybe his chance of securing an Érard concert through Robert gone, too.

Robert paused at the door, looked back at Léon in surprise. "Aren't you coming?"

"Coming?" Léon asked. "Coming to what?"

"My birthday party!"

Robert rapped a complex rhythm with the golden lion's head clapper, then dipped in when a valet opened the mahogany door. The valet peered at the carriage, uncertain, while he waited for Léon to make up his mind.

Léon startled into action, patted his jacket pocket to make

sure the tie pin birthday present was still there, wrapped in its brown paper, then grabbed the Delafosse picnic basket and stepped into the street—and right into the puddle Robert had leaped over.

Shaking out his shoes, Léon gave the driver his last coin and sent him back to the depot. Then he tucked the basket under his elbow and greeted the valet who, after giving Léon's wet shoes a pointed look, allowed him in and closed the door.

The house was full of warmth and light. All the candelabras were lit—in the daytime!—and their light mixed with the bright grays of the autumn sun to give the interior the appearance of midsummer. The jeweled tortoise ambled around a corner and off into the garden.

From upstairs came the sounds of loud whispers and moving furniture. *I'm invited this time,* Léon reminded himself as he prepared to walk up the same staircase he had once snuck up with Marcel. Still, he felt like an intruder. He shook out his coat and placed it on a bone hook while Robert sat on a bench nearby, his valet working off his tight leather boots. "I'm meant to be surprised, I think," Robert said. "I assume you were meant to keep me away for long enough that he could get in to prepare the stage."

"He who?" Léon asked. "Keep you away from what?"

Robert's eyes narrowed as the second boot came off, and the valet began to bend and soften a pair of buttery leather slippers. "You've played out this scheme long enough. There's no need to keep up the ruse."

"I honestly have no idea what you're talking about."

Robert's eyes narrowed even farther, then he found something in Léon's face that made him throw back his head and laugh. "I thought you were the shepherd and me the sheep, but we're both sheep! How delightful! Or perhaps you're a goat. You're more a goat than a sheep, I think."

He dismissed the valet and got to his feet, then threaded his arm through Léon's and tucked their bodies tight against each other, hip to hip. "Baa!"

"I swear," Léon said, "I have no idea—"

"Baa!"

"Baa," Léon said.

The sheep headed up the stairs.

The receiving room, which had held the party where Léon had first met Robert, was closed shut. "Woe is me!" Robert proclaimed loudly. "How sorrowful am I to be all alone on this day of all days, my birthday!"

With that, he turned the knob and threw the door open.

Léon gasped.

"Surprise!"

It was the set of *Around the World in Eighty Days*. Or at least pieces of it. A great cresting wave, the basket of a hot-air balloon, and a desert backdrop. Three belly dancers from the show were gyrating in front of it. Well, two belly dancers from the show, Léon saw now—the third was one of the male dancers, only wearing the belly dancer costume, a skirt of gold coins and a gauzy glittering chemise.

The rest of the room was full of faces Léon recognized

from Robert's earlier party—the countess and Sarah Bernhardt and many young men in tailored suits. Léon dropped behind Robert, to shield himself from view. "What is this? I've never had a birthday party with a set before!" Robert exclaimed, reveling in playing the bad actor.

In response, Sarah Bernhardt climbed up onto a wooden wave and swung around it, leg extended out like a showgirl.

The explanation was clear, but Léon's mind still refused to accept it. This was the set. From the show he'd seen with Marcel. Transported to Robert's house. Marcel had rejected his idea and then done a version of it anyway. It was all impossible, and yet it was all true. He didn't even realize he was still holding the picnic basket until it dropped from his hands and clattered on the parquet floor.

Robert sailed forward into the room, turning in a circle, hands to his chest. "Are we in the Pacific? Why, I do believe we're in the Pacific!"

The room was full of laughter and cheering and young society people clamoring to get close to Robert, which meant no one noticed the upturned basket or the shaking young pianist squatting by the door, assembling apple cores and greasy napkins and empty bottles so he could heap them back into the panels of cracked wicker. Tears warped Léon's vision.

He rubbed them away with the back of his sleeve, and the unpleasant sensation of rough fabric catching on the soft skin of his eyelids turned his shock into anger. That anger found a target when he heard a mellifluous voice from the other side of the room. "Do you like it? Do you really? I knew you would!"

Marcel. Worming his way back into Robert's graces.

Léon kicked the basket, denting the side in and sending the contents scattering across Robert's ballroom floor. He stalked around the edge of the room, young gentlemen and women giving him nervous looks as they parted.

Marcel was with his friend Lucien from the Saussine salon, both of them telling a story—probably about how they got the show's set moved—to Robert. Marcel gesticulated wildly, all the better to make sure he held the count's attention. It was only barely working—Robert was already looking over Marcel's and Lucien's shoulders to see who else was there.

Léon pushed through a circle of gossiping guests to stand directly before the trio of young men. "How *dare* you, Marcel?"

Robert already had his arm out to put around Léon, a smile on his face—he'd probably been about to tell the story of the picnic—but then went still once he noticed the anger radiating off Léon.

Marcel kept his face carefully composed. "Léon? What's gotten into you?"

"What's gotten into me? How *dare* you, Marcel?" Despite his intentions, hot tears appeared on Léon's cheeks.

"I'm sure I don't know what you're talking about," he said, with a *can you believe this is happening?* look to Lucien.

"This party was *my* idea—I suggested it! And you said Robert would *hate* it."

"Léon, this is unwise," Marcel said. "Everyone is staring."

"Let them stare! They should hear about what you did!"

The male dancer came to stand beside Marcel, all toned arms and legs and bangles. Marcel put his arm through his. "This is my friend Claude. He helped me arrange all this."

"Hello there," Claude said, glittering.

"Please do explain," Marcel continued to Léon. "How were you going to arrange this? Were you going to steal a set? You don't have the connections or the money or the . . . anything to pull this off."

"Who's this gem?" Claude asked, holding his hand out to shake Léon's.

Robert cut in, a tender expression on his face. He stood right before Léon, inclining his forehead toward him. For a moment it was like they were alone together again. "Léon, you've given me a wonderful birthday already. I feel perfectly ambivalent about surprise parties, as anyone who has seen into my soul well knows. You don't need to try to take ownership of . . . this."

The trio of pit musicians from the show was still playing, but Léon became aware that the conversations in the room had all stilled. He kept his back to the crowd, knowing that his courage would fail if he looked in their faces. "I'm not taking ownership of this," Léon whispered. "I'm just . . . Marcel lied to my face, Robert. I wanted to take you to this show."

"Is that all?" Robert said, laughing. "Marcel Proust, lying—that's hardly anything to notify the papers about."

Marcel laughed heartily. But the light had left his eyes.

"Now, let this go, Delafosse," Lucien said sharply. "Nothing good will come to a boy like you throwing out baseless accusations in high society."

"'A boy like me'? What does that mean?" Léon asked.

"He means that charm is not an infinite well, even for those who are the best at it," Marcel said. "And you are not the best at it."

The energy in the room had turned cold. All it would take was one word from Robert for him to be ejected forever. He had only Robert—Robert, inconstant Robert!—to count on for help. Léon couldn't appeal to him now, couldn't risk having the count snuff out the warmth of his light. Especially not when his future depended on it.

So instead he turned to Marcel. "You snake. I never want to see you again."

"So long, then," Marcel chirped before pointedly turning his back.

"Goodbye, Robert," Léon said, his voice husky. He spun and stepped toward the exit, nearly colliding with the crowd of staring guests. A mixture of expressions on their faces: sympathy, indifference, contempt. "Excuse me," he mumbled as he pushed his way through.

The Delafosse picnic basket was crouched flat in the corner, like an abused dog, surrounded by a spray of wicker shards from when Léon had kicked it. He couldn't clean it up, not in front of all these staring eyes. He'd dream up some explanation to give his mother later. Passing the basket by, he descended to the entrance hall, his damp shoes squeaking on the wooden floors.

Robert's valet startled to his feet when Léon approached. "Is everything all right, sir?"

Léon wordlessly pointed to his coat. His face impassive, the valet took it down from the bone hook and held it out to him.

Slipping one arm and then the other into the worn and familiar lining, Léon felt a poke against his ribs: the small box that he'd carefully wrapped in paper and string that morning.

He let out a long breath, reached into the pocket with trembling fingers, and pulled out the package. "I'm sorry, sir, would you be willing to give this to Robert?"

"You mean the Count of Montesquiou?" the valet said.

"Yes, the Count of Montesquiou," Léon corrected, face flushing in embarrassment.

The valet's expression softened as he accepted the package. "I'll be sure that he gets it," he said. "If it's all right by you, I'll leave it on his dressing stand tonight, so it will have his full attention."

"Thank you," Léon said. "That's kind."

The valet went to open the front door but paused. "Do you mind if I speak to you directly?" he asked, using the informal *tu*.

For a moment, Léon thought yet another insult was coming his way. Then he saw the earnestness in the valet's eyes. "Yes, I think I'd like that, actually," Léon said, surprising himself by laughing.

The valet was a whiskered, middle-aged man, with a chapped red face and kind, bright blue eyes. He gestured at the house and its upstairs rooms, with the party reverberating. "It's not easy for men like you and me in this world. We get no room for mistakes, and if we fail, we can't turn to our family for help getting us back in. We got our one shot and that's it."

Léon nodded. There was no mistaking Léon for a gentleman, that was for sure, and the valet clearly knew it.

"But you have more going for you than most of the boys who come through here. You have your talent and the way that Robert looks at you . . . He's not the warmest soul, our Robert, and you've unlocked something rare in him. A kindness, I guess you could call it? You and me, we both know we could easily be those urchins begging on the street outside. All it takes is one word from someone like the count. But that word can also get you what you need. Getting a favor or two is really the only shot we got. The system has us blocked out, so something like Robert's fancy is the best option we have. It's worth taking it when and if it comes our way."

"Okay. Thank you," Léon said.

The valet paused, his hand on the door handle. "Here's what I'd do, son. I'd send him a card tomorrow, when it's just an ordinary day and not his birthday. Don't try for nothing fancy. It's better that you don't. He'll be asking if he's got a card from you all day, I know it. He'd love to get some sweet little word."

"Thank you for the help," Léon said, knotting his scarf. "Really."

The valet shook the little box, the brass tie pin rattling inside. "I'll put this at his bedside. I promise you, he'll be glad for it."

Léon stepped out of the Montesquiou home into the bustle of the streets. He trudged past the old woman selling flowers on the corner and went off to the conservatory, where he could find the mercy and comfort of his piano, at least until the closing bell.

12.

IT TOOK A FEW HOURS IN A PRACTICE ROOM FOR LÉON to find calm. His latest composition took him to a still quarry pond, heavy sky above cool air, lying on moss beside a boy with red hair. As he played through the coda, his lips were on Félix's, something that had never happened in real life. It was just what the sonata needed—surprise, heat, resolution. Once he'd finished marking up his music, this familiar practice room, with its old wood and its piano with the rattling C-sharp, felt more of a home than Robert's house or even his family's Paris apartment. Léon closed the keyboard cover and stood, stretching, the corners of his mouth pulling into a long smile, like he'd woken from a nap with tortured dreams to find the monsters hadn't been real after all.

He startled. Charlotte! He hadn't seen her since the birthday lunch—she'd be dying to know how the picnic went.

Léon shrugged into his coat as he made his way down the conservatory's narrow, creaking halls, left its dim gaslight for the only slightly brighter sky.

How would he present the day to his sister and mother? A successful lunch, a horrible party, a betrayal followed by the valet's unexpected encouragement. He decided he wouldn't tell them about what Marcel had done. It would only upset them, and since he didn't quite know what he was going to do next, he'd rather not have them jumping all over him, deciding his next course for him. He paused in front of the apartment door, preparing for the onslaught of his family.

There was no onslaught.

His mother and sister didn't even notice him come in. They were at the far end of the apartment, peering into a chest.

Léon padded over. "What is it?"

"It's my traveling chest, you dolt," Charlotte said.

"What is it doing out?"

"I'm traveling."

Léon nodded. "Okay, great. Very helpful, thank you." He watched as his mother folded one of Charlotte's chemises and placed it gently in the chest. "No, not that one, only new Paris clothes," Charlotte said.

"There aren't that many new Paris clothes. I'm afraid André will have to occasionally see you wearing clothing that he's already seen."

"Why are you getting to see André?" Léon asked. "Is he coming to visit?"

"Léon, where is your head? I'm *packing a chest.*"

An embarrassment to high society and now cut out of the intimate doings of his family—it was too much. Léon cried out. "Maman, you're letting her visit André? I thought this whole bring-Charlotte-to-Paris maneuver was about protecting her 'immortal chastity.' Now you're helping her pack *chemises*?"

"Whose side are you on here?" Charlotte sputtered. "Did I not spend the whole morning helping you prepare for your birthday picnic with the count?" Her voice softened. "Oh, right, how did that go?"

Before Léon could answer, her attention had returned to her traveling chest. "No, I think I should pack the blue-and-white dress and wear the gray, not the other way around. Don't you think so, Maman?"

"It went well," Léon said, his voice trailing off as he realized he didn't have either of their attention. "Both of you, stop packing for a moment and explain to me what's going on."

"I got a new letter from André," Charlotte said. She plucked a stack of curling pages from the writing desk. They were covered in blue ink, blotches and energetic underlinings everywhere. She thrust them at Léon. "Here, read."

He took the stack and flipped through. There had to be twenty pages. "Can you give me a summary?"

"His father died," Madame Delafosse said.

"Oh," Léon said. He'd never much liked André's father, who had often sent Léon home without bread because he was reserving the baguettes that remained for his favorite customers. Then again, that didn't mean that Léon wanted him dead or anything. Just to be nicer.

"That means André is running the bakery now," Charlotte said, eyes gleaming.

Léon gave a quick glance to their mother, who nodded in confirmation. This changed everything. Before, André had been a boy. Now, he was a businessman and a central figure of the town, with good prospects ahead of him. Marriage would have been out of the question before, but now . . .

"Charlotte!" Léon said, embracing her.

"I really can't believe it," she said, with another look to their mother to make sure that her good luck was still holding.

"How did he die?" Léon asked, searching through a bowl of plums for the ripest.

"Léon," his mother scolded.

"Heart attack." Charlotte beamed. "Really awful."

"Charlotte!" Madame Delafosse said, sitting heavily in a chair.

"Maman. André's father used to take a belt to him every day after dinner, just as a way to unwind before bed. I know it's not very kind to be glad that someone has died, but I'm still going to keep my mourning of André's father to a quiet minimum."

"In any case," Madame Delafosse said, "we now have to get Charlotte back to Vernon as soon as possible, before someone else gets her hands on André. We don't want Odile stepping back into your territory."

Charlotte scoffed. "Odile Toussaint? Maman, she might be worried about *me*, but I'm not worried about *her*."

"Odile is very pretty. You can see why I'm concerned," Madame Delafosse said to Léon with a conspiratorial look.

He nodded gravely.

"I refuse to be pitted against a member of my own sex. I simply refuse!" Charlotte said.

Madame Delafosse chortled in response.

"Are you letting Charlotte travel alone?" Léon asked. It was then that it fully sunk in that there were two chests out. His mother's was already closed and battened. "You're both going?"

"My father was working and living full-time at a mine in Tannerre-en-Puisaye at age thirteen," Madame Delafosse said. "I know you can get yourself back and forth to classes for a week or two."

Léon looked around the apartment. He knew where to buy his bread and vegetables and cheese. He knew where to empty the pots, how to handle the hissing radiator. His mother was technically right. But still, he was surprised to be offered this independence.

"There are six francs under the chipped plate, enough to see you well into next month. I know Professor Marmontel will help you if you have any big problems. You'll send me an update in the morning post every day, and you'll concentrate on your practice and compositions. I know you will, darling."

"Why does it sound like you're leaving now?"

"Not now. The train's at 7:20, so we're leaving in three hours."

"You're not serious! Are you two really abandoning me?"

Charlotte whirled on Léon. "Spare me. I will never, not in my whole life, get what you're about to get: time on your own, actual independence, no one looking over your shoulder or caring what the lower half of your body might be interested in, or who is interested in it. Maybe once I'm old and wrinkled and can't conceive babies and André has,

I don't know, fallen into a well and disappeared or some-thing, then I'll get a shred of independence, but even then, everyone would push me to live with some other spinster cousin to prevent this freedom that you're getting just as a matter of course. So don't go looking at me for sympathy. I'm not even allowed to ride a bike, for God's sake, or don't you remember?"

"Not that that stopped you," Léon said darkly.

As he watched Charlotte finish her packing, Léon realized she was right about one thing: an incredible, freewheeling openness was in front of him. Of course Charlotte was right. She was always right. He'd wake up when he wanted. He'd practice when he wanted. He'd spend a day eating only soft bread and a hunk of chocolate. He'd stay out late.

Or not spend his nights at home at all.

Charlotte was piling stockings in her arms, each of them thick with darning repairs. He pressed her against him, the stockings a fuzzy lump between their bodies. "I really am so happy for you, Charlotte."

She went rigid, then relaxed. "Thank you. You should visit as soon as you can, okay?"

"You'll invite me to the wedding?"

"Not so fast. Who knows if there's going to be a wed-ding?" Charlotte said as she dumped the stockings in her traveling chest. It was heavy enough now that it made her bed sag—the bed that would soon be empty.

Of course there was going to be a wedding, barring something wild and unforeseen. Léon had seen the way that

Charlotte and André looked at each other. All André had to do was ask for her hand and it was done. Since he needed help running the bakery, he'd be asking soon. André's father would have forbidden such a lowly union, but he had no say in it now.

"If there *is* a wedding, of course I'll be scheduling it around you, Brother."

"Charlotte, I'll miss you."

"Thank you. I'll miss you too. Now, um, I need you to sit on my traveling chest so I can latch it."

Just a few short hours later, he went to the Saint-Lazare station with them, helped muscle Charlotte's and his mother's baggage onto the train car, waved goodbye, and walked slowly through the streets of Paris back to the apartment. When he closed the front door, the sound of it echoed in the empty space.

He folded the two extra screens, unscrewed the legs from his mother's and sister's beds, and propped them up against the wall. He stood in the middle of the wood floor and looked at the apartment. *His* apartment, at least for a while.

He sat at the writing desk and selected a piece of pink vellum. He refilled the well with deep blue ink. After considering his words for a moment, he began to write.

Dear Robert, the letter began. *On this, the first day of your eighteenth year, I unexpectedly find myself at home alone.*

13.

ROBERT'S EXCITED REPLY CAME IN THE EVENING MAIL, and when Léon woke up the next morning, he found the count in the dawn street below his window, leaning serenely against a lamppost, reading a slim, clothbound book.

"This is really too grand," Robert said as he followed Léon up the stairs. "I hadn't realized how tired I was of my own life until you offered me a different one. I'll love being here. It's so delightfully plain!"

Léon was worried they wouldn't know how to be in his apartment together, but Robert had brought his favorite pens and papers and a tin box of tea leaves, and soon got to writing. He worked through the day, occasionally trying out a word or a phrase on Léon. He stayed in the Delafosse apartment while Léon went to the conservatory for his tutorials and was there waiting when he returned. They had dinner at the brasserie on the corner to finish the day, after which Robert headed home, whistling. "Tomorrow morning, get some croissants for us before I arrive, I left some money on the counter," he called over his shoulder.

He'd left twenty francs on the counter—enough for a thousand croissants.

They spent a week that way, each day the same. Léon

enjoyed the daily trip out for pastries, the morning sunshine on his face, fresh air in place of the stale cigar scent Robert left behind in the Delafosse apartment. He'd walk to the good boulangerie—not the one right at the bottom of his building but the one two blocks over, that made its croissants with real butter and not shortening. Then, with the delicate pastries adding barely any weight at all to his knitted sack, he returned home.

Even though Léon's croissant run took only ten minutes, Robert somehow always timed his arrival so that he would appear before Léon got back, the long line of his body leaning against the front door. They would embrace, then head upstairs to get to work—Robert on his poems, Léon on finishing his sonata and preparing for his music history exam.

Today Robert lingered behind Léon on the stairs, letting the metal coffee canteen Céleste had prepared ring out against the bars of the twisting banister. The pitch was low from the heaviness of the liquid inside. They didn't say a word to each other as Léon unlocked the door and opened it, Robert slipping in first. The reedy count adventured through the Delafosse apartment like he was in some fabulous underground cave, feet light, eyes attentive, delicate gloved fingers running over the grime between the kitchen tiles, breathing against the dusty window as he glanced out at the mortals going about their business in the street below.

Energized, Robert lay on Léon's bed, took out his leather book, and began to scribble.

Léon followed behind, heating the cups on a ceramic tile

he'd placed over the gas flame, pouring in coffee and adding some of the frothy milk that had arrived that morning, the bottles lining the wooden crates in the building entranceway. He delivered Robert's cup to his side of the Delafosse apartment. The count didn't acknowledge it, concentrating on what must have been a tricky turn of phrase. He chewed on the end of his pencil, evidently far beyond ordinary human concerns like food and drink, but Léon knew it was only a matter of minutes until he'd smell the coffee and would be sipping.

Today, Léon sat down at the piano.

Robert had had it delivered the day before, conspiring with the concierge to keep the delivery secret from Léon until he walked in and saw his new instrument, right where his sister's cot had been. The piano was shiny and solid, its notes a little bright and shallow from the upright frame, but perfectly adequate for practicing at home.

He tested the keys for their weight and feel. He bent back the cover of his étude book, so it would lie flat. Then he played.

Léon would look up between movements, listening to the scritch of Robert's pencil. When he was sure Robert's attention was in his poetry, he'd work on his own compositions, playing them from heart and then settling into the task of converting them to notes on inked paper. It continued to be Félix who entered his mind when he was composing. Maybe it was just because Vernon was so far away from here, from everything that worried Léon in his everyday life. Léon's mind went to their walks by the lowing cattle, the tall, stiff grass poking at their skin even through their heavy cotton clothing, the clouds drifting across blue sky. The drops of sweat that dotted the fabric over Félix's chest. He continued to kiss Félix when he imagined his latest piece, and the perverse joy of that, secret to anyone but him, made his heart—and the notes—race. He lifted Félix's shirt in his imagination, lay the side of his head against his friend's bare belly. No one could know this secret desire, but the sonata itself knew somehow. *A breakthrough,* Marmontel had called it when Léon played the latest version for him.

Once they'd both worked long enough to take a pause, Robert would read a few lines out loud, and Léon would play him a few lines of his composition. Never the Félix scenes—those felt too private. Then it was back to silent labor. On most days this process could repeat for hours, but today they were interrupted by a knock on the door.

It was the countess, but not as Léon had ever seen her before. She wore a man's linen suit, the fabric was tailored tight to her curves. Her nails and face were unadorned, and she somehow had made her breasts vanish; they must have been bound beneath fabric. She'd rolled and pinned her hair, hiding most of it under a jaunty cap. Robert gave her the jostling sort of cheek kisses that men usually reserved for each other. "Hello, Beckwith."

Beckwith winked at Léon. "Lovely to see you again, Léon Delafosse."

"Won't you come in?" Léon managed to say. Normally he'd

use her title, but that was apparently not what one did with Beckwith. He stared at her, agog.

Beckwith came in, did a full turn, taking in the apartment, before she saw Léon's stare. "Do you like my suit?"

"I do, Countess," Léon said.

"Not today, I'm not. I'm a count if anything, but I'd rather just be Beckwith."

"Shall we get started?" Robert asked briskly.

"That is a fine idea," Beckwith said, laying a basket on the table. "I brought lunch." Out came metal tins with boiled fish, cooked lettuces, fresh berries. Léon lost himself in the surprise of it all before he startled and busied himself getting down plates and glasses, rubbing any smudgy bits with his sleeve before setting them on the table.

The food was pushed to the edges of the table and ignored, because Beckwith had also brought along a calendar and empty sheets of paper, three charcoals, and what appeared to be a leatherbound address book.

"Excellent," Robert said, rubbing his hands.

"What's happening?" Léon asked.

"Your future, darling," said Beckwith.

"Oh!"

"Robert is your patron, but I've decided that I will be your patron *saint*. I couldn't miss out on all this fun," Beckwith said.

Robert arranged the blank pieces of paper around the calendar. "I feel like Napoleon carving up Switzerland!"

Léon was more worried about Beckwith's glass, which

was oily and had an old strawberry seed stuck to the rim. Maybe no one else would notice. He could hope.

"We start you with the Dénons," Robert said. "That's an easy invite, and they always have the Levains at their at-homes, which means—"

"Access to the Bismarcks, and with them come the Battersbys, with the Érard as the official stamp of society approval at the end of all of it."

"The Battersbys are the barons of some English place, which means they could get us to Queen Victoria, who would get that severe and muddled look hearing our Léon play, the one that means she's actually enjoying it very much."

"Five steps to Buckingham! The one thing I would add, though, is an initial stop at your family's very own new pavilion near Versailles, Robert. Léon's performance at the Saussines made enough of an impression that we need to erase the memory, restart him as *yours*. His rise should begin with *you*. If your party is grand enough, it will."

Robert thought about it, then nodded. "That does sound wise."

At first it felt wonderful to have them caring about his future so passionately, but as their conversation continued, the feeling turned sour. He was a creature to them, that they could drive forward like they would a beloved ox. Léon felt hot within his shirt, and he was speaking before he knew what he was saying. "Don't you think you ought to check with me about all these plans?"

Beckwith startled, as if Léon had just flung something. "Don't you *want* to play for the Queen of England?"

Léon paused, the flush of his irritation fading. Beckwith was too beautiful to stay irritated with for long. "Yes, of course."

Beckwith laid a hand on his arm. "Oh, good. Then it's settled. You're right, Léon, we should provide you with options. How about this? We could take five different steps and land you in Boston with Isabella Stewart Gardner rather than in England with Queen Victoria. Robert, what do you think of that?"

Robert shuddered. "An ocean passage. Green is not a great color for my skin. Before I forget, Léon, some logistics. I've gotten my father to open you an account at Mallet. On the first of each month, his bankers will add fifty francs to it. It is for you to use as you need, to prepare yourself for the season's events culminating in the Érard concert. At the end of the term, we'll also deposit enough money for you to pay for the next at the conservatory, if continuing your education still seems a wise use of your time. When you're traveling with me, you won't need to pay for anything, of course. But I suppose from time to time you might not be with me."

"Let us all banish the thought!" Beckwith exclaimed. "You're too adorable together."

Léon had been hovering with a handkerchief, in case he spied some dirt that needed wiping away. He lowered himself into a chair and leaned over the table, handkerchief fluttering to the floor, forgotten. It was all coming true. A patron, and a plan. His family would be secure. Those calm, blissfully unaware moments when he was lost at the piano, those might never be taken away from him now. "I wonder—well, do you think I might be able to secure enough seats to the Érard recital to invite, not just high society, but other sorts of people? Who don't help get me closer to playing for the Queen of England?"

Beckwith snickered. "Ah yes! Let's get your fellow students good and jealous."

Léon shook his head. "No, I don't want all my friends to hate me, thank you. I was thinking of my family. My mother. My sister and her boyfriend . . . or fiancé, or maybe husband, depending on the timing." His mind went to Félix too. But his time with Félix was so private; he didn't want it to be witnessed and ruined by so many others. Besides, Félix couldn't spare a day to come to Paris just to hear Léon play.

Robert and Beckwith shared a look. Then Robert nodded. "Of course. We'll set aside however many seats you need."

Beckwith consulted the calendar, marking it with delicate strokes of charcoal. "The Érard concert would also fit quite naturally between the Levain and the Bismarck salons."

Robert cast a glance at Léon, then gestured expansively to the seating chart on the wall. "I sent that plan to Madame Delafosse to convince her to give her son up to me, and it's for none other than the Érard. This has been meant to be from the start. I'll get the necessary letters sent out in the evening post. It's as if this is all foreordained, I could swear it."

"Now, about the Stewart Gardner possibility," Beckwith prompted.

For the next hour Robert and Beckwith settled into the calendar, marking up dates and drawing arrows from option to option, all leading up to the spring, where one date was blacked through—the one when they'd decided Léon would play for the Queen of England. He dreamily chewed on a piece of smoked fish as he looked at that charcoaled square. "What happens after this?" he asked.

He'd interrupted Robert and Beckwith midstream. They turned to look at him. "What happens after *what*?" Beckwith asked.

Léon tapped the blacked-out square, his fingertip purpling with wet ink. "After I play for the queen?"

Robert laughed. "You want to know what you'll do *after* you play for Queen Victoria?"

Léon nodded. It did sound a little funny when Robert put it that way.

Beckwith closed her eyes and clasped her hands before her forehead, like a fairy prince casting some spell. Then she opened them. "That's when you do your American tour, I do believe. Stewart Gardner and then more! Not just Boston but New York and Philadelphia."

Robert's eyes opened wide. "Would you believe I've never been to the New World at all, not once?"

"Nor have I!" Beckwith exclaimed. "We'll romp right through, like pioneers. We'll eat, what is it, cornbread? I was just reading this morning that they're about to add a new state called Wyoming. How exotic! Can you just imagine?"

Robert leaned in conspiratorially. "You know, I did meet the Stewart Gardners the other month. They spoke excellent French and wore fashionable clothes. It was all very surprising. Isabella is just the beauty she's said to be."

Beckwith clapped. "A Delafosse tour of North America! Delightful. Where *do* you go after you play for the queen? It's an excellent question, and now we have our answer. We go to Boston!"

"And after that, perhaps Wy-oh-ming!" Robert said with a wink. "We'll need to get our shotguns and stagecoaches ready."

"I don't understand why you're doing this for me," Léon said. The question came out of nowhere, surprising even himself.

Beckwith held up a finger to stop Robert when he started to answer. "Let me handle this. It's a fair question from your pianist." She selected a slim piece of smoked fish, laid it out on her plate, then proceeded to ignore it. "If you haven't noticed, dear Léon, our lives are a little shallow and also a little boring."

She held her hand up to silence Robert before her cousin could even begin to protest. "Robert has his poetry to broaden him and help him touch the Beyond, of course, but even that might not be enough. He would never admit it, of course, would you, Robert dear? Léon, a young elfin creature like yourself, entering into our lives from such humble beginnings, is a cause for much celebration. We have too few concerns of our own, you see, to make our existences worth living otherwise."

Léon wasn't sure how to take that, and it must have showed on his face.

Robert smiled gently. "All Beckwith means is that it feels nice to care for someone. It is nice to care for *you*, Léon."

"There!" Beckwith said. "Much better said. Thank you, Robert."

Léon's gaze wandered to his shiny, new piano, his first gift from Robert and surely not his last, filling the space where his sister's bed used to be.

14.

Dear Léon,

~~I assume you heard the news about your Charlotte's wedding.~~ I will be looking forward to seeing you at Charlotte's wedding. Not much has changed here to tell you about, but maybe I can tell you all the things that are still the same and that will make you laugh.

Father has slipped further into the drink, and I feel like I am in charge of the farm now. It is not the life I'd imagined for myself, but it also has plenty of pleasure in it. I have more ducks than ever because Father is not here to tell me to sell the males.

If you let me know what coach you will be taking back here, I would like to meet it.

Your friend,
Félix

Dear Félix,

I will be taking a train home! The time for coaches is past. I will be on the one that arrives at 1:30, but don't worry about meeting me. I'm fine hiring a porter for my case. I will tell you all about train travel and the excitements *of Paris when I see you at my sister's reception. (I hope she has invited you. I'm sure that of course she has.)*

I look forward to hearing all about your ducks and about Cécile of course.

Can you believe Charlotte is getting married? Her love affair with André has worked out in the end.

Your friend,
Léon

Today would be Léon's second time taking a train. After his initial conservatory audition, whenever they'd had to travel between Vernon and Paris, the Delafosses had done like most people of their station did: bought seats on a coach and took the bumpy carriage trails from town to town and through dense forest. Unless they needed to speed Charlotte home to marry a certain eligible baker, of course. That called for the train.

So did traveling home to attend his sister's wedding. It didn't hurt that he was currently getting fifty francs a month deposited into his bank account. He was now the sort of person who took a train.

Léon rushed through the grand glass-and-iron entrance of the Gare Saint-Lazare, stopping briefly at the counter to buy his ticket before hurrying to his platform. He still had fifteen minutes until the train left, and he wanted to be nicely installed and reading his music theory book before the whistle blew. He intended to get the full train experience, to sink into the noise of the conductors gossiping, the custodians sweeping, the stokers shoveling coal into the hissing locomotive.

He'd been late leaving the Érard rehearsal. Robert had unexpectedly brought the tailor to fit him for his recital suit, and each time Léon tried to inch his way toward the door, there was a new measurement to take, a new color swatch to drape against his skin, a new shoe to try from a bottomless steamer trunk of samples. Finally, Léon had succeeded in begging his way out the door and rushing into Robert's carriage.

Now, at the station, Léon had enough time to really think about where he was heading.

Home to Vernon. For the first time in almost a year.

Home to Vernon. For his sister's wedding.

Home to Vernon. Freckles and a sweet, old horse.

He realized he was arriving empty-handed. Shit. He had plenty of coins jangling in the pockets of his crisp, new suit, so he stopped at the station florist to pick out a bouquet of cheerful wildflowers set in a jar of blue-tinted glass. A man nearby was selling prints, and Léon flipped through them until he found one in sepia of a somber, old man riding a penny-farthing. It wasn't quite a wedding card, but it would make Charlotte laugh. That was good enough, wasn't it? He would think of something to write on the back while he was on the train.

Whistling, he overpaid the vendor and turned around to go to his platform—and nearly ran straight into Marcel Proust.

Léon set his case down. Marcel was staring at him, hands

folded in front of his waistcoat and an amused expression on his drooping face. Next to him was an older woman, half of her face covered with an intricate lace shawl. It couldn't hide her dancing eyes.

"Hello there, Léon Delafosse," Marcel said.

Léon nodded curtly.

Marcel blew out a stream of air, enough to send the ends of his mustache flying. "Léon, this is my mother, Jeanne."

For a moment Léon thought she wasn't going to acknowledge him. But then she looked his way. "Léon Delafosse? The composer? France's Mozart?"

Léon could feel his face flush. "I think 'France's Mozart' might be overselling it," he said. "We actually met before, a few weeks ago, when I visited Marcel after he . . . after Robert de Montesquiou's party."

"France's Schubert, then," Marcel said, winking.

For a searing moment, Léon still hated Marcel.

Then he saw bits of himself in the gossip columnist's hopeful, nervous eyes. He was just an awkward person trying to get ahead, to be loved, and he was working hard at it—just like Léon was. And Marcel might have won the battle of Robert's birthday, but hadn't Léon won the war? Couldn't he afford to forgive him?

He'd hated Marcel like a brother. Which meant he also loved him like a brother. Léon tipped his hat and gave the old woman a warm smile. "It is a pleasure to meet you, Madame Proust."

Amid the bustling crowd, Jeanne rapped her cane on the

tiles of the station's floor, then pointed it toward the tearoom across the street. "Léon Delafosse, you are coming with my son and me for a hot tea. I won't accept a no."

"That's very kind of you," Léon said, shifting the jar of flowers from one sweating palm to the other. "But I have a train to catch. It's leaving in a few minutes."

"Back to Vernon?" Marcel asked. "There's a train every two hours on the Rouen line now, you know. Or maybe it's every three. In any case, they're frequent."

"Yes, but this is for my sister's reception. She's being married at mass tomorrow."

"Those Rouen line trains are never on time. Are they, Maman?" Marcel asked.

"Never on time," Madame Proust said, shaking her head. "My train last week was at least two months late."

Léon laughed despite himself. He gave Marcel a meaningful look. *I forgive you. I'm not foisting you off.* "Maybe another time."

"Maybe *this* time," Madame Proust said. "For you see, I really do insist. Your sister will understand. Marcel and I were just discussing his trip to England. He was supposed to travel with his cousin Lionel, but Lionel was called up early for his military service, and Marcel needs a friend to travel with."

Léon could see Marcel was at a loss for words. He looked beseechingly at his mother, then when his eyes returned to Léon's, they were filled with a soft sort of fear. He was being exposed, or something had been said that could make him be rejected. Léon wasn't sure what was happening here, but there was more than was being stated.

A train whistle blew. People started rushing toward a train. Léon's train.

"This trip is important," Madame Proust continued, "because we have secured a visit to the Kensington palace for a reception. We don't know if the queen will be there, but members of the royal family will be. Lionel is quite gifted as a singer, so his performance was the context, but that context is gone. And that performance slot is open now. When we withdraw Lionel, we could suggest another. Do you understand my meaning?"

"You want me to go to England with Marcel and play for the queen?"

"*Maybe* the queen," Marcel quickly amended.

"What I want," Madame Proust said, "is for you to come to tea at the tearoom across from the station. Perhaps the subject of playing for the queen will come up. Or perhaps I just want to spend time with a handsome young man such as yourself. What can I say?"

"*Maman,*" Marcel said, scandalized. He started toward the ticket counter. "Come, I'll find out when the next train is."

"It's in two and a half hours," Léon sighed. "I already checked, in case I missed this one." He would be late for his sister's reception. But playing for the queen would unlock everything for him, and Robert hadn't yet managed to secure a date for it. Wouldn't having two avenues to Kensington be better than having one? Surely Robert would want him to pursue this opportunity as a fallback, if nothing else. Léon wavered, then set the wildflowers down on the ground beneath the big station clock. Maybe they would still be there when he got back from the tearoom. If they weren't, he could buy some more.

"Now, about that Érard recital," Marcel said, linking arms with Léon on one side and his mother on the other as they headed to the tearoom. "Tickets sold out the first day, but I was hoping you might be able to help out an old friend."

15.

BY VERNON TRADITION, EVERYONE UNDER EIGHTEEN who wasn't busy with chores or schoolwork or kissing met the trains from Paris. The loud chug of the steam engine and the plumes of black smoke were too appealing to ignore. Just the previous summer, Léon had been one of those teenagers hooting and running alongside the train, standing under the bridge and cheering as it rumbled over. Now he was the person riding the train. In the first-class carriage no less. It was quite a thing.

He stepped down from the car with a new English wicker suitcase in his hand. Everyone else who got off the train was scooped up by waiting family, greeted by tears and hugs and handshakes, then off to a waiting horse carriage or the dusty footpath into town. Léon was left to make his way alone along the platform, his new black shoes ringing out on the chipped stones.

Once the local young people had chased the departing train, shouting with every shriek of the steam engine, they came back around and saw Léon making his way through the station hall and onto the streets of his hometown. Cécile, dusky and pretty, put a hand on the rough cotton waist of her pants and cocked out her hip, arm out at an angle, like a teapot. Or, Léon realized with a startle, in a parody of a cultured gentleman. A parody of him.

She didn't recognize him. Not with this smooth, trimmed hair, the tailored wool jacket, the Italian shoes. Léon set down the case and smiled. "Cécile? Claude? Jean?"

Cécile's mouth fell open. "Léon? *Our* Léon Delafosse?!"

He nodded, grinning.

They surged forward, stroking his sleeve, mussing his hair. Claude took up his case, turned it upside down to look at all the joints and fastenings. "What happened to your steamer?"

"The trunk's back in Paris," Léon said. "I'm going back on the evening train tomorrow. Rehearsals for a big concert I have next week." He regretted saying "big" as soon as he did. Jean and Claude looked suitably impressed, but Cécile was having none of it.

"Excuse me, a big concert, well, well! Next it will be off across the Channel to have tea with Queen Victoria."

"Actually . . ." Léon said, his voice trailing off.

"Come *on*," Claude said, his eyes shining. "Are you serious?"

Léon nodded, then thought for a moment about the correct words in English. "It is lovely to meet you, Your Majesty."

"Yes!" "Thank you!" "A biscuit, please!" "What time is it?" Cécile, Jean, and Claude added in English before running out of phrases and falling into laughter.

Cécile bowed low. "Where are we going, Milord Delafosse? To your house?"

"No time," Léon said, looking around for Félix. But of course he wasn't there. Léon had missed the train he was supposed to be on, and Félix couldn't spend the whole day waiting around. "I'm heading to Charlotte's reception."

"Oh, you mean the new wife of André!" Claude said.

"Not until tomorrow, she isn't," Léon said. "That's what I'm here for."

Coming through the trail that snaked through the forest, hoofbeats. Hoofbeats!

A figure approached, a gentle mare clopping along beside him. He was taller and thinner than Léon remembered.

He pulled Clémentine to a stop and dismounted. For a moment his face was too shadowed by the sunset to make out, and then it resolved. Pale skin, save for a long sunburnt nose, red hair choppy and scattered. Félix.

"I saw them going into the inn for the party hours ago," he said. He'd always been the quietest of the village boys, quieter than even Léon. He was still that boy, even if his features were a man's frame now. "Hi, Léon. I was worried you weren't coming."

Félix seemed nervous, keeping most of his attention on the dusty ground.

"It's good to see you," Léon said.

Félix nodded swiftly.

"I know I'm late," Léon said, pulling his gaze away from Félix. "Did you come to the earlier train too?"

Félix shrugged. Of course he had, but he didn't want Léon to feel bad. "I grazed Clémentine all morning," Félix said.

"She's getting on in years, but she's got enough energy to carry the two of us. We can ride to the inn together."

"Really?" Léon said. "Thank you. I'm feeling like a bad brother, and I'll get there faster on a horse."

"It was my turn to ride Clémentine with Félix," Claude huffed. "But it's fine, Cécile and I can walk."

Cécile stood demurely beside Clémentine, caressing the horse's broad haunch while she peered at Félix. "It's too bad she can't take the three of us. I do like to ride her too, Félix. You know that."

Félix blushed furiously.

"Sorry, everyone. You'll get many chances to ride with Félix, and I have only this one," Léon said.

"Gentleman's privileges," Cécile said darkly.

Félix stroked Clémentine's flank, a mild dappled gray. "You get on first," he said to Léon. "She likes me to be at back and holding the reins."

Léon handed his suitcase to Félix, then mounted Clémentine, settling into her saddle and stroking her strong and soft neck, smoothing her mane so it fell neatly on one side. Félix handed him back the case, and Léon clutched it to his belly as his childhood friend mounted behind him, his legs wiry and tight around Léon's hips.

Cécile raised a hand and curved it toward them. It was a wistful gesture, half a wave, half a goodbye.

They started away from the station, the gravel path switching to ruined paving stone, Clémentine's iron-soled hoofs ringing out as she went. Léon realized he'd missed the jerky, jostling rhythm of riding a horse. Robert's and Marcel's carriages didn't feel anything like this.

Félix's sunburnt hands snaked under Léon's own jacketed arms. When Léon looked down, he could almost imagine those hands were his own. They rode in silence, Léon taking in the shifting muscles of Félix's forearms, the bone of his wrist, the scab on the back of the right hand, soil beneath the nails that hadn't been bitten to the quick. He imagined what Félix's hands would feel like if he placed his own hands over them, his hands that were kept soft by their different sort of work. In the early evening air, he could detect Félix's breath wafting over his shoulder, sweet and just a little milk sour.

"Thank you for your letters," Léon said.

"I'm always glad when you write back. Everything seems to be going so well for you, I'm surprised you have the time to write at all."

Léon held his breath at that. His letters were all cheer, all the time, exaggerations of every good feeling with none of the bad ones. He wanted Félix to be proud. He wanted Félix not to ask too many questions.

"There are a lot of rumors about what happened to you," Félix said. "Not that I believe them."

Léon's heart quickened. For a moment he told himself he wouldn't ask. But that quickly proved impossible. "Like what?"

"That you'd never return for summers anymore, that your family had lied about the conservatory. That you'd been made a knight. That you were living in sin with a count, pretending to be his nephew. That you'd killed off a competitor at the conservatory, slashed him right across the throat."

Living in sin. The truth was somehow both duller and more salacious than that. "Those are all untrue, I'm afraid," Léon chuckled. "Though I am living with a count, basically, ever since my mother came back here to help prepare for the wedding. He's my patron. Not as old as that makes him sound, though."

"Robert de Montesquiou, am I remembering the name right?" Félix asked after a pause.

"Oh! Yes, that's him."

"You don't mention him in your letters."

Léon nodded. Félix was right. Léon had avoided anything that might make Félix suspect he was an invert. The worst thing he could imagine was his best friend with his face twisted in disgust, telling Léon he couldn't see him anymore. Félix coaxed Clémentine onto the forested route. This way was longer but avoided the bustling town square. "Is he . . . everything that's said about him?" Félix asked.

"Probably, and then some more on top of that."

"Are you afraid to be with him?"

"Afraid? I don't know what you mean." Though of course Léon did know what Félix meant. He knew precisely. There was a generous quality to Félix's voice, though. His friend was curious to know, not judging. Léon realized he'd never seen Félix disgusted by anything, ever. "I'm not afraid at all. Here in Vernon, it feels like there are so many ways to become hated. Do you know what I mean? That you can be wrong in so many ways, and we spent our childhoods trying to be the correct sort of boys. But there's a society in Paris, the count's society, where you can instead say 'I am me; I am this thing,' and whatever that thing might be, no one gives you up for dead, no one starts praying for your soul, no one says you're not a man or not a person. There are plenty of ways to go wrong in Paris, don't mistake me, but it's not about being something immoral. Like, I met a countess who sometimes wears men's suits and calls herself Beckwith. And I met an actress who is playing Hamlet."

Félix let out a long breath. His thighs were passing heat to Léon's as they rode.

"Hamlet is usually played by a man," Léon explained.

"I know that," Félix said. He shifted the reins from one hand to the other. In the process his arm pressed firmly into Léon's side, then relaxed down by Clémentine's flank. "You don't have to answer me if you don't want, but what exactly do you mean by 'this thing'?"

It had been a long day, and Léon was suddenly afraid. Something was about to be put in words, and if it did, then it couldn't ever go back to being nameless. It would exist outside of him. What if saying something aloud now would mean never seeing Félix again? Would Félix then tell his mother if she asked why he never came around anymore? Would it turn everyone he'd ever known in his childhood against him? But it wasn't that that worried him now. It was losing Félix, these legs wrapped around his hips, these arms that looked like they would be just a little salty if Léon licked their thick skin. Maybe one day those arms could be wrapped around Léon's body as they woke up in a country bed with sun streaming through a window.

"Léon?"

He couldn't put words to it—not yet. The chance that Félix would still accept him didn't outweigh the crushing risk. "I don't think I know what I meant either," Léon said. "I'm sorry. I guess I'm tired and not making sense."

"Okay," Félix said. "Let me know if you're ever ready to speak about it. Because I'm ready to hear it."

"Thank you," Léon said. A white butterfly had landed on Clémentine's ear. The moment Léon moved to cup it with his hand, the butterfly flew off.

Félix coughed, and his voice took on a brighter tone. "I can't believe your sister is getting married! Settling down with the town baker no less. Well done, Charlotte. Who doesn't love André?"

"Yes, he's a good match for her. She's lucky," Léon said. His voice sounded fake. He was happy for his sister, but for the moment he was sad—to have been so close to actually expressing his heart to Félix and yet not done it. Was there ever a time when he could be this relaxed with Robert? With Marcel? He'd thought so, he'd have said so this very morning while he dressed in Paris in his smart woolen suit, but now he wasn't so sure. What had changed, except this quiet farm boy and this dappled mare and the thrushes calling within the woods, a butterfly on a horse's ear, Cécile looking at them both like she'd realized something that was too deep and too true even to start to fight against?

They'd arrived outside the inn where Charlotte was holding her reception. It glowed orange in the twilight, cheerful voices and laughter warming the night air. Léon caught himself. He memorized the feel and look of Félix's legs and arms, knowing it could be the last time he felt them. Then he slid down from the horse, ankles tingling as he hit the ground on his hard Italian soles.

"Thank you," Léon said, giving Clémentine's neck a stroke. When he looked up at Félix, the boy's eyes were fixed on Léon's. There were an intensity in them, an intensity Léon couldn't name, but—unless this was just in his mind?—he sensed one feeling coming through: *I am this thing too.*

"Do you want to come inside?" Léon asked, clutching his suitcase like a shield. "There's not a guest list or anything. My sister would love to see you, I know. You know everyone here better than I do, anyway."

"No, I have to get back. I've had Clémentine out all afternoon and my father needs her. I should be there too, because we're tilling in what's left of the light and my father's not as strong as he used to be," Félix said.

"Okay, then, I understand," Léon said. He scuffed the ground with the narrow tip of a polished shoe. "Thank you for the ride, Félix."

"Let me pick you up from the station again, next time you come, if your new life doesn't carry you away from here forever," Félix said. "You can write me to let me know. I'll put it on the family calendar, and they can't stop me from coming, even if it's harvest. No matter what, I will meet your train."

"Thank you," Léon said, unexpected tears in his eyes. "Félix, I . . . I miss you."

"Congratulations, Léon Delafosse," Félix said, before whispering something into Clémentine's ear. Whatever he told her remained secret. The two clopped off into the evening dark.

Léon watched Félix leave, his back swaying side to side as Clémentine clopped along. Had he been a coward not to push the conversation further? Or had he made the only choice he could, to keep his true nature a secret? He didn't know. But he did know that his heart lurched as the night insects' drone became a throbbing swell, as the dark arms of the pine trees reached around the trail to secret Félix and Clémentine away.

Years ago, Léon had toddled through this very same restaurant after Charlotte, who was a year older and knew it, spinning expert cartwheels between tables. The Delafosse family had come to this inn once a month, whenever their father had received his pouch of coins, spending some precious francs on a meal out. They'd strategized for days about which of the inn's five dishes they would each order. Of course Charlotte had chosen to have her wedding reception here.

The physical memory of Félix still alive in his body, Léon opened the front door and slipped inside. The beer must have been flowing for a while, as not one but two drinking songs were underway at the same time, the voices all sloshing against one another. Charlotte was on one side of the hall, André on the other, red in the face and singing like it was an act of war. The courses had all been served long ago, the narrow wood tables covered with fingerprinted glasses and dirty dishes. Léon looked to where Charlotte had been sitting and saw—yes—there was a clean place setting at her side. A place setting that had been for him.

Léon approached the bartender. "Store this back there for me, would you?"

She looked at him warily as she placed his case on the shelf beside the ceramic bottles of local brew. "Welcome back, Léon. We've missed you."

He glanced in Charlotte's direction. "Am I in trouble?"

In response, she poured him a stein of cider and pushed it across the bar.

Léon took it and sipped. He removed his tailored jacket and folded it carefully, stowing it on a nearby stool before looking out at the crowd.

Before, his family and home had just been *his*, too familiar to describe. But tonight, he saw them as a stranger would. Skin and hair worn dry by sun and fields, hands roughened, ankles thickened, accents ringing with country vowels, good Sunday dresses—each woman's only dress—gussied up however they could: sleeves rolled up, ribbon stitched around hems, stains disguised by brooches and scarves.

Charlotte had pulled her inky hair back with a strip of gray cloth, had applied the lightest amount of rouge on her cheeks—or maybe that was just an effect of the wine and the singing—and must have lost one of her stockings early in the evening. She shouted a bawdy song, voice screeching whenever she stretched to any note outside her minimal range. She must have dropped something on her hand in the last few weeks; two of her fingernails were purple.

Léon skirted the edge of the crowd, hoping to stay out of view. He removed more and more of his tailored wool suit as he went, unbuttoning his collar, putting his cider down for a moment so he could pull his crocodile-skin belt from its loops, roll it up, and tuck it in his pocket. He picked his stein of cider back up and continued his way through the boisterous and drunken crowd, toward his sister. As he did, he looked for his mother and found her—staring right at him. She stonily returned her gaze to the reveling crowd, pointedly ignoring him.

Charlotte, though, might be ignoring him only because she hadn't seen him yet. As Léon picked his way through the crowd, offering one-word greetings to the people who recognized him, he watched Charlotte serenade André and his friends, then catch his eye and send him an expression of such private affection that it made Léon blush from the intimacy of it.

Now Léon was beside his mother. He kept his gaze down. Her feet looked red and swollen in her Sunday shoes. "Hello, Maman. I'm sorry I'm late."

"You decided to come," she said. "I had started to think that you wouldn't."

"Of course I came," Léon said. "I wouldn't miss this. I just got the later train, that's all."

"Well, you nearly *did* miss it."

Now irritation flushed his throat. "I said I'm sorry. I got pulled away, prepping for the Érard concert next week. This is the party and not the wedding, right? Charlotte is getting married in the church during tomorrow's mass, right?"

"Yes, of course. You'll be here for that. Just like we'll be at your Érard recital when you tell us to be, right on time."

"I understand, Maman. You're making yourself very clear," Léon said, rolling his eyes.

She kept her gaze down. "It's good to see you. I've been worried about you."

"I've been writing twice a week. I've been telling you that everything is good."

"Yes, but is it? Good?"

"Yes," Léon said. His temperature was rising. Of course it was good! Look how much he had going for him. Why wouldn't it be *good*? She was the one who left him all alone in Paris, and now she was mad at him for pulling it all off, despite having no help from his family?

Léon's mother put her arm around him and drew him in. Her shirt and neck smelled like soil, wine, linen. Home. Her voice hitched as they embraced. "Go say hello to your sister. She's been asking about you all night. And take those cuff links off. What are those, polished stones? You look like a dandy."

Léon undid his cuff links as he disengaged and made his way to Charlotte, who was still belting a song to her fiancé. André cheered from the other side as he noticed his soon-to-be brother-in-law. Then Léon was beside Charlotte. He realized he had never bought a second set of flowers to replace the ones he'd left in the Gare Saint-Lazare. Why had he come all the way out here without a present for his sister? Idiot. He tried to smile extra widely to make up for it. "Congratulations, Sister."

When Charlotte first turned to Léon, she had a giant smile on her face, flush with the high of the party. Then she realized who had interrupted her and the smile dropped, fury flashing in. Her eyes drooped, and the smile returned, more measured but with unmistakable love. Léon might have been late to her party, but she was still his Charlotte, and she still loved him.

"I'm so happy for you," he said.

"Léon, I—" She dropped whatever she was about to say and instead wrapped her arms around him. "You came. You came!"

"Yes, of course I did," Léon said. He was late, yes, but he'd arrived on the day he'd said he would. Why did both his sister and mother assume that he might not come? Had everything changed that much?

"Come on, let's go outside," Charlotte whispered, her cheek slick with sweat against Léon's. She grasped his hand

and pulled him toward the exit, calling out as she went: "André, I'm going outside with Léon!"

"Have fun! And hello, Léon! Everyone, that's Léon Delafosse. Léon is my *brother*!" André called. He was just as Léon remembered: a pleasantly soft middle, wide and gentle eyes, and thinning hair that at the moment was sticking up ludicrously, matted by the sweat of the party. He was also quite drunk.

"Hello, André!" Léon called as he let himself be led across the restaurant, tripping across friends and family and strangers who slapped him and Charlotte across the back. "Congratulations!"

Then they were outside in the cool air, right where Félix had just recently departed with Clémentine. Her hoofs had left prints in the sod.

Charlotte fanned herself with her hand. "I'm going to look a mess tomorrow for the church ceremony, but I don't care, Léon, I don't care! This, *this* is my wedding, Léon. This party. It feels that way. The church stuff is something else, something weirder, for everyone else but not me, do you know what I mean?"

"It's a good party," he said. "I'm so happy for you, Charlotte."

She took his shoulders in her hands. "I want you to know I'm not mad. I'm not mad. I'm just glad that you're here. My brother. You're my brother!"

"Ha. So I hear. How much have you had to drink, Charlotte?"

"Enough!" She twirled under the cloudless night sky. "But I think I'd be drunk even without wine."

"André looks just as happy as you," Léon said. "Which is hard to pull off because you're absolutely glowing right now."

"It's been such a whirlwind. I mean, it's out of a romance novel, isn't it? Forbidden love, sent to different places to stop us from seeing each other, then circumstances change and we're sent crashing into each other. We joke about it, André and me, how we're not really the types to have this kind of story. It's more for the likes of you."

"The likes of me," Léon said, chuffing his foot in the soil. "I don't know about that."

"I don't totally mean it as a positive, Brother," Charlotte said.

"Don't worry yourself there, that came through clearly."

"What has been happening?" Charlotte asked, sitting down in the wet night grass. "You write us letters, but there's too much good in them. I never believe it when people say that everything is great. I don't believe anything that anyone says unprompted. Nothing makes me more nervous than 'everything is fine.' If it were, I don't think you'd feel the need to say it, do you know what I mean? It's my pet theory that we only state things absolutely like that if they're untrue."

Léon crouched beside her, so the grass wouldn't stain his pants—their imported fabric probably cost as much as this whole party. "I get what you're saying, but everything really is fine." This tack of conversation was making him feel a little sad. Just a few minutes ago he really had felt fine! Why wouldn't his sister take his word that it was true? Sure, he could come up with a list of frustrations if that's what she wanted from him, but who didn't have a few frustrations?

Maybe, someday, he would be able to tell Charlotte about his desire for other boys. Maybe she, out of all people in his life, would still speak to him. Maybe. But why test it and risk losing her? If he kept saying he was fine, then no one would ask any questions, and he could hold on to the pieces of happiness that he had.

He certainly wouldn't tell her about it tonight, the evening of her party, which ought to be all about her making everyone proud by marrying an industrious local boy. "I'm so happy for you, Charlotte," he said again.

She laid her hand on his. Her fingers were wet with dew. "I know you are." She patted the grass. "What are you doing, crouching like that? Come and sit the right way with your soon-to-be-married-and-boring sister."

"No, I'm fine," Léon said. Just that week, he'd been at the Pavilion Montesquiou, Robert's new mansion in Versailles. A Spanish tailor had been taking his measurements, to craft this perfectly fitting suit from bolts of fine Italian wool. He was not going to ruin it by sitting on the grass in Vernon.

"I see," Charlotte said, wrapping her sleeves tight around her, tucking the edges under her fingers.

Léon began to unbutton his jacket. "Are you cold? I can—"

"No, you keep your nice jacket on," Charlotte said.

"It *is* nice, isn't it?" Léon said. "I don't know if you've noticed the lining, but it's this green silk—"

"I don't care about your lining, Léon."

"Oh," Léon said, stung. The half-moon fogged in his vision.

Charlotte sighed. "Show me the silk."

Without quite meaning to, Léon sank into the grass, his pants instantly wet. The wool would dry. It probably wouldn't be stained. Sulkily, heart racing, he opened one side of his jacket so his sister could see the lining.

Charlotte ran the back of her hand along it. "I think that's the softest thing I've ever touched, and I've touched baby pig ears."

"Right?"

Charlotte sucked in a long breath and held it before releasing it noisily. "You know, sometimes I like to put a daisy chain in my hair and jump along the riverbanks. It doesn't make me the Queen of the Fairies."

"What is that supposed to mean?" Léon asked. But he knew exactly what that was supposed to mean.

"You're still a Delafosse. You're still from here. You can't just hurl us all to one side."

"I know that," Léon said quietly.

"Just because we don't know our way around high society, doesn't make us all idiots. I'm not *worse* than you by having this life I have."

"And just because I don't want to get my pants wet in the grass doesn't mean I think I'm better than you! Just because I'm in a better *place* doesn't mean that I think I'm a better *person*."

"A better place. Nice, Léon. Thanks."

"Come on. I shouldn't have to pretend with you. It *is* better. You've talked forever about how awful this poor provincial town is, the same old routines day after day, bread and work and sleep and bread and work and sleep. You said you were excited to get to Paris, even if it took you away from André."

"I did say that," Charlotte said, her lips tight.

"You can be Charlotte here, but I can't be Léon. I can't be myself in Vernon. I'm not like other boys. I can't handle it here. Anyone who sticks out gets all this gossip and, and all this *condemnation*. Even missing a day of church here gets you a bad reputation. Maman didn't want you to even ride a *bicycle,* Charlotte. Oh, that reminds me. This is for you." Léon pulled the card he'd bought from the train station out of his jacket pocket, the one with the man on a penny-farthing.

Charlotte glanced at it and then absently placed it to one side. Her mind was on other, more fervent, things. "She still doesn't want me to. Not that there even *are* any bicycles in Vernon yet." She ripped up a handful of grass and scattered it on top of the card. "Hey, Brother. You know I'm not going to gossip about you. I'm not going to condemn you. No matter what anyone says, no matter what you do."

"You make it sound like everyone is gossiping about me."

"Well, yes," Charlotte said. "That's because they are. Mainly because they're jealous. Ignore them. You can't have a beautiful Italian silk lining in your jacket without a few consequences. It's totally worth it, though."

Léon placed his hands over his face. "Mom had me take out my cuff links because they made me look like a 'dandy.' Is this 1890 or 1870? I swear!"

"You can't live here being who you are. I understand, and you don't have to say why unless you want to. And you need to dress up to get ahead. I also understand that. You need to act a certain fancy way. But just know that if it all gets too exhausting to do all those things out there that you think you need to be doing, you can come here and be no way at all. You can just be my brother."

"And teach piano in some hovel, like Maman?"

Charlotte's eyes flashed. "Yes. You can teach piano in some hovel. Lots of people have it much worse. Even a few weeks ago, you probably felt like you were our family's only hope to keep us all out of the poorhouse. You weren't wrong. But now my circumstances have changed. André and I can care for Maman. You don't have to perform a role you don't want just for our sakes. We'll be okay. Do what's right for *you*."

Léon didn't know how to answer. He'd told himself for so long that he was doing what he had to for the sake of his family. And he remembered that night at the Saussines', how he felt like he was doing something artificial, when all he really wanted to do was make music. But he didn't just want to play music anymore. He wanted to be someone important in the world, too. Was that so wrong?

"I *am* doing what's right for me," Léon finally said. "You

know what they call me, Charlotte? Der Mozart von Frank-reich."

"The Mozart of France? Is that German? Am I supposed to be impressed?"

"It would be nice if you were at least supportive."

"Queen of the Fairies, Léon."

"You keep pretending that I could just be myself and everything would be okay. That's ridiculous. If I'd just been myself, really been me, they wouldn't have let me in the door. I wouldn't have gotten a patron. I'd have been kicked out of the conservatory. You and Mother would have been in the poorhouse. That's not an option."

"That's what I'm trying to say. You can be yourself here."

"No, I can't, Charlotte. I cannot. You don't understand why."

A long gaze passed between them. "Oh, my brother. Oh, Léon. I think I might understand why."

Léon shocked himself by crying. Great big tears, shaking shoulders. He'd been trying so hard for so long, not letting the veneer crack, not having a moment to relax. To exhale. Except for when he was at the piano; there was nowhere else he could exhale. Not when he was unnatural here and uncultured there. Charlotte was wrong. There was nowhere he could just be himself. Léon struggled to put words to it. "I'm wrong everywhere I go," he said. "I'll always be wrong."

Charlotte wrapped her arms around him, and together they fell in the dark, wet grass. Her breath smelled like wine. "You could never be wrong with me."

"Don't start to hate me," Léon cried into Charlotte's shoulder. "I couldn't stand it if you hated me."

"I could never. Never."

Léon cried for a while. "It's your wedding reception, and I'm making it all about me and sobbing into your nice dress."

"It's not a nice dress, and you know it. But your apology is accepted anyway."

"Thank you," Léon said, his voice hiccupping.

"Maybe if you were mean to André."

"What?"

"If you were mean to André, then maybe I'd hate you a little. But not if you were mean to me."

Léon laughed. "Okay, I won't." He paused. "Who could ever be mean to André?"

"No one. He is wonderful," Charlotte said. "I'm the luckiest girl in the world."

"I don't know about that," Léon said. "I just meant that being mean to André would mean not having anyone we could go to for morning bread, and who would ever want that?"

Charlotte laughed. "I'm marrying the baker. I'm going to be so fat, Léon."

"It will suit you," Léon said. "All things suit you."

"Especially you," Charlotte said.

"Shall we go in?" Léon asked, sitting up, shivering in his wet woolen suit.

"Not yet," Charlotte said. "Not yet. This, this right here, is the party I was waiting all day for."

16.

LÉON ROLLED OUT OF HIS BED UPSTAIRS IN THE PAVILION Montesquiou, pulled on a satin robe, scuffed his feet into slippers, and padded over to Robert's room. He had so much to do that day that he'd been worried he'd oversleep, but nerves had tricked him the other way and woken him up before dawn. He was getting fitted for his suit that morning, then it was Léon's first trip out of the country—they were heading to London so he could sit for a portrait. They would come back on Friday so he could be ready for his big Érard recital on Saturday afternoon.

As ever, Robert was up before him, his long form propped up on purple Japanese pillows, revising poems. Ink-globbed pages were strewn about his bed, blotting sand dusting the ebony floor. Once the two boys were out of the house, the maid would have her morning's work cut out for her, brushing sand out of each seam. Léon stood in the doorway. "Are you ready?"

"I've discovered something really quite extraordinary. Did you realize my initials spell out *ephémère*?" Robert replied. "F.M.R., how wonderful."

"I did not," Léon said. "Come on, my fitting is at eight,

then we have a train to catch at ten thirty. It's one of those days. We have to get moving."

"My muse will not be rushed," Robert said crossly, tossing a stained page to the floor. It unexpectedly took flight, making a back-and-forth motion before landing on Robert's nose, staining it adorably.

Léon crossed over, kneeled by the count's bedside, licked his thumb, and stroked the ink off the sharp tip. Robert watched him, smiling as he went nearly cross-eyed. Léon had learned that this was the sort of physical intimacy that was allowed between them—affectionate, caring, but nothing more than especially close cousins might do.

"Do you want to stay here and work?" Léon asked. "I can go do the fitting and then return to pick you up."

Robert looked at the pages strewn about and then shook his head. "The muse is combative today. I'd much rather stop trying to wrestle her and walk out with you instead."

Léon stood, holding out his hand. "Then get your robe on, grand poet."

The Pavilion Montesquiou was in Versailles and so was the tailor's hut. It was only a five-minute walk, and if they took the goose paths, they never had to touch a street, which meant they could stay in their house clothes.

Unlike in Vernon, the animal paths of Versailles were surrounded by brick buildings, the brooks and creeks engineered to pass under sculpted bridges. The walk with Robert was full of wit and banter, unlike the silent communication Léon had with Félix. It was hard to imagine that the Léon who was here was the same one who'd been in Vernon just a few weeks earlier. There were so many ways to be a person.

He missed Félix. He also liked this.

Once they arrived, their sheepskin bedroom slippers were dark with dew. They kicked them off in the tailor's doorway. "This was once the cottage of Marie Antoinette's falconer," Robert said. Léon wasn't sure he believed him. It *could* have belonged to Marie Antoinette's falconer, and that's all that mattered to Robert.

The tailor was a stately older Valencian, who waited patiently while Léon shucked his robe behind a screen. Robert sat on a velvet stool in the corner, smoking his morning cigarette and offering commentary as Léon flipped through bolts of fabric, testing the colors against his bare skin so the tailor could decide which had the best effect. After they finally selected a rich red black, Robert brought his gaze from the window outside and shook his head. "Absolutely not. The Érard hasn't moved to electricity. This recital will be gaslit. You must provide more color. And a weave that reflects whatever paltry light manages to hit you."

The tailor offered a cobalt blue instead, and it was decided. There was no talk of money as Robert and Léon left. They merely picked up the suit from the last fitting—this one in mustard wool—and made their way back along the crowded goose paths. There was a standing Montesquiou account everywhere they went; Robert's father would pay the bill.

They took the train to Calais for a choppy Channel crossing (Robert belowdecks the whole time, arm over his eyes,

Léon at the stern, listening to the roar of the steam engines as he looked in wonder at France from the outside), and then they'd arrived in Dover, England.

Robert had reserved at the guesthouse he always stayed in. The front desk clerk greeted him by name the moment the two young men arrived. Léon said "thank you" in English and felt very proud of himself.

Dinner was at a pub, where Léon ate his first shepherd's pie. Everyone there spoke English, of course, and Léon used his "thank you" on as many people as he could. He and Robert staggered out arm in arm, singing in falsetto, getting scowls from some local toughs lounging against a low wall across the street.

Léon immediately went quiet, but Robert did not. "Damn them," he said, whirling his lacquered cane and tilting his hat to the toughs in a mock greeting. They glowered back. "Damn the English in general, actually," Robert concluded before whistling his way down the street to their hotel.

Léon hurried to catch up.

"Regressive puritans," Robert muttered as they made their way up the creaking stairs. "You wouldn't believe the laws they still have on the books here."

Their room had twin beds against opposite walls, made up with lacy, old-fashioned linens, like they were child princes on a fairy-tale journey. Léon was unsure what to do with himself when he returned from the hall bathroom. As he removed his clothes in front of Robert for the second time that day, he thought about leaving them off. Of looking at Robert frankly instead of keeping his gaze trained on the floor.

Léon plucked up his courage and did just that, standing naked by his bed for a long moment. What would it feel like to have Robert's delicate hands on his body, to cup Robert's jaw in his hand, to kiss those lips? It would be vile and wrong and against God, but that "truth" was feeling less and less real the more time he spent in Paris. Even if it was the sin he'd been taught, the alternative had begun to feel worse: To be a body alone in this world. Alone forever.

He waited for Robert to notice him.

But Robert did not notice him. Well. He had to have, but he kept his gaze on the ceiling, as he lay on his own twin bed, hands laced primly over his chest. "Good night, Léon," he said, all while staring at the ceiling. Still fully clothed, he leaned over and turned down the gas of the bedside lamp.

The portrait sitting was in Chelsea, and they had all morning and half the afternoon to get themselves there. No rushing today.

All the same, when Léon awoke, he found Robert moving about the room briskly, adjusting and repacking everything in his case, mussing and fixing and re-mussing his hair in the room's mirror. Léon found ways to be busy too, pretending to read over sheet music in bed, while his mind spun out over the night before. Did Robert hate him now? Had putting the idea of sex out there, even if silently, changed things forever, made Léon unworthy of patronage or maybe even friendship?

Come morning, Robert translated the *Times* headlines for Léon over a breakfast of soft rolls and cut fruit. Then the men were on a train to the painter's studio.

All around him were conversations in English, going impossibly fast. The fashions were different too: the men's hats more rounded, the women's dresses more dull. Léon caught himself staring more often than was probably polite. Each time he was caught he'd blush, embarrassed by his Frenchness. Could they tell just by looking at him?

They got off at St. Pancras station, where they hired a brougham to take them to Chelsea. Robert gave the driver a crown and got shillings in return. Léon examined the coins all the way. Queen Victoria was on most of them. He read the Latin words on the edges out loud, Robert laughing at his pronunciations.

They arrived at a townhouse. A collie sat on the stoop, stern and ferocious until she burst into happy panting and hopping about when she recognized Robert. "Hello there, Ellie!" he exclaimed.

The front door opened, and a mild, bearded man appeared behind it. Ellie barreled in, nearly knocking him down. "Welcome, gentlemen. The studio is in back, as you well remember, Sir Montesquiou."

"Oh I'm a knight in England now, am I? How delightful. Hello, John," Robert said.

The bearded man laughed. "In this house, you are a knight and a queen all at once. You may be anything you like here, actually."

"Thank you," Léon said. His two words of English were getting pretty worn at this point.

"Hello, Léon," the painter said in near-native French. "I'm John Singer Sargent. Thank you for sitting for me. I've been looking forward to this."

The men passed through a small dark foyer to a glassed-in courtyard full of shrubs and one large tree. It was a gorgeously overgrown English-style garden, here in the middle of London—a curated wildness. Léon stroked the tops of the thistles as they stepped along footstones to a structure that was half-hut and half-greenhouse. His mind started composing a new melody as he thought how to capture the feel of the garden in a city, a chaos that somehow wasn't tense at all.

In the hut was an easel. On the easel was a blank canvas. It made Léon nervous, like he was being called on to perform. But he wasn't playing the piano today. That would have been easier than just . . . sitting. Being.

"Is that what you're intending to wear?" the painter asked, looking curiously at Léon's dingy white collar, his loosely tied cravat.

"Oh no," Robert said. "We've brought a gorgeous mustard suit. It's the color of an overdue harvest. It will give you hay fever just to look at it."

They tried the suit, but Sargent frowned. "I'm afraid the color is off. Léon should be the star here, not the suit. Here, keep on the white shirt you were wearing, Léon. There, and now take this."

With that, the painter placed his own jacket on Léon. He clipped some clothespins on the back, so it looked fitted. The smell of Sargent wafted up from the coat's wool. Homey scents: Ellie the collie, and something like a fried egg, and two different colognes.

Robert arched an eyebrow, displeased. Sargent looked delighted, though. "We should feature Léon, not his patron. Your largesse should be in the background, not the spotlight, my dear Robert. You know that is true, even though you'd prefer it weren't."

Léon hadn't even considered that—that the expensiveness of the mustard suit, its outlandish color, was a sort of stamp of ownership from the count. Sargent, a stranger, had just protected him from something. Robert flicked his fingers in the air. "Fine. This is getting tiresome. You decide what to wear, Léon. It's your portrait after all."

That didn't feel true. Léon hadn't arranged it, Léon wasn't paying for it, Léon wouldn't own it. Robert was soon off wandering the garden, smoking, peering up at the low gray clouds, pointedly leaving them be. It was just Léon and this gentle painter. "I prefer the plainer look," Léon confessed in French.

"A very good choice," Sargent said with a layered, sweet smile.

They chose a pose, Léon with his hand on his hip, thin mustache arranged over a questioning mouth, the natural waves of his blond hair brushed into as much order as possible. As the painter began charcoaling in the broad strokes of the portrait, tinkering with perspective and scale, Léon's mind tried to capture the chaotic urban garden in musical form . . . though with the undercurrent of worry from the night before back now, as the Count de Montesquiou continued to pace. This would be a music quite unlike his sonata, which had been born from walks with Félix. Not better, not worse. Different.

"Something dark just entered your face and made it more interesting. That's the perfect expression," Sargent said. "Whatever's happening in your mind, this is it. Try to keep it up."

Léon swallowed and kept his mind where it was for as long as he could tolerate it—divided between thoughts of two different young men.

Maybe it happened because Sargent had made Léon sit there for such an extended period, thinking about his body and Robert's body and Félix's body for longer than his mind would have naturally allowed. In the carriage ride and in the train back to Dover, he kept thinking of his body against Robert's. He studied the curves and angles of the count and wondered what they would feel like under his hands, under his mouth. It was lust, partly, and also a sense that it would be freeing to finally have his wrongness laid open. To stop wondering and just do and be and consider the consequences later.

Robert and Léon checked into the same guesthouse, ate in the same pub, Léon ordering the same shepherd's pie— peas and Worcestershire sauce, what a wonderful combo, the French could learn something from this! There was even one of the same toughs lounging against the same low wall across the street, though when he was alone, his expression was different. There was no scowl. There was no smile. There was hunger and an open stare that made Léon's heart race. He looked to see if Robert had noticed, but the count was hurrying down the street, whistling, whisking his cane through the air like he was batting away arrows.

Still feeling the heat of the tough's stare, Léon returned him a questioning look, wondering for a moment what it would feel like to have one of those strong hands against his mouth, before he caught up to Robert. His whole body was alive. He was desperate to touch and be touched.

Time slowed on the stairs up to their room. Léon watched the lean body of the count moving down the dim hallway as he arrived at their door, as he did a flourishing half-turn fit for a dancer while he waited for Léon to follow with the key. As Léon placed it in the lock, he felt an unexpected pressure on his back. Robert's hand. Robert, his hand on the back of Léon, waiting for him to unlock the door to their room.

Surely that was a sign that Robert wanted this too?

It was the same humble, creaking chamber they'd had before, with its twin beds for runaway princes. Léon felt a flaring sort of heat—not an emotion exactly, but something more primal than emotion. A need. As they passed into the chamber, he turned and seized Robert's lapels. He brought his lips toward the count's. Robert laughed and threw his chin back before Léon could kiss him, exposing his long neck. "Knave!"

Léon crouched, arms out like a wrestler. "This is how we are in England, Governor."

"Heaven forbid," Robert said, kicking the door shut behind him. He started working on his sheer calfskin gloves, giving each finger an initial tug before returning to give a second tug. Léon sat on his bed, the mattress sagging in the middle. He clutched the feather pillow to his chest as he watched Robert dismantle himself.

Once Robert had removed the gloves, he undid his tie and opened his shirt. "I do like undressing myself from time to time," he said, speaking quickly so Léon couldn't interrupt. "I wouldn't dare be seen traveling without a valet in France, but here in the land of barbarians and Celts, no one much cares very much about the *de* before Montesquiou."

"I could help you," Léon offered.

"Your position is court bard, not dresser," Robert said.

"Yes, milord," Léon said in English.

Given how much Robert's whims ruled the day, Léon had always assumed Robert would be the aggressor, that he'd eventually spend his life fending off (or giving into) Robert's advances in order to benefit from his money. He'd been waiting for it all to begin, the balance of their transaction to be drawn. Not with dread but not excitement either.

But it was never going to happen, he realized as he clutched the pillow. Robert was never going to pursue him—and he realized now that he'd wanted it to happen. That he wanted to be with Robert.

It would be up to the bard to seduce the king.

He got up from the bed and took two careful steps to Robert, who was sitting on his own bed, working on the buttons of his vest. Robert glanced up. "What are you doing?"

Léon sat beside Robert. He took the count's long hands and placed them around his own waist. He ran his hand through the wave of Robert's dark hair, let it lay firm on Robert's slender neck, felt a pulse and thin muscles cording beneath his fingers.

He drew his lips to the count's. Robert tremored but did not pull away. Léon deepened the kiss, parting the count's lips with his tongue. It was the first time he'd ever kissed anyone like this. It might have been Robert's first time being kissed like this. It wasn't like with Marcel, when the kiss had been the destination. This was a kiss that was part of sex. They were in a new land, doing new things.

Léon moved his mouth from Robert's lips and roved over his face instead, caressing eyelids, forehead, ears, neck. He snaked his hand beneath the cotton of Robert's parted shirt, his own breath hitching at the sudden sensation of skin and heat.

Robert held his hands up in the air, as if his body had seized up, his fingers twitching. Then he placed them around Léon's waist, pressing tentatively into Léon's hips, and then with more force. Léon felt himself rocked back onto Robert's bed, and the count was wandering his body with hands and mouth. The white shirt he'd worn to the sitting at Sargent's studio was on the floor.

The moment they were down to their undergarments, Robert got under the thin blanket and sheet, bringing them up to his chin. Léon sat at the foot of the twin bed, confused. "Are you okay?" he asked.

Robert nodded, lips tight, like a kid who hadn't learned the word for a certain feeling yet.

Léon laid a hand on Robert's leg, the sheets and blanket a barrier between their skins. "Are you sure?"

Robert nodded more vigorously.

Léon shook Robert's leg. "Gahr, you!" he said. He didn't know why. Something had to be said, and that was what had come out.

What Léon had wanted to do was tussle, to roll around and enjoy the physical pressure of each other's bodies, like he'd once done with Félix in a field of sunburnt wheat. If he were back in Vernon more often, he and Félix might tussle in a different way now. Not as children but as men. The feeling of Félix's strong legs wrapped around his own had said that they might. But Léon was increasingly aware that Robert was never going to tussle. That the Count de Montesquiou did not tussle.

Léon retrieved his clothes from the floor. "What are you doing?" Robert asked.

Léon held his shirt and pants up to his bare chest. "I don't know. I guess I'm confused."

Robert opened his sheets where he lay, patting the bed beside him. "Come here. Lay next to me."

Shivering, Léon arranged himself beside Robert in the bed. The count's soft chest hair tickled Léon's back. Robert lowered the blanket against them. He wrapped his arms around Léon. "Like friends keeping warm," Robert said.

Not like that at all, Léon thought. Though that didn't matter much, since the feeling of Robert's chest against his back made him sigh with pleasure.

What were they doing with each other? Had they already committed a sin? It didn't feel like it. But did lying in this bed mean that Léon would never start to desire women, that something would click shut in his life, that any conventional hopes were done for?

Robert didn't say anything, and Léon didn't either, studying the count's body with his own. The conversation was continuing without words.

Would they sleep this way? Could they? The bed was uncomfortably narrow, but Léon hoped they might fall asleep; not since he'd left Vernon where'd he'd napped with Félix by a pond had he slept with another body alongside his. He missed the tangle, the reminder that he wasn't alone.

If they did stay in this bed together, Léon wouldn't possibly sleep. His heart was racing.

Léon could almost feel the combined energy of their brains, puzzling in silence. Gradually, Robert's hand on his chest began to move, to travel over Léon's torso, his belly, to snake along the line of hair leading to his crotch. Then his hand was on him. Reaching back, Léon had his hand on Robert. Together, they stroked each other until they were done, until the sheets were wet.

Léon sighed in pleasure, wiggling his body against Robert's. The count didn't move.

Léon reached back and placed his hand on the back of Robert's head. Robert jerked his head away. Léon turned to look at him, propping his head up on his wrist. Robert's eyes were pressed shut.

"What's wrong?" Léon asked.

When Robert opened his eyes, they were flooded with tears. "Go away."

"I'm sorry?"

"Get out!" Robert said, his voice suddenly sharp.

The force of his words shot Léon to his feet. Like he was under attack, he seized up his discarded clothing, draped it over his body. The old shirt and pants made for shabby armor. "Do you really want me to . . . leave?" Léon asked, turning slowly in the middle of the room.

Robert curled his body into a fetal position, head against his knees, and dragged the bedding over him so only the crown of his head was visible. A sob escaped, muffled by the fabric.

Léon couldn't leave. Robert could leave anywhere he didn't want to be, but Léon was in a foreign country, without any money to his name. "I'm going to just get in my bed over here," Léon whispered.

Léon got under the blanket and sheet, lay his head on the

pillow, and stared up at the ceiling. What had just happened? "Can I do anything to help you, Robert?" Léon called out.

The sobbing was over. All that came from Robert's half of the room was a horrible stillness.

"I'm sorry if I did something wrong," Léon said. "Please just tell me if I did something wrong."

More stillness. His stomach curling tight and low, Léon swallowed a sour taste in his mouth as he studied the cracks in the hotel room's ceiling. "Please, Robert, talk to me," he tried again.

"I want to go to sleep" came Robert's voice. "If you won't leave like a decent person, at least let me do that."

"Okay," Léon whispered. A weird kind of guilt flooded him, a different feeling than his shame. Had he done something to Robert? Had he attacked him, somehow? Hadn't that been Robert's hand that had reached down his body, that led to the wet patch in the middle of Robert's bed? Wasn't this his doing?

Was everything over now? Would he and Robert part in the morning? What would that mean for Léon's concert at the Érard on Saturday? His tuition bill for the fall?

The morning room was empty and bright. There was no sign of Robert. His bed was neatly made, his bag packed and gone. Léon's own bag was square on the luggage rack. Robert had placed it there while Léon was sleeping. An act of mercy.

Léon dressed quickly, dread twisting his insides, and staggered down the stairs. He had no idea what time it was, but their passage across the Channel was scheduled for eleven that morning. Robert had the tickets, but he was gone. Maybe Léon could talk to the shipmaster, explain that someone else had his ticket for that crossing. If he didn't get on that ferry, he had no money and would have to wait until . . . until what? Until he'd begged enough money to get himself back to France?

He staggered past the breakfast room, tucking in his shirt and scuffing his feet into his shoes as he went. Something caught his eye: a blue cane. He stopped and found Robert, alone at the guesthouse's best seat, by the window with a view of the sea, the *Times* open before him. He was bathed and coiffed and dressed in his impeccable fashion, like he was sitting for his own portrait.

"Good morning, Léon," he said, only barely raising his gaze from the paper. "You're finally up. Come, I'll translate the headlines for you."

17.

IT WAS A THREE-ENVELOPE MORNING AT THE PAVILION Montesquiou. That was Léon's very favorite sort of morning—except for a four-envelope morning, which was of course even better. He accepted the cards from Céleste and stepped out the glass door in back to sit on one of the white metal chairs in the aviary. Green parrots screeched above, and goldfinches flashed yellow among the branches.

In such a charming setting, he could almost forget that the most important concert of his life was that evening.

The first letter was from Charlotte.

Dearest Léon,

Maman and André and I received the tickets you sent us for the Érard recital. We are so very excited. You mentioned that you would be staying in Versailles and would meet us at the stage door an hour before. That is perfect, since André will need to use your bed at our apartment before we release it to the new tenants. It's good that the plan works for us, because given the pace of the mail you will probably receive this response the day of your concert.

The Érard! You've made it. We are very proud of you, Léon.

Love,
Charlotte

Within the same envelope was a slip of plain white paper. Léon almost missed it. It fluttered out and became instantly soggy on the aviary's humid ground. Léon read the writing quickly, before the ink smudged into nonsense.

Dear Léon,

I keep thinking about our ride together when you were in Vernon. I don't have your gift with words, and I know you probably have many new friends who can express themselves better than I do and who are much more interesting. But none of them care for you as much as I do.

When I see you next, I would like to try to put words to what I could not say when we rode. Maman and I cannot rely on my father anymore so the farm has become my duty. My life is lonely but very full. All at once. I hope you will come to Vernon again soon.

Your friend,
Félix

Léon looked up instinctively, to see if he was alone. Of course he was, except for the parrots and finches. He read the slip again, the words crammed onto the scrap of paper. *I would like to try to put words to what I could not say when we rode.* That could mean many different things, of course. But Léon's racing heart told him that maybe—maybe—it could mean that his heart was like Léon's, that he felt the desire for Léon that Léon felt for him. That he loved in the way of the Greeks, as Marcel would put it.

Félix had never enjoyed school, but to have it taken from him must still hurt dearly. Léon imagined him in his farmhouse, his only company his surly father and his mother, whose mind had faded. Without Léon there, Clémentine would be his closest friend. Except for the times Cécile Boicos came by.

Once the Érard concert was over, he would find time to visit Vernon.

Dear Léon,

It is done. Our trip to England, the one on which you're replacing my cousin Lionel—you're replacing him in all ways! After much work, Maman has managed to swap you into his program. Instead of Lionel's voice, it will be your piano playing at the recital at Kensington Palace in two weeks' time. Of course, being herself, Maman also has hopes this will finally bring us up from middle class into the upper. And equally of course, being myself, I hope the same, for the sake of the immortality of my writing. No one wants to read a novel from the middle class. Can you imagine?

The Érard tomorrow, and then Kensington Palace so
soon after—your future is made. Please remember to
acknowledge me on your inevitable ascent to grand fame.

With generous amity,
Marcel

"Robert, Robert!" Léon said, rushing from the aviary, nearly releasing a green parrot into the house in the process. He pressed the door closed and dashed up the back walk, finding Robert at the breakfast table.

Robert was using his long fingers to battle his croissant down to crumbs and then pushing those crumbs around his plate, all without eating a single morsel. Not a good sign as far as mood. But he'd perk up when he heard Léon's news.

"Kensington Palace, in two weeks!" Léon said as he staggered in, waving Marcel's card.

"What are you talking about?" Robert asked.

"A performance date, thanks to Marcel. I'm replacing his cousin Lionel."

Robert crossed his arms over his chest, pulling his silk dressing robe tight. "You're not playing in two weeks. You're playing in four days. Beckwith arranged it yesterday."

Léon stopped still, mouth open. "I can't have my English debut four days from now and also two weeks from now."

"No, you most certainly cannot. You'll have to decline the invite from the young *arriviste* Monsieur Proust. He'll find some other way to claw his way into the upper class, I have no doubt."

"You booked an English recital. Why didn't you tell me?" Léon asked.

"I just said, this only happened yesterday. Getting you to England was always the plan. Beckwith finally managed it. I didn't want to tell you until after your Érard concert. You have enough to worry about." He pushed his plate back so hard that it knocked over his teacup, sent it rolling across the table to clink against the sugar bowl. "I had planned a special moment, a dinner out and a grand reveal of your future ascent. And now I find that *again* I'm sharing you with oily Marcel Proust. I don't like the sensation."

Right beneath Robert's words, Léon knew they were both thinking of their fraught night at the Dover hotel. They'd never discussed it. Léon was tempted to bring it up again now. But Robert had made it clear he wanted nothing of the sort. They were to pretend it never happened. "I'll have to tell Marcel that I can't do it," Léon said, still stunned.

"Yes. You had enough temerity to double deal, you'll have enough to figure a way out of this. Write him a letter. Keep it short and keep it clear. What were you *thinking*, Léon? You don't want to swap out for someone's *cousin*. That's no way to debut in England."

"I didn't double deal. That's not fair. I just heard out Marcel's offer."

"I don't have time to continue discussing this," Robert said, standing up. "It's the first Saturday of the month, which means I have to lunch with Father."

In the run-up to the Érard concert, Léon had completely forgotten about Robert's dreaded monthly appointment. That explained Robert's bad mood. And, well, those sobs in the Dover hotel. "I'm sorry. I forgot," Léon said.

Robert lit a cigarette and took a long drag. His words were chatty, but he avoided Léon's eyes. "Ugh, it will be cold meats in heavy sauces, scowls of disapproval across the table. Both of us trying to think of something to say, asking questions and fearing we'll be asked a question. Try being a poet child to a stockbroker father. He had three sturdy and prosperous children, and a sturdy and prosperous wife, and they all died. What survived was *this* fey creature." Robert gestured to his long, fine body and popped his eyes open dramatically.

"Once your lunch is over, we'll have a great evening, so great that you'll forget all about it."

"How can we? He'll be there!"

"He's coming to my recital?" Léon asked. He'd known the hall would have plenty of strangers in it, of course. But he hadn't known it would have this particular stranger in it.

"Yes, we've set aside those house seats for friends and family. And he did fund this whole thing, Léon. Who knows, my father could be sitting next to your mother and your piano teacher. Can you imagine it?"

"Oh," Léon said, chewing slowly. "That's quite a thought."

Robert tilted his head backward. "Time to go. Mustn't keep Father waiting."

Léon laughed. "You're being very brave about this whole 'lunch out' sacrifice."

"Thank you, thank you." Robert stood, then laid a careless hand on Léon's shoulder before he headed out into the cold. "I'll see you there. You will be wonderful. Of that I'm certain. And write that card to Marcel right away."

That evening, Léon sat on the piano bench in the great hall of the Érard, parting the curtain with his foot so that he could peek out at the arriving guests. His mother and Charlotte and André were the first ones there and looked as nervous as he felt, shifting in their seats and speaking tensely to one another, reading and rereading the five lines of the program. Well, not André—he was excitedly pointing out elements of the Érard's ceiling and proscenium, making sure Charlotte and Léon's mother noticed every cupid and sun.

Léon's instructors and some of his classmates arrived next, taking up the scattered spots left over for them at half-price, dotting the hall. Léon remembered that day years before when he'd walked into the conservatory audition chamber, a child.

Reynaldo Hahn arrived, with a terrific front-row seat that he had gotten through a benefactor. He was close enough to see Léon staring through the parted curtain, gave him a warm wink. Léon waved back.

Marcel arrived next. He was alone, stroking his soft and drooping mustache. He examined his ticket, clearly confused about where to go, then recognized the countess and went to greet her, perching on the raised seat of the chair beside hers. She entertained his questions but clearly heard a voice she preferred and turned to see Robert behind her. She greeted him gaily, while Robert looked pointedly at the seat Marcel had taken. Marcel moved down one seat.

Robert was right about the scowl; his father was here, and Monsieur Montesquiou was a somber, glowering force. He stared angrily down at the seat Marcel had taken, then pointed to his ticket. Marcel moved even farther down, looking furtively around.

By then he'd made it to the end of the row of reserved seats. Marcel perched on the last available chair, unsure whether it was his to take. Unsure whether he was on the list of intimates.

He was not on the list. Léon had forgotten to even consider it. Robert had put the names together, and Léon had fought for his family's spots, then let it lie. He wasn't bankrolling the concert, after all, and was more than happy to let Robert handle all the social maneuverings.

Finally, minutes before the performance was to begin, Madame Saussine came walking down the aisle, greeting friends as she passed through the crowded hall. Then she came to Marcel's seat and glared at him while he read his program. Léon watched him startle and then apologize profusely, dashing to his feet and showering Madame Saussine with what appeared to be long compliments, very Marcel sort of compliments, full of dashes and semicolons. She accepted them all, then took her seat, and Marcel slinked to the back. Léon watched him take a second-rung stool, the top of his head barely visible. He probably couldn't see the stage at all.

Poor Marcel. Léon had done this to him. Unintentionally, but he had. And he was about to do much more, once Marcel received that terse, little card declining the invite his family had gone through such lengths to get.

He would make it all up to him somehow. For now, Léon had to focus on his concert. He forced his gaze away from the audience, away from Robert's scowling father, away from distant Marcel, and away from his nervous family, who had sacrificed so much to get him here. He would focus on Schubert—the very piece he'd auditioned with, that had once made the professors erupt into applause. Starting with that sonata had been Marmontel's idea, as a nod to history. He'd follow with a nod to the future by performing his latest composition, "Soirs d'amour," that had come to him while sitting for Sargent's portrait, then his own first sonata, that he called the "Félix Sonata," if only in his mind, and then to Chopin and Liszt and Debussy, daring to put himself alongside the great modern composers. Marmontel had said he would compare favorably, and Léon's teacher was not one for empty compliments.

Léon closed his eyes. His heart was racing, and his hands were slick. Some of the runs in his own composition tested the limits of his agility; sweaty fingers would be a problem. He ran his palms along his pant legs, wishing fashion allowed them to be absorbent cotton rather than this wool. He forced his mind to country paths, to Clémentine grazing, to a boy lying flat on the sun-warmed earth.

On the other side of the curtain, the audience hushed. Léon heard Robert's voice address them.

"Thank you, everyone, for coming. My dear Léon is overjoyed to have the opportunity to perform for you tonight, and I am overjoyed to have played some role, be it ever so small, in making it happen. As most of you know, I have always had an eye for beauty, as evidenced in my own poetry. In *Les Chauves-souris* I explored my interest in voices that broke through ordinary life and into the Beyond. My poems about beauty, though I like to believe they will still be beloved by many, will unfortunately be made hollow and meaningless by the performer you are about to hear. It will be my humble destiny as the Count of Montesquiou to serve as the lowly servant for the angel soon to descend among us."

Polite and confused applause. Then the curtain parted.

A stagehand lowered the chandelier over the piano. Léon looked up, remembering too late that Reynaldo had advised him not to, and its dozens of candles dazzled his vision, making it harder to distinguish anyone in the audience. He was actually grateful, since now he could concentrate on his performance. The Schubert began to unfold. As planned, the recital would go for only an hour, with no intermission. As if they were in a private home, not a recital hall.

Schubert: the late-summer walk with a boy and horse, peace and no need to strain.

The last movement of his sonata: the time the summer before when Léon had walked to Félix's home in a thunderstorm, only to find him running from his house in tears, his father yelling drunkenly at him. Following him and holding him wordlessly as the tears flowed and finally subsided into hiccups.

Chopin: an adventure on a bicycle, Charlotte pumping her legs wildly as pigeons scattered into the trees in the Jardin de Luxembourg.

Liszt: a picnic on an old gingham cloth, a candy-striped count smiling despite himself.

Debussy: two men kissing on a tin roof, with no worry or anxiety or fear between them. A scene that had never happened.

Léon played through in a transported state, his nerves only elevating his performance. He flubbed a single note, in the Debussy. As he finished the edgy, new "Prelude to the Afternoon of a Faun," rewritten for solo piano, Léon kept the pedal down so Debussy's music would reverberate through the audience.

The clapping began.

Léon stood, overwhelmed, as waves of applause shook the stage, demolishing the peace of the Debussy. He clasped his hands, bowed, and when he straightened, saw that some of the audience had stood. More followed as the applause continued, then most of the hall was on its feet. A man in the balcony shouted, "Bravo, bravo!"

Robert looked around in delight, his own gloved hands

making little claps, too soft to produce any noise. Then he made his way up toward the stage, cane in hand. He laid it on the stage floor, then began to hoist himself up. This was unplanned. Léon rushed to help him, holding a hand out to lift Robert. Murmurs joined the applause. Robert dusted himself off, then took on a surprised look around and dutifully bowed. The applause grew more strained.

Léon made a gesture of thanks to the crowd and started offstage. Robert wasn't done, though. He went down onto one knee before Léon, as if worshipping him. His face flaming red, Léon stopped and stood there awkwardly, staring into the audience and not at the count.

He didn't know what to do. The applause was rapidly dying down, and the murmuring was now louder.

Léon looked out, as if someone he knew might be able to beam advice through their eyes. The first person he saw was his mother, her face shifting from joy to confusion and something like fear. Charlotte and André were only shocked, mouths wide-open.

Madame Saussine had her gloved hand over her mouth.

Léon's eyes finally landed on Robert's father. He'd been stony before and was even stonier now. While the audience shifted uncomfortably in its seats, he stood, placed his hat on his head, and walked up the aisle to leave the hall. He passed by Marcel's stool. Marcel was wide-eyed, scribbling in his notebook every detail of the unfolding scene.

Finally Robert got to his feet, handing Léon his cane. Léon took it, unsure what he was supposed to do. Then he extended his other hand to the count. He guided Robert by the wrist, and together they floated backstage, the curtain whooshing shut behind them.

Robert clapped, a manic gleam in his eyes. "That went so well. Perfection! They loved us."

18.

ON MONDAY MORNING, LÉON FOUND HIMSELF LYING IN bed awake. The concert had been followed by a reception and then a smaller party at Robert's Paris apartment, and Sunday had been spent recovering from both. Now, it was Monday, which meant any coverage of the concert would be in the papers. His future was being printed at that very moment, and once the papers were delivered, all he would have to do was go out, buy some of them, and find out what it was.

His room was far above Robert's, near the maid's quarters. He watched the dark street below through the gauzy curtains, listening to the sounds of the rousing house and waiting for the first light of dawn to hit the window.

Then the sun was there, lighting the curtain's bottom edge, and he knew it wouldn't be too early to get himself the day's newspapers.

He dressed and tiptoed through the downstairs rooms, hoping the creaking floorboards wouldn't wake Robert. Then he was out the front door and onto the quiet morning street.

He greeted the corner baker arranging the day's bread and then passed by the old woman selling flowers. It would be a few blocks still until Place Solférino, which had the nearest newspaper stand, and he felt the before-ness of the moment, that he still didn't know what the future would hold. If the reviews were terrible, this might be the last time he'd feel good for a while. If the reviews were great, then a whole world was about to open—one where he'd have a career, receive commissions for his pieces, play grand halls.

He often bought his omnibus tickets to travel to the conservatory from this newsvendor, so they knew each other. The man waved as he saw Léon arriving. "Four reviews, Léon! I pulled them out for you."

"Four!" said Léon, running the last few feet to the kiosk. "That's more than I expected."

The newsvendor tapped a stack of papers next to the register. "Twelve sous, please."

Léon counted out the coins and clutched the stack to his chest. The one on top was still damp from the printer. "Thank you!"

As he made his way home, Léon ran his hands over the smooth paper, wondering what words were beneath his fingers.

Then he was inside Robert's still-wakening house. He sat down to a pot of hot chocolate, bread, and butter, served by Céleste. "My future is inside here!" Léon said as he laid the papers on the table.

"Are those your notices?" Céleste asked. "I'm sure they're terrific."

"Thank you, Céleste," Léon said, letting out a long breath. He leafed through the top paper. "Ah, here it is."

... and on the other side of the city, the noted young Liszt interpreter Léon Delafosse played a promising combination of classical piano work and compositions of his own, which shared the dreamy and evocative mood of Claude Debussy, who rounded out the recital.

"I'll take it," Léon said, and thumbed through the next paper.

A rare event transpired at the salle Érard on Saturday, as the young ingenue of the Paris Conservatory, Léon Delafosse, offered an afternoon concert that was open to the general public—should they have been able to get a ticket to the sold-out performance, offering them a chance to see the young star that until now has been closely guarded by elite society.

Léon yelped in glee.

A standing ovation was the fitting end to the sold-out Léon Delafousse recital at the Érard on Saturday. Frequent readers of this section should look for future opportunities to see this rising young star before his bookings inevitably take him farther and farther from our own shores.

"Delafousse," Léon murmured to himself, chuckling. "Why not?" He turned to the final paper, *Le Mensuel*. He started with the arts listings, looking for his name or the

Érard's in boldface. He was disappointed not to see it, but then noticed the large article on the opposite page, heading up the section.

AN ANGEL BESTOWS THE GREATEST ECSTASY ON HIS BENEFACTOR

The salle Érard was the site of great intrigue—not entirely of the musical sort—on Saturday, as the beautiful young pianist Léon Delafosse displayed the talents for which he is deservedly known. The sold-out audience was treated to an altogether more transporting performance at the recital's end, when the angel's flamboyant patron, the Count Robert de Montesquiou—known more for his decadent parties than for his slender poetic talents—made an impromptu appearance on his knees. He offered the knob of his cane to the beautiful creature, who caressed it with great care, before receiving the shower of the count's blessings. The discomfort of this conclusion, more Moulin Rouge than salle Érard, was only the higher for the truth it revealed: the ravishing young man has talents far greater than musical. Montesquiou's cane is more than a mere affectation; it is the erect post to which this young angel's elegant hands cling as he negotiates his rise.

—Anonymous

Léon closed the paper sharply and instinctively, as if he'd just seen a tick crawling along the center crease. His face flamed. "Oh my God," he said, his hands on his cheeks. "Oh my *God*."

"Is everything okay in here?" Céleste asked, ducking in. "How were the notices?"

"Very good," Léon said carefully, without removing his hands from his face.

"I'll tell Robert," Céleste said. "He's just waking and he'll want to see them, I'm sure."

"Yes, of course," Léon said absently, mind still reeling. "Or no—" But Céleste was already gone.

The fruit vendor was continuing to hawk wares in the street outside, and the sun was continuing to shine. But once Paris society read the day's papers, the sun would stop shining and the world would snap shut. He'd thought it was dread filling him, but it took him a few more moments to realize what it actually was: shame. Shame worse than he'd known he could feel, that was no longer in the back of his thoughts but was screaming from the center. Forevermore, the world would think of him only as a social-climbing pervert.

Robert glided into the breakfast room in his bathrobe, sashed tight over his slender waist. He selected a cigarette from the tray on a console table inlaid with a scene of a Japanese temple, lit it, and took a long puff before he sighed in pleasure. "The notices? Did they love it?"

Léon nodded vaguely and pushed the papers across the table. He debated throwing the last one out the window or ripping it into shreds and eating them until he gagged, but there were thousands more copies on newsstands across the city. There would be no avoiding the news.

He watched Robert read the first three articles, voicing aloud the phrases he enjoyed. He folded each one sharply and placed it in a neat stack before finally getting to the last. "'Delafousse,' that's a new one. I do think one of these *might* have mentioned me," he said.

"Well, one does . . ." Léon started to say before words failed him. He simply went quiet.

Robert sat far back in his chair, a smirk on his face. Then the smirk went brittle and left his eyes and finally his mouth. He leaned forward, lips forming the syllables of the words he was reading. He put the paper down and stared at Léon, his expression blank.

"What do we do?" Léon whispered.

Robert peered around the breakfast room as if it were the room of a stranger, as if he were seeing it all afresh: his basket of canes, the expensive imported cigarettes, the handsome young pianist living in his home, sharing breakfast with him, wearing his robe, on whose face Robert had been publicly accused of spraying his affections.

Robert's own face was unmoving. Only his eyes altered, turning red and wet. "Who would do this?"

"I don't know, it could be anyone," Léon said. As Robert began to cry, Léon was in shock. Only in their Dover guestroom had he seen Robert express a feeling like this, one that wasn't an emotion and ironic commentary on that emotion wrapped into one. He wanted to hug him, so they could comfort each other. But that would only confirm what the world had decided about them. Would prove their perversion. Even in the privacy of this room, he was too ashamed to touch Robert. And he knew that Robert didn't want him to.

So Léon folded his hands tightly in his lap while he watched Robert cry. He wanted to cry too, but what Léon felt most was fear. Every instinct told him to run as fast as he could, to get himself as far away as possible. Steal an ax, hide in the woods, drink river water, and forage berries. Live in the society of deer and wolves. He could cry later. What he needed to do for now was survive.

Robert tried speaking, but his throat wouldn't allow it. He coughed and hung his head back, taking long breaths.

Léon got to his feet. "Robert, are you—"

Robert looked directly at Léon for the first time that morning. His glassiness was gone. "You have ruined me."

"*I've* ruined *you*?!" Léon said. After that, he couldn't find words. He gestured around the room. Robert was the one with wealth and status and connections. The power to make choices. And he was accusing Léon of ruining *him*? But even though he was outraged, some cruel voice in Léon's heart also said that Robert was right, that Léon had brought this perversion into his life and was to blame for everything.

"You and your wide eyes, innocently climbing up society, using my connections and my power and my fame to maneuver yourself into the Érard recital and playing Kensington

Palace, and then putting me in the perfect position to discard. You've ruined my reputation, and now you'll move on to the next benefactor. Wasn't that what you mapped out? Was this something you and that weasel Marcel had planned the whole time? Take down the black rook and move on to the queen? Worship the knobby cane of some greater artist? Someone whose poems aren't slight and inconsequential?"

"Marcel?" Léon said.

Marcel. Of course this had been Marcel's doing.

"You didn't think I would recognize his oily prose, did you?" Robert asked. "He's always loved to point the finger at other men's inversion and hide his own. As if he's not opening his trousers for sailor boys every night in the district."

The review had Marcel's fingerprints all over it. "What he's done to you, he's done to me," Léon said. "He's ruined us both."

"Oh, you'll be sought-after now," Robert said, relighting his cigarette, which had gone cold in the ashtray during all the upset. "Maybe not for your skills at piano, though."

"Stop it," Léon said, then clamped his hand over his mouth. He wanted a bolt of lightning to fall right now, to give him what he deserved and turn him to cinders, so this could all be over. "Please stop it."

The brass bell above the mantel wiggled and tinkled. Someone was at the front door.

Robert's anger turned to fear. He fixed Léon with a desperate gaze. His hand reached out and held Léon's. The palm was wet with sweat. *The end is come. Save me.*

The two young men went still, as if they were prey animals. Céleste greeted someone at the door. Her steps scuffed as she approached the breakfast room. They whipped their hands away from each other. Céleste paused at the entrance, startled by the expressions on their faces.

She had a blue calling card in her hand. "What is that?" Robert asked.

Gaze down, she brought the card to Robert.

He seized it, read it, flipped it over to see the other side was blank, and then cast it to the table. The thick cardstock breezed right off and onto the floor.

Robert got to his feet, cinched the robe tight, and headed upstairs. "Paul," he shouted to his valet, "in my room now. And call for the carriage."

Before he headed up the stairs, he whirled on Léon. "At least our end is quick. The guillotine's blade has dropped."

In the quiet of the room, Léon breathed until some of the panic left his system. Then, hand trembling, he flipped the heavy blue cardstock over with his toe and left it on the floor, as if too much contact with the paper might poison him.

Robert. Come to my house as soon as you receive this. Without your "angel."
  —Father

19.

LÉON DREW THE CURTAINS CLOSED. FOR THE FIRST HOURS of the morning he sat near the window of Robert's Paris home, staring numbly out of the narrow gap where black velvet didn't quite meet black velvet. He wasn't sure what he was expecting—his mother and Charlotte storming back from Vernon to disown him, an angry crowd with pitchforks coming to bash in the door, drag him into the street, paint "abomination" on his body with hot tar?—but there was only the usual bustle of a Monday. The well-to-do glancing at their reflections in shop windows to fix hats and bonnets; vendors dragging donkeys dragging carts; youths lounging about and looking for trouble to remind themselves they were alive.

Eventually, Léon mustered the energy to go upstairs to his room. He was struck by how little evidence of himself was in it. A humble wooden brush, a stack of sheet music, a drawer containing the few simple clothes he'd arrived with, that he hadn't worn for months (he kept his new tailored clothing on a special rail in Robert's closet). He wished he had an image of Charlotte, his mother, or Félix to look at and feel some scrap of closeness. But he wasn't Robert; he couldn't afford to commission a painting or a daguerreotype. All he had was the memory of his family in the street after the Érard concert, filled with happiness for him as they headed off to get a stagecoach back to Vernon. What would they think of him now? Léon wandered the rooms, conversing with the paintings of Robert's ancestors, with their severe faces, watching this young interloper who had wrecked their legacy.

He didn't even have a piano to distract himself with—Robert's grand was at the Pavilion Montesquiou in Versailles. He could go to the conservatory to practice, of course, but that would mean stepping outside. *Léon Delafosse,* they would say, *how dare you show your face? Get him!*

Léon's stomach growled. This was one way to fill a void. He'd eat and eat. He waited for Céleste to put on her bonnet and then called to her, "Would you, perhaps, pick me up some cheese and bread while you're out?"

"Of course, love," Céleste said. "There's heaps of cheese in the downstairs kitchen, left over from your reception after the concert. I'll get you some nice fresh bread. The loaves we have are a bit stale."

"Oh, right," Léon said. "Thank you. I'll go downstairs." He passed numbly around the balustrade of the servants' stair.

"Are you quite all right, our Léon?"

Léon nodded and went downstairs to eat cheese.

Once he'd stuffed himself so much that he was in a stupor, he waddled back upstairs and risked parting the curtain to get a better view of the street. Robert would have to come home at some point, and when he did, he'd bring news of what his father said. Léon could find out if he was being cast in the pit, if he would need to move out, or if all was somehow forgiven, that a dandy count with a hundred canes and a jewel-encrusted tortoise could give up conventionality entirely and shrug off an accusation of immorality. What *was* a count capable of? Léon didn't really know.

They would be heading to England tomorrow, to prepare for the royal reception.

Would they be heading to England tomorrow, to prepare for the royal reception?

Robert didn't come back from seeing his father, not that whole day. But Céleste did return with fresh bread, so Léon headed downstairs to eat more cheese.

The next morning, Léon drew a basin of water and washed his face. Like on any ordinary day, even though he didn't know if this one would end with him imprisoned in Robert's house like a monster or having journeyed to England so he could play for the queen in full glory.

Amid the awful quietness of the house, he dressed in the outfit Robert had chosen for him, a fancier version of the classic black-and-white of his Sargent portrait, dingy old fabrics swapped out for brilliantly brocaded versions of themselves.

Dressed and packed, he sat in the front room and continued his watch over the street. He smoothed his hands over his pants, opened a book, and read for a while, switched to a magazine and then a newspaper, then returned his gaze outside.

A clatter rose in the street as a familiar carriage approached. It was green and black, gilt along the edges. Robert's glossy horses drew it, and the familiar brooding groom was seated on the lip.

Léon went to the front door and eased it open as the carriage came to a stop.

The door didn't open.

Normally, the groom would have dismounted to open it, but today he just gestured to Léon. "Get in."

Valise in hand, Léon opened the carriage door, prepared to greet Robert. But there was no one inside. A sheet of paper lay on the red seat.

Would it say to go back to Vernon, never to return? Léon crept inside. While he lifted the note, the groom shut the door. He fell onto the seat as the horses whipped into motion.

Léon,

I am detained. I will be at your reception with the queen, but you will need to finish your sitting with Sargent yourself. Go to him today, and meet me at the Albemarle Club at 11 in the morning tomorrow.

F.M.R.

Under the heavy paper were tickets. Train to Calais, ferry to Dover, train to Chelsea. Francs and crown coins beneath.

"Let's go," Léon called to the valet. But of course there

was no need—the carriage was already in motion. It didn't matter whether Léon asked for it to be or not.

Sargent's maid helped Léon with his valise, then gestured him into the chaotic overgrown garden. The painter smiled kindly as Léon approached, Ellie the collie twining around his ankles, eager for a scratch. "You must be exhausted from your journey, and I know you have that important reception tomorrow. I'll let you rest, but I wonder if you might sit for me right away, if for just a short while? The sun's about to set, and it's my only chance to see your skin in proper daylight."

"Yes, of course," Léon mumbled, and took his stool.

Sargent paused where he was preparing his palette. "Are you quite all right?"

Léon nodded. He fiddled with his collar and sleeves.

Sargent held up his brush, then put it back down. "Try to relax, Léon."

Was his shame stamped on him now? Would no one see him as a person, the person he was, as Léon, and instead he was now this imposter creature? Léon rubbed his face, put on a smile.

Sargent raised his brush to the canvas again. He peered at the image he'd started, chewing the end of his mustache. His all-seeing eyes moved from the canvas to Léon's face, then returned. He set his brush down, wiped it clean with a rag. "The light's not right after all," he declared. "We'll finish in the morning. Don't worry. You'll have plenty of time after to prepare for your recital. Did Robert book you into a hotel?"

"I'm not sure, actually. Are you sure . . . I haven't done anything wrong?" Léon asked. His lip quavered. "That it's really just the light, and not the way I'm sitting, or that I look tired, or something about me in general?"

Sargent moved around the easel to stand before Léon, extended a hand to help the boy up. "You've done nothing wrong." He looked deep into Léon's eyes. "Of course you haven't. Absolutely nothing."

"That's good," Léon said, his voice hitching. Sargent helped him to his feet. He couldn't be so totally wrong if someone was willing to touch him. Léon managed to smile. "I'm sorry. I've had quite a few days."

"Would you like some dinner? We have a spare room, if you'd like to stay here. I wanted you to meet my Albert, but he's out at his discussion society tonight, so it's just the two of us. I hope I won't be the worst company."

My Albert. The words tumbled in Léon's mind as he followed Sargent inside. They walked to the dining room, where the painter lifted a silver cover from a cold meal of sliced ham, pickles, cheese, half a loaf of dark peasant bread. "May I ask how old you are, Léon?" Sargent asked.

Léon thought for a moment. It was such an easy question, and yet his mind was so distracted. "Seventeen."

"Ah, over half my lifetime ago, then. I remember seventeen. I don't miss it. All these fresh and giant feelings. I'm less pretty now than I was then, but I'm much happier. Not that I was ever very pretty. I paint prettily, that's the best I can do."

Sargent set a chipped plate before himself and an unbroken one before Léon, then filled two goblets with water from a pitcher. "Please, start. You must be hungry from your journey."

Léon was famished, but the feeling was weirdly abstract. He lined some pickles up on his plate and stared at them.

"Léon, something is happening with you. How can I help?"

Léon wanted to tell Sargent everything and to tell him nothing. There was a chance that this could all blow over without anyone noticing. Maybe no one read that paper. Maybe the print run had been botched, and they'd only distributed that one copy that he and Robert had read. And the copy that Robert's father had read. Maybe they'd only distributed two copies. Maybe that was true.

"Are you nervous for your performance tomorrow?" Sargent asked.

"No, actually," Léon said, surprised to discover he was telling the truth. "Performing is the thing I'm least nervous about."

"I'm going to assume this is related to why Robert isn't here with you." He held up a hand. The lifeline was filled with dried black paint. "Don't tell me anything you don't want to tell me. But let's put dinner on pause for a minute. I want to show you something. In case it helps."

Léon followed Sargent through the dining room and down a long hallway. "As you can probably tell from my accent,

I'm American. I was born in Italy, though, and lived in Paris for years, so I suppose what I really am is a mutt. A mutt who speaks French, lucky for you. When I lived in Paris, I became famous for my portraits. It's what I love, and it pays well. Trying to capture the souls of people. Failing mostly but succeeding sometimes." He chuckled. "'Capture the souls of people.' That's a little more sinister than I intended."

It was so kind of Sargent to chatter, to fill this space with *you are worthy of being spoken to.*

Léon stepped into a dark-wallpapered room, framed canvases leaning against the wall. Sargent brought him to a large tableau in the corner, covered in a sheet. He whisked it off, spraying them both with dust.

It was as though a beautiful woman had just entered the room, she was that realistic. She wore a thick black velvet dress, deep off the shoulder, her pure white breastbone and neck leading to a light face and red lip, staring over her shoulder like someone had entered the room, someone she didn't know how to feel about. She was beautiful and sharp and sad and maybe a little bit afraid.

"Who is that?" Léon asked.

"Mademoiselle Virginie Gautreau, though she's known only as Madame X now. A darling of high society who wanted her portrait to be daring. Too daring by half, it turns out. She would burn this painting if she could, which is why I've hidden it away here. I painted this years ago, when I was at the height of the Paris scene. It was around the time I met Robert, though he was just a little boy back then. I was ready to push further, hit bigger, push envelopes, and ask questions. You could say I was cocky, I guess. She walked in with this dress on. She chose it. This is how she *wanted* to look. I should have pushed her to wear something more conservative. It was too suggestive, too dangerous. It made people uncomfortable, and uncomfortable people turn that feeling outward on others. It was a big scandal, and I had to leave Paris. That's why I live here now."

"All because of one painting?" Léon asked. "But it's so beautiful. And it doesn't seem that scandalous, at least not to me."

Sargent shrugged. "I'm still proud of the painting. I don't regret the art. But at the time I felt really low. Like everything I'd worked on was for nothing, like there was no future for me. And here's the thing, Léon: in a way I was right, and in a way I was wrong. *That* future was done for. I lost my most important and well-connected friends. I embarrassed myself and my family and Virginie. But as one future closed, another began. The second future was slow to start, but it had more room to grow. Another future will always begin. I'm doing more honest work now, here, than I could ever have done in Paris society. I'll live on through portraits like yours."

Léon knew Sargent was trying to tell him something. It's like he was predicting a downfall. Can pity be offered in advance? Coming from as soft a man as Sargent, it felt kind rather than presumptuous.

"If it all ends, it doesn't really end. That's all I'm trying to say," Sargent continued. "Paris society is fickle and judgmental. It raises up heroes only because it so enjoys to tear them down as villains. There are fewer options for men . . . like us, I know. We can't fall back on family. The streets are closer to us than they are for conventional people. If you need to, you can always come stay here. Whatever happens, Albert and I have a spare room you can use until you get back on your feet. If it ever came to that, you could leave France and never return. It would be hard, but you would survive it."

"I'll keep that in mind," Léon said, swiping at his eyes. "Thank you. Right now, everything looks okay, though. I'm playing at the Kensington Palace tomorrow after all."

"Yes, of course you are, and that's wonderful. I wish I could come, but Albert and I have planned a beach trip to Brighton," Sargent said as he lofted the sheet back over Madame X. He laughed. "Hopefully I won't let Virginie get as dusty between viewings this time."

"I'd love to come talk to her again," Léon said, leaning down to pet Ellie.

Sargent started down the hall, then stopped, clasping his hands over his chest. "I'm not sure if you're referring to the fallen lady or the dog, but the answer is yes either way." He took a deep breath. "Léon, there's something I want to say and I'm just going to say it: I know Robert, and I'm sure he's taking as much credit as he can for your success. But I also remember your playing last time you visited. It's your talent that's gotten all of this for you. Not

Robert's connections. Those might have helped, but they're not the reason."

"Thank you," Léon said. "Really."

"I might regret saying this, but it's possible that Robert wants you to be good and is terrified you'll be great. He might only want you to rise so far and no higher. Some people are like that. There, I've said my piece."

Léon's stomach growled. He would think on those words. Later. It had been a long day.

Sargent noticed the sound. "There's that appetite," he said. "Let's go eat."

20.

LÉON WAS OUTSIDE THE ALBEMARLE EARLY. HE'D GOTTEN up at dawn to sit for Sargent, then made his way over on foot. As he stepped inside the club's heavy front door, he was wrapped in a solemn hush, almost silencing the noisy tumult of the streets outside. A suspendered man behind a counter asked Léon what his business was, and when Léon told him he was meeting Robert, the man asked him to wait in the lobby. Robert's name was enough to allow Léon to stay, but it got him no farther inside.

He settled in to wait. How would Robert react to him? Warmth or coldness? Léon knew which one he thought he would get, but still, he hoped for kindness. Léon watched men in top hats come and go, linger in conversation by the door. Their English went by too fast for Léon to catch much, but he assumed it was talk of business deals, of travel, of wives, of politics. Finally a pair of men came by speaking French. They were hushed, conspiratorial, perhaps speaking French to cover their conversation from eavesdropping ears.

"There'll be a new position open at the club now, I wager."

"Yes, hit play in the West End or not, that sodomite won't be getting out of jail anytime soon."

"To think it all started in this very club."

The other man laughed. "We like to say the Albemarle is for 'extraordinary men.' Perhaps we ought to have clarified precisely what we meant."

Léon's breath shallowed, his limbs tingling. Was this Robert? Had Robert been arrested? His mind went to their night in the hotel room, that stained sheet.

"It breaks my heart, though I dare tell only you that. I always enjoyed my conversations with Oscar. He always had something amusing to say, unlike the sorry rest of us."

The man tugged on his black calfskin glove. "Four or five amusing things, I'd say, when one would have sufficed. That's really the core of his problem."

Ah, this wasn't about Robert.

"He ought to have fled to France when he had the chance" came a voice from the edge of the room.

Robert was in spectacular form, finely tailored in red silk, like an elegant take on a cooked crab.

The two men nodded their heads.

Robert must have seen Léon, but he didn't make any sign of having done so and certainly wasn't going to introduce him. Instead he twirled his cane—this one with a Union Jack on the knob. "It's really a queer dark sort of poetry, isn't it? Being me, today. Oscar Wilde is going to prison. *I* am France's Oscar Wilde. It is like my shadow, my English shadow, is being detached from my body and sent away to suffer. Like Oscar is the portrait, and I am his Dorian Gray!"

Léon couldn't understand why Robert was making a mocking performance out of all this, and so loudly. What

would either of them do if they someday wound up surrounded by ruffians in a prison cell? Oscar Wilde would
surely die in prison. A man like Oscar would die in a place
like that. Any of the three of them would.

Léon's eyes darted around the quiet club room, small
groups of men in hushed conversation, reading the paper,
maybe reading the very same article, all about the sodomite
Oscar Wilde, wondering the same thoughts about the other
sodomites that might be walking free among them. Léon
wanted to leave. But he couldn't say anything. He hadn't
even been introduced.

The two men obviously didn't know what to say back
to Robert either. They busied themselves retrieving their
coats from the check.

Robert laughed in their direction. "I suppose I ought to
have worn black today, not this tarty red."

"Good morning, Robert," Léon said quietly.

When Robert finally turned toward him, Léon could see
how very exhausted he looked, his face both oily and flaking
with dryness, his eyes sunken in purple pools.

"Come, Léon," Robert said. "Get your jacket."

Léon put his fingers to his lapels, confused. He was still
wearing his jacket.

Robert began to whistle "Greensleeves," of all things.
He removed a wad of newspaper from his bag and tossed it
into the fireplace, watching it go up in flames. Léon could
only assume that it contained the article on Oscar Wilde
and imagined Robert at breakfast, folding it again and

again while he ate his scone, planning just what he would do with it.

Then Robert took up his English cane (that saucy pink Union Jack gleaming from the handle) and headed to the brougham stand outside. The attendant—a handsome, straw-haired lad—asked if Robert had a carriage he could fetch. Robert did not keep a carriage in London, though, and asked for a cab instead.

Once the straw-haired boy had opened the door and helped Robert in, the door hung open in space. Léon was meant to follow. He got in, thanked the boy, and watched him seal the door shut.

Robert was sitting primly, trying not to touch any surfaces, as the tired horse pulled them clop by clop closer to Kensington Gardens. Léon thought of Clémentine, Félix and Clémentine, managing the family farm on their own.

He cleared his throat. "How did . . . how did the conversation with your father go?"

"I do not wish to speak of it," Robert said primly.

"I understand," Léon said. "If you decide you want to—"

"I will not decide that," Robert said. His face was so sharp, so resolute. But how could Robert possibly feel resolute? He must be this same puddle of shame and uncertainty; why pretend otherwise, when he was alone in a carriage with Léon? Léon watched Robert watch as town houses were opened up, chamber pots were emptied, as cooks and nobles and street cleaners freely made their way in a country that imprisoned men for loving one another.

Robert removed a glove and held up his hand idly, pointing at the gold ring he always wore. "I had this made when I turned seventeen. Encased in the gold is one of my own tears. I wear it always."

Léon stared out the window, heart racing. He'd noticed that ring long ago, had no idea that it supposedly had one of Robert's tears inside it. What was he supposed to say to that?

Robert called for the driver to stop outside Kensington Gardens, and the two boys made their final approach on foot. Robert gave his name to the guard at the ornate gate before passing toward the palace entrance and making his way to the conservatory, a sort of fancy greenhouse with one wall all of leaded glass and a roof bursting in light blue paint and sculpted cupids. Léon stopped to admire it, but Robert kept right on going, marching up to the door. Through the glass Léon could see beautifully dressed people, milling and nibbling and gossiping.

Robert shrewdly took in the crowd while he waited for Léon to catch up. "No Queen Victoria, of course, she couldn't really be troubled by something like this," he said once Léon was near. "Even without that salacious tidbit in *Le Mensuel* it was foolish to have hoped she might come, but there's a good representation of famous names nonetheless. Even if I hadn't recognized their faces, we would know that from the fact that those six guards are stationed along the outside of the conservatory glass."

Léon hadn't noticed them; the men wore tailored suits like anyone else. The only signs they weren't regular guests were that their hands were crossed and they weren't talking to anyone.

"This is where we part," Robert said. "The English style is that you arrive while the party is in mid-swing. You don't wait for an introduction; you just take to the piano and sit. Wait for thirty minutes, then make your entrance and play."

Léon dug his hands into his pockets. "Robert, we haven't talked, not at all really, since that article came out."

"We will talk, don't worry," Robert said. "Now, I'm going in the entrance for guests, and I'm going to enjoy some conversation while we all wait for you to show your face. *You* go around to the other side of the conservatory. You'll find a plain door. That is where the musicians enter. Just explain that you're the young French pianist and they'll let you through. Don't enter for half an hour, though, remember."

"Thank you, Robert," Léon said. "I . . ." He let his voice trail off.

Robert was already stalking toward the entrance.

Léon blinked under the sunshine. There were swans gliding over a pond, toddlers learning to walk on gravel and clover. It was a normal day. His concert was still happening.

But Robert was totally inscrutable, and dread was heavy in Léon's stomach. He was tempted to return to Sargent's home, get into the guest bed, and pull the sheet over his head.

Instead, he dutifully made his way around back, found the gray door. It was locked, so he knocked. A young woman wearing black, with hair frizzling out under a cap, answered. "Hello, can I help you?"

"I'm performing today," Léon said in French.

"Oh, another one?" the woman replied in French. "Come through."

She waved him in and then stalked down a narrow dark hallway. Léon sped to keep up. "That accent of yours is proof enough for me," she said over her shoulder. "Come, come, watch your step, here we are."

She stopped before a wide set of double doors. "You know what to do from here, I think," she said.

"I believe I do," Léon said. "Thank you."

Sounds of conversation passed through the doors, hushed words in English, occasional laughter. How long had it been? Léon wasn't sure. He wasn't supposed to play for half an hour, Robert told him, but that didn't mean he couldn't join the room, feel the mood of the party so he could better decide when to start.

Léon cracked open the door and slipped through.

There was a flash of gray wool. He'd clearly startled whoever was on the other side. "I'm sorry, monsieur," Léon said in French, "I didn't mean—"

"What sort of business is this?" the man said in English. He was joined by another man in a dark wool suit—they were two of the guards that Robert had pointed out. The men hemmed Léon in with their broad bodies, keeping him pinned at the entrance.

"I'm sorry, excuse me," he said. "I'm supposed to play here today."

The men looked at each other and then at Léon. Some of the tension left their bodies. "What's your name?" one asked in English.

"Léon Delafosse," he replied. He pantomimed playing piano.

"You're not the pianist," the other man said in French.

"I'm sorry, but I am," Léon said. He nervously crunched his hat down on his head, so it bent his ears. He needed it to feel like a helmet.

Suddenly, thankfully, Robert was there. He draped an elegant arm over the shoulders of one burly attendant, who evidently knew him. "Is there a problem here?"

"Robert!" Léon said. "Tell him. He doesn't have me on the list. There's some sort of mistake."

"There's some sort of mistake," Robert repeated, smiling blandly at the attendant.

"Sorry, milord, I didn't realize he was with you," the guard said, stepping to one side.

"Thank you," Léon said. "I'm glad that's been fixed."

"I am as well," Robert said absently. "Léon, you're late. You have to start now."

"What do you mean, I'm late? You said to wait half an hour."

"I said no such thing, I'm sure of it. It's all right, don't worry, no one's angry, but you should start now before anyone gets restless."

Léon's gaze darted from the piano and back to Robert. "Are you sure? I was hoping to—yes, of course, I'll start."

Sweat broke over his brow as he hurried over to the piano. He said "excuse me" over and over as he worked his way between a cluster of women in varying shades of pink. They broke off their conversation, shocked and scowling. They would understand why he was in a rush once he began to play. Then everything would be fine.

Finally he was at the piano. More and more people began to mutter darkly as he pulled out the bench and sat.

Not daring to look up and see everyone staring at him, Léon began to play. Music would make everything better. At Robert's encouragement, it was a song of his own composing, more daring than anything he'd yet played of his own, more in the vein of Debussy than Schubert.

Just as Robert said they would, conversations stilled.

Léon played his étude in G major, which began briskly, a walk on a loud and cheerful beach, sun hurting the eyes and children crying over spilt ice cream.

He had just arrived at his favorite part of the music, the measures he'd written once and then altered time and time again, until he'd gotten them just right. He was on that beach in the mind of the music, shaking out a crisp new towel, only a trace of cloud in the sky—

The piano lid shut on his fingers. He yelped, blinking as he looked around the room.

One of the guards had shut the piano on his fingers.

Beside him, reluctant and abashed, was Reynaldo Hahn.

Léon struggled to process. Reynaldo Hahn. Was here, in Kensington Palace. At the same time as Léon.

Léon's mouth opened and closed. This made no sense.

"Léon, why are you playing at my recital?" Reynaldo asked, bewildered.

Léon shook out his stinging fingers, ears rushing with the noise of his own racing blood. He could only barely make out Reynaldo's words. It was like Reynaldo—everyone in the hall—had suddenly gotten very far away.

More men in dark gray wool were saying things to him in English. He probably couldn't have understood them in the best of circumstances, and he certainly couldn't now.

Reynaldo was still speaking, moving to the end of the piano, a hand on it, as if reclaiming stolen property. Léon looked at him, then at the three men—who, from the set of their lips, had switched to French—and his face began to flame. He still couldn't make any sense of what was happening.

"Léon, if you just leave, I'll try to explain that there's been some mistake," Reynaldo whispered.

The enormity hit him. He looked at the dozens of faces staring at him, whispering, at Reynaldo Hahn, the star conservatory pianist. Who had scampered his way right up salon society, who was welcome at dinner as well as at the keyboard. Léon had been set up. He was not meant to play here today.

Then, as he felt the blush on his face continue to deepen to scarlet, Léon looked out, appealing for help. His lips formed two syllables: *Robert*.

Léon finally found him, almost hidden by the folds of the long crepe curtains at the window. It was less like Robert was attending the event than that he was haunting it.

Léon gestured hopelessly to Robert, still beyond words. *He will explain.*

Robert sprang into sudden motion, took up his cane, and crossed the conservatory in three long strides. The whispering crowd made room for him.

Léon looked at him gratefully.

"Have you no shame?" he asked Léon.

He turned to the men and women of the English court, arms extended. He spoke in English. "This is scientific proof that *les rats de Paris* and the rats of London are one and the same species. Having nuisanced his way into all the houses of Paris, Monsieur Delafosse has moved on to the houses of London. You should join me in casting out the rat. If he has no warm place to sleep, he will die in the cold and leave us all be."

21.

LÉON COULD ONLY BARELY UNDERSTAND ROBERT'S words—they came too fast in a foreign tongue. But he knew how they felt, and he saw the reaction of the crowd. Gasping, whispering, laughter, scandalized stares at Léon, or, for most of them, very deliberately not looking at Léon at all. The ultimate dismissal.

He looked for support in Reynaldo, but his friend's expression was a different sort of shock: *Léon, how could you think you'd get away with this?*

Robert stood with his hands on his hips, staring down at Léon, the red of his suit shockingly bright in the springtime sun glancing through the conservatory windows.

Léon's brain caught up. The situation was actually simple. He'd been publicly assassinated.

There wasn't an easy way out of the room—the crowd covered the exit. Léon placed a hand on Robert's elbow. "Why have you done this?"

Robert snapped his arm away, scoffing. "Look, he's in *love* with me now."

Léon slapped away the tears that stood in his eyes. He almost found himself saying *I'm sorry,* but he caught himself.

He had been betrayed. What words were there for that? If there were any, they were not *I'm sorry*.

Léon swung his legs around the piano bench and stood, nearly tripping himself in the process. After another furious swipe at his eyes, he shoved through the crowd to the exit. The guards looked to the hostess, but she made a delicate wave of her hand: *Let him go*.

As Léon opened the door, he heard Robert's voice addressing the crowd in English: "Forgive me, and more importantly please hold none of this against the talented young pianist you are about to hear, whom you were meant to hear. France has more and better to offer than what you just witnessed."

Léon was in the hall. A moment of breathing heavily into his hands, then a few more steps and he was outside, past the guards and into the Kensington Gardens. His steps became jerky, his limbs numb. He made it to a great shady elm and collapsed at the base before erupting into tears.

It was over. He didn't even have his bag, which was back in the palace hallway. He was in a foreign land, with no benefactor and only whatever money he had in his pocket to get him home.

Home? Where was that? Would it still exist once word got out?

He knew he had the right to be angry, but that feeling didn't come. All he felt was shame. Not to have done wrong but to have *been* wrong. Robert had aired some awful and essential truth about him, and the world had seen it.

He maneuvered around the tree, so that the bulk of its trunk shielded him from view of the palace. Maybe conversations were continuing while Reynaldo performed; maybe they were deciding what to do about the intruder who'd tried to take over an innocent and charming young man's recital.

Léon, he told himself, *you don't want them to come outside and find you here.*

He got up, brushed leaves and flower petals from his pants, and began to walk.

He started by skirting the edges of the garden, the baffling sounds of English all around him. Would anyone speak French back if he asked for directions? He couldn't risk talking to anyone, in case they yelled at him or cut him down. He was too dressed up not to attract attention, but even the supposedly admiring gazes seemed to be hiding anger behind them: *How dare you pretend to be more than you are?* Léon chose the paths that would take him near ducks, not people. Even they seemed to be taunting him by being so carefree.

By the time he'd made it to the end of Kensington Gardens, Léon's tears had dried. He paused by a pond to take an inventory of his pockets. A few French centimes, one English crown, his passport, and his return ticket on the ferry from Dover.

Léon's crossing wasn't until the morning. He'd have to spend the night in England, somewhere.

The closest he had to a friend here was Sargent. Léon couldn't afford a cab ride there, not when he'd need that crown for his train ticket, but he'd ridden that way this morning and could retrace his steps. He thought.

It was afternoon by the time he reached Sargent's door, and the sky was starting to spit rain. He knocked, first politely and then with his whole fist. He felt like the mother of Quasimodo, begging to be let into the cathedral at the beginning of *Notre Dame de Paris*. *Sanctuary, please give me sanctuary!* There was no answer. The painter must be out.

Then he remembered: Sargent had said he was leaving for Brighton. He wouldn't be home for days.

Léon stopped a nanny pushing a pram. "Saint Pancras station?" he asked.

She said something lengthy in English, pointing to a passing omnibus. He shook his head. He couldn't afford that. He might not have enough for his train ticket to Dover as it was.

The woman pointed in a general direction, and Léon was off.

Every few blocks he'd ask directions from someone new, until finally he was at the familiar Saint Pancras station. He stood for a moment outside of the great hall and then entered the bustling line at the train window. "Dover," he requested in carefully enunciated English. The agent said some amount back. Léon pressed his crown coin under the window. The agent shook his head, tapped the counter. Léon showed his empty vest pocket. The agent shrugged, passed back the coin.

Léon had to get home. He couldn't be trapped in England forever.

Smiling tightly, he left the counter and made his way to the Dover train. He boarded without a ticket.

Léon didn't dare take one of the wicker seats—he figured that if he kept moving, maybe no conductor could check his ticket. His feet were sore from all the walking in his narrow, wooden-soled dress shoes, but the train trip was only three hours. He could manage it standing.

He stood near the door to the car, and when the conductor blustered near, he stepped into the second-class toilet, feet up on the seat so his shadow at the bottom of the door wouldn't betray him. He waited.

It was well past sunset by the time he arrived in Dover. Léon couldn't think what to do. His ferry wasn't until the morning, but still he continued toward the terminal. It had to be close to midnight when he got to the docks. A few grizzled and storm-nipped sailors gave him long looks as he passed. He couldn't sit down and wait out the night here, that was becoming clear.

Léon would walk. He would walk all night if he had to.

One of the grizzled men tailed him from the port area, and Léon picked up his pace. His feet had to be bleeding now; each step he took sent pain up his legs. The man followed for a few blocks, Léon imagining all the while the ways this could go. A friendly greeting, a mugging, a rape, a murder.

Then the man yelled something in English and stopped walking. Léon didn't risk turning around. He sped up even more.

The city of Dover eased into farmland. When a creek

crossed the dirt road, the water glittering in the moonlight, Léon followed along it. He could see the water, but not the ground, and his feet landed on soft clay, slipping him up to the knee in the cold water. He pulled himself onto the bank and couldn't make himself get up. He pressed his eyes against his wet knees and, shivering, rested as best he could.

When dawn finally came, he retraced his steps. His wet feet in their wet shoes were too painful, so he pried the shoes off, carried them in his hands, and went barefoot. In Vernon he'd had calluses enough to walk barefoot to town and back, but those calluses were long gone. The bleeding wounds on his soles were soon caked brown with mud.

He hobbled into the ferry station. He knew how he must look: dirt streaked his white shirt and his pants were still wet; the chill spring air had done little to dry them. He'd tried but failed to wedge his swollen and bleeding feet back into his shoes. The ticket agent avoided Léon's gaze as he placed his damp ticket in its own spot on the podium, separate from the other passengers' dry tickets.

Léon had a reservation for the first-class portion of the ferry, but when he went to enter the attendant said, with a pitying smile, "I'm sorry, sir, I can't let you in here like that."

Face on fire, Léon took a corner seat by the window in second class, training his face furiously outward, hoping no one would come over and ask what was wrong and if he was in trouble.

When the ferry blasted its horn and started moving, Léon filled with relief. He had a ticket for this passage. No one could kick him out. At least he wouldn't be trapped in England.

Once the ferry had arrived in Calais, Léon spent his remaining money on the train fare into Paris and a half-price ham-and-butter sandwich from yesterday's stock at the station boulangerie. He spent the journey mustering the courage to fight his wounded feet into his shoes, gritting his teeth each time a leather seam bit into a bloody blister. Once the shoes were on, the pain diffused, and he found he could put weight on his feet.

He was in Paris now. But where would he go? His mother had released the Delafosse apartment to new tenants after the Érard concert. The conservatory wasn't in session, and besides, he couldn't sleep there.

Who had he ever known? Who could he appeal to? His mind went back in time, thinking over everyone he'd met in Paris, who'd ever been sympathetic to him. He could plead his case, find out if he might have some foothold to restart his career.

He didn't know where his teacher Marmontel lived, or he'd try there. Whose homes had he been to?

Society functions. Glittering ballrooms.

Léon winced, both at the pain in his feet and his sorry prospects. That article accusing him of unnaturalness with Robert would soon be joined by the news of his public shaming at the Kensington Palace. And look at him, bedraggled and pathetic. What house would open its doors to him? He wasn't even allowed to sit in first class on the ferry, when he had a ticket for it!

Still, he had to try.

He made his way to the Île Saint-Louis, the home of the Saussines. Madame Saussine of the dove-gray dress, of the kind eyes, who'd once had such pride to introduce Léon to her guests. *Please, madame, let's start over,* Léon might tell her. *Pretend I never chose Robert de Montesquiou as my patron. Let me play for you again. I'm still your Léon Delafosse, can't you see?*

The tidy grounds of the Saussine house were shut away behind their formidable gate. Léon gave it a clatter, but it wouldn't open. He busied himself studying a poster for *Around the World in Eighty Days* glued to the scaffolding next door while he waited for someone to come or go. Finally a servant emerged from the house and unlocked the gate.

"Excuse me," Léon said, hat in his hands. "I'm sorry to bother you, but I was hoping to speak to madame."

The servant looked him up and down. "Madame Saussine? Is she expecting you?"

"No, but she knows who I am. Please just trust me. She'll listen. Please tell her Léon Delafosse is here to see her. The pianist."

"Léon Delafosse?" the servant asked. Léon watched the boy's face as he tried to place Léon's name.

Léon searched his pockets, coming up with his soggy ticket stub from the ferry crossing. He held it out, pointing to the name printed at the top. "Here, that's proof. That's who I am."

The servant looked at the name, then up the street wherever his business would have led him. He sighed. "I'll be back in a moment." He returned through the gate, making sure it had locked securely behind him.

Léon waited, suppressing shivers, kneading the brim of his hat.

The servant came back. This time he did not open the gate. "You must leave," he said. "The lady will not see you nor will the rest of the house. You will not be seen here."

"Did she . . . did she give a reason?" Léon asked.

"You must go," the servant said.

Face burning, Léon left.

The Giuffre house, where Léon had played a New Year's concert, was a similar story. His name was accepted acidly and then he was refused. At the Villeneuve home, no one answered, not even the lowliest servant—though the curtain by the entrance trembled as someone stared out between its edges.

It had been a day and a half since he'd been in a bed, and he'd had only that stale sandwich to eat. It wasn't that he was hungry—food was far from his mind—but the world had started to wobble from the lack of it. The pain from his legs had become an ache that was all he could think about when he was aware of it, then was gone from his mind for long periods.

Before he knew it, his feet brought him toward Marcel

Proust's home. But he stopped himself. Marcel had been the architect of his downfall. Léon wouldn't give him the pleasure of witnessing him like this. He wouldn't give Marcel the chance to wriggle his way out with wordy excuses. He'd rather sleep in the gutter.

His scalp was itching intensely. Maybe it was that his skin was crawling with fatigue or maybe he'd managed to catch lice or fleas when he spent the night by that creek. "Have at me, boys," he whispered as he continued his way along the wobbling street. The world went bright for a moment, and he held on to a lamppost until he was steady again.

There was only one place left to try. The place he lived. Or had lived.

Robert was probably back home by now. He might have gone straight to the Pavilion Montesquiou in Versailles, or maybe he was spending a day in Paris first. There was a chance.

Léon began his walk across Paris. Maybe by the time he got to Robert's apartment, he'd have thought of what words to say to him. *Robert, is this because of your father? Did he threaten to disinherit you? Surely you didn't really mean what you said about me.*

He took a rest every few blocks, sitting on curbs amid busy streets, head between his knees, testing the swollen flesh of his ankles. When he passed the Jardin de Luxembourg, he took the opportunity to splash cold fountain water on his face until an angry swan chased him off.

Then he was on Robert's block. The old flower vendor

was in her usual position at the end, peddling her wares. She offered him a rose. "Free, free!" she said, shaking it so hard a petal fell. Léon was sure she didn't know he was the sinful boy from the newspapers, otherwise she wouldn't risk speaking to him. He was also sure that she'd use the free flower to compel him to buy a dozen more. Everyone just wanted to wring what they could out of him. Well, the joke would be on her—he had almost no money. He shook his head and kept walking. He stopped in front of Robert's house. It was dark and still.

Léon tugged the pull chain beside the front door. The bell rang through the quiet house. Léon stepped back and looked up at the building, the ballroom where he'd first met Robert, the roof where he'd unexpectedly spent the night a lifetime ago. He rang the bell again.

Finally the door cracked open. It was Céleste.

Léon stepped forward. "Thank you, I'm so glad you're here."

Céleste didn't fully open the door. She leaned so only her head was visible, the maid's bonnet bright in the afternoon light. She looked up and down the street, seeing if she was being watched. "Léon, you can't be here," she said.

Léon shook his head, pointed down at his wrecked body. "I have to be, Céleste, I have to be. I don't have anywhere to go."

"Robert left me clear instructions before he left for London. You're never to come in here again."

Léon placed his face in his hands.

"I'm sorry."

"I don't know where to go," he said, his voice muffled by tears.

"I am sorry," she repeated. "Léon, if I let you in, we'll both be out on the street. I can't afford to lose this job. Please, I'm risking it even by speaking to you."

"Can I—if Robert isn't even there, can I come in and wash up? And maybe rest for a bit?"

Céleste shook her head and closed the door.

Léon stood under the chill and blinding sky, undone.

He could wait here until Robert arrived, whenever that was. He could rail against him, against Marcel. But he had no power here. Without money, without a reputation, there was no winning move.

He staggered down the street.

"Free, free," the flower vendor said to him. Léon stopped in front of her. She held out the rose.

He took it. He couldn't muster the energy to say no. He looked down at the white flower. A ladybug wended his way between two of the petals.

Léon sat on the sidewalk.

The flower vendor adjusted the cart's umbrella so that it protected his eyes from the worst of the sun's glare.

Léon was only distantly aware of motion near his lap, then he felt a light weight. There was a handkerchief-wrapped bundle on his knee.

He gingerly unwrapped it, revealing a stuffed pastry so greasy it was translucent.

Léon parted it, revealing spinach and funky cheese inside. He brought half to his mouth, and then found himself eating ravenously. He thought he'd save the second half, but then he was eating it.

More motion in his vision. The woman had placed a fifty-centime piece on his knee.

He looked up, holding the piece out to her. "I can't take this."

The old woman crossed her arms, shook her head. *I won't take it back.*

Léon stared down at the piece. Half a franc wouldn't fix his problems. It would only prolong his suffering.

He held the piece out again. The flower vendor shook her head and gestured to the corner. Léon followed the course of her arm. The telegraph office.

He looked down at the piece again.

Fifty centimes. The price of a telegram.

22.

AS THE AFTERNOON DARKENED TO DUSK, THE FLOWER vendor invited Léon home. Her name was Antonia, and she lived on the edge of the northern slums, in a neat and tidy one-room apartment that—she explained in broken French—she sometimes shared with her son and daughter. The son was off working a fishing ship, and the daughter was a chambermaid in a hotel, so it was just Léon and Antonia for the night.

Antonia rolled up the oiled paper shade and lit a votive candle, either to fight the ratty odor coming from the walls or to pray to the Jesus etched into the glass. She offered him some of her son's clothing, and Léon sighed in relief to get his damp dress suit off, to wrap his tortured feet in clean and soft—if much darned—socks.

He went downstairs and spent his last coins on two skewers of lamb from a street hawker, and by the time he brought them up the old woman had set a simple table. The tablecloth was the same gingham colors as the picnic blanket Léon had once used to entertain Robert.

They ate in silence—the woman didn't speak much French, and Léon didn't speak whatever language she did speak, which he was coming to suspect was Greek.

His eyes, already half-lidded, began to close before he'd even finished his skewer.

Antonia tried to offer him her bed, but Léon refused, pointing repeatedly to the floor. He did allow her to place her blanket on the worn floorboards, softening his resting place. Léon was asleep before she'd even had a chance to blow out the Jesus candle.

He was awakened by the sound of her shuffling in the dark, the striking of a match and whoosh of a gas burner lighting, the smell of coffee. He joined Antonia at the table, where she pressed a mug into his hands. Its tin soon turned searing, so he gripped the handle with his napkin in order to drink.

He warmed his clothes near the burner, then he stepped behind the pantry curtain to change back into his recital clothing. He kept Antonia's son's socks, and the extra cushioning made his own shoes tolerable. The socks he had been wearing—black Italian wool, purchased on Robert's account—he left drying on the edge of the wicker basket with the rest of Antonia's son's clothing. He could have them.

They stepped out into early morning Paris. Antonia led him down the quiet streets of the slums. They'd arrived in the dark last night, but it had been a bustling, loud dark. This time before dawn was the only hour of true quiet in the city. Antonia knocked on a broad warehouse door and waited patiently.

Out came a burly mustachioed man, who greeted Antonia in Greek (or maybe it was Turkish?) and came rolling out a wooden cart already loaded with crates. Where the wood had splintered, Léon could see flowers, their colors reduced to grays in the near black.

Antonia took the cart in her hands, but Léon prized the handles from her. She accepted his help, and together they headed down the cobblestones into Paris, Antonia leading the way and Léon clattering along after, doing his best to avoid ruts and potholes.

It took at least an hour to make it to Robert's block on the Rue de l'Université. It must have taken that long to go the opposite direction the night before too, but Léon had been beyond noticing. He thought to the long mornings spent waking in leisure in Robert's rooms, when they used to complain about the racket in the street below. Some people had been up for hours just to produce that racket.

Antonia positioned the cart. She was particular about it; there were certain grooves in the cobblestones that she clearly preferred. Then she went about opening the crates, inspecting the flowers, nodding approvingly at some, casting others back in with a tsk. She took up a bucket and handed it to Léon, gesturing to the public water pump at the end of the block.

Still in a stupor from the day before, he walked the bucket down and took his place in line among charwomen and servants. He pumped for the woman in front of him, and she worked the pump for him. Bucket filled, he sloshed his way back down the street.

A curtain moved.

Robert's apartment. The second floor—his bedchamber. A long, handsome face staring down, sharp nose, expression unreadable.

Léon, stained recital clothing, hair greased down on his head and still showing the shape of Antonia's floor, waddling down the block with a dented bucket.

He didn't stop. He returned his gaze to the cobblestones and kept it there until he'd arrived back to Antonia. He helped her fill the smaller buckets that contained the roses, the lilies, the chrysanthemums.

He forced himself not to look back at the house at number 30. He never would again.

Late morning. Léon was no help selling flowers—so he sat near the cart, chin on his knees, watching people pass by. Brooding.

When the sun had reached midday, Antonia brought out two wrapped sandwiches—a small kernel of cured fish in the center of each, but mostly bread and oil—and they ate them while the sun warmed their faces.

Léon folded the waxed paper so Antonia could use it again. It was pleasingly soft and had clearly been reused plenty of times before. When he handed it to her, he saw, out of the side of his vision, horse hoofs. They clopped along, then stopped before Antonia's cart. She might finally have a customer.

He looked up.

Clémentine groused along the curb, lipping a filthy lettuce

heel and rejecting it, probably searching for dandelion weeds to eat. Riding her was a familiar person. Deeply familiar. Mussed red hair, sunburn and freckles, soft and open smile. "Félix?" Léon said.

He made a mock bow, then gestured to the bustling city around them. "This is . . . a lot, isn't it?"

Léon nodded, eyes wet. "Yes, it's a lot."

Félix stroked the horse's flank. "She's had a long walk. We left as soon as you sent word. It took us the day to get here."

"You came . . . through the night?"

Félix nodded, ran a hand through his thick hair. "Does it show?"

Léon laughed. "Yeah, a little." He pointed to his bedraggled outfit. "I'm not in the best condition either."

"I thought life in the city was supposed to make you *more* glamorous."

"Watch it."

Antonia eyed them curiously. "This is Antonia," Léon said. "Antonia, this is Félix. From my home."

"Hello," Félix said. Antonia nodded.

Léon stood, his arms awkward by his sides. He wanted to ask Félix to get down from the horse so he could embrace him, but . . . that idea of embracing anyone had gotten so complicated recently. So he tried to act normally, even though his heart had dropped right out of his rib cage. "I sent the telegram to Charlotte," he said. "I thought that she'd be the one to come help."

"I'll let her tell you, but she has reasons not to travel."

"She's . . . pregnant?"

Félix shrugged. "I know nothing, I told you."

"And you traveled through the night to get me."

"I've never been to Paris, and I've always wanted to see it, and we've already done our spring planting, so Clémentine is well rested, so . . . yes. I guess I did. Your sister and mother were scared by your telegram, Léon. It sounded bad."

"Thank you for coming," Léon said. "And all through the night too. Thank you. I don't know what else to say."

"Do you . . . want to come home?"

Léon nodded.

Félix stroked Clémentine's flank. "She might be slow, but she never tires out. She won't notice skinny you joining me up there. If we want to make it to Vernon by night, we should head out now."

"Okay," Léon said. "I'm ready. I don't have a bag or anything." He leaned in and whispered in Félix's ear. "Do you have any money? Antonia saved my life, basically."

"I have a franc," Félix said. "Your sister gave it to me. It's for our lunch on the way home."

"Okay to go hungry? I'd like to give it to her."

"We passed long brambles of raspberry along the way," Félix said. "Clémentine was upset that I didn't let her stop and browse. We'll take a break on the way home, have a nap in the sun, and eat some raspberries. There was a brook nearby too, to get us and Clémentine some water. So sure."

"Thank you," Léon said. He accepted the coin from Félix

and pressed it into Antonia's palm. She didn't resist, just pocketed the coin and put her hands in prayer.

Félix patted the space in front of him. "Are you ready? Like old times?"

Léon nodded. He gripped the pommel and swung his tired body over. It settled into Félix's perfectly, like two halves of a nut had been rejoined.

Epilogue

1895

A MORNING IN LATE SUMMER, QUIET AT THE FARMHOUSE except for the drone of the bees. Léon is standing at the front window, drinking a chamomile tea brewed from garden clippings.

The upstairs bed is laid with fresh linens, scented with lavender from Félix's garden, so fresh that Léon has just found a praying mantis walking across a pillow. He carries it out the back door.

The house is ready. No amount of wandering its rooms will make it more or less so. And yet! That's what Léon keeps doing. Making sure.

The evening Félix brought him back from Paris, they'd parted ways, Léon going to live with his mother. He got the front bedroom, now that Charlotte had settled in with André. But then there had been that terrible winter, when Léon's mother had died, followed by Félix's father, and Félix was overwhelmed with the farm.

It had happened slowly at first, and then all at once. Léon lives here now.

There are still four hours until their guests arrive—and that's if everything goes well, if the train and ferry are on time. Léon prepares lunch for Félix's mother; her soft, old teeth hurt so much these days that she is eating mostly porridge in her upstairs bedroom. She hasn't been up yet today, but Léon knows that is because she is marshaling her strength to make an appearance that evening.

Léon sits on the foot of her bed while she eats, watches out the window as Félix swings his scythe against the tall yellow stalks of wheat. They sold half the land and kept only a small field, enough to bring their grain to the miller so Léon can bake all year, but even farming this reduced plot is shirt-drenching, backbreaking work. Léon canceled all his teaching appointments for harvest week, but Félix insisted that he put them all back. "We need the money," he said. "And your students need to know you're always there. It's good business."

And so Léon is bathed and neatly dressed, standing in the front room with a tea, while Félix labors outside under his wide straw hat, skin pinking beneath the August sun.

Léon's first student of the day is just arriving, on foot, her music folder tight in her grasp. Louise. She's one he inherited from his mother, before that winter day when she collapsed on the front walk, never to get back up. Louise is charming and talkative, probably a little in love with Félix. She never practices and she never improves. Léon adores her. "Hello, Louise!" he calls out, waving.

"Léon, hi!" she says, running up the last steps to the house and taking her place at the piano, chatting about bluebirds and school lessons and church and is Félix around today?

Léon taps the music. "Chopin, Louise, Chopin."

After a tinkling and discordant hour, Léon's next student

arrives, and then the next. He is glad to have the distraction, so he doesn't just sit and anticipate the evening's guests.

By the time his teaching afternoon is over, the sun is orange and halfway down the sky.

Félix comes in, fetches a tin jug, then fills it again and again from the pump out back, quenching his thirst. He grooms and feeds Clémentine in front of the barn, then comes to join Léon inside. "Students done for the day?" he asks, picking bits of hay from his thick hair.

"Yes," Léon says beside the kitchen sink. "And I think I just have time to—"

In two strides, Félix is next to him, embracing him. The sweat from his torso is already seeping through Léon's shirt. "I was going to wear this . . ." Léon gives up resisting. Instead he lets his lips meet Félix's, presses his body against his, clenches his open hands against Félix's shoulders, wet with sweat.

Léon pulls back, loses his fingers in Félix's damp hair. "Now you bathe."

Félix wiggles like a wet dog, spraying Léon even more. "Join me?"

Léon laughs. "I think I'll have to."

Two hours later, around a long table out back of the farmhouse, cicadas are throbbing. Félix's mother dozes at the head, in the comfy armchair they brought out expressly for her. Félix, his usual quiet and patient presence, is sitting at the other end, asking endless short questions to Albert, who gives endless long answers. Léon and John Sargent are in the middle, facing each other across the table.

"I'm sorry about Albert," Sargent says. "Once he's started, he keeps going. He even talks in his sleep."

"He's delightful," Léon says. "I'm glad to finally meet him."

"Me too," Sargent says. "I'm so glad this happened. When Claude Monet wrote inviting me to Giverny, and I discovered the nearest train station was 'Vernon,' I thought—it couldn't be! The place where that young pianist was from?"

Léon lifts his glass in a toast. "And now I'm back. And Giverny is right over the hillside."

"See, what did I tell you?" Sargent says. "Assassinations are perfectly survivable. Well, the social kind are."

"Maybe . . ." Léon says, "maybe it's even all for the best." He goes pensive. He'd never willingly go through something like that again. But he does love his life now. Being him for his sake, writing music for music's sake.

"How's . . ." Sargent glances at Félix's mother. "How's the reaction, to . . . What am I trying to ask . . ."

Léon knows precisely what Sargent is trying to ask. He watches the slow rhythm of Félix's mother's chest to make sure she is asleep. She can't hear much even when she's awake, anyway. "I moved in to help Félix manage his farm. We're partners in that. I'm sure people are talking. If we were strangers here, I think we'd have run into trouble by now. But we know everyone in Vernon, for better or for worse. Most people could take or leave me, to be honest, but they all adore Félix. It's a small town, and if people in a small town like you enough, they're perfectly willing to turn a blind eye to anything. Everyone here has something that needs a blind eye turned to it."

Sargent laughs. "Albert and I require blind eyes from everyone we meet. Three or four of them at least."

"How long do we have you?" Léon asks.

"We're hoping to stay a week or two here, until we outstay our welcome. If it's all right by you, I do want to spend the days with Claude, painting his flowers. Maybe while I'm out you can teach Albert how to farm or at least bake." Sargent breaks out laughing, crying before he manages to rein it in. He wipes his eyes. "Farming might be out of the question, but he does clean dishes and pump water. That's about all I can promise. Then we continue down to Provence and into Italy. A bit of a grand tour, really. We think we're unique and then we go and do what everyone else does."

"It sounds lovely. Maybe Félix and I will manage something like that one day."

"You could come with us, if you like."

"Farming and teaching keep us here, I'm afraid." Léon yawns. "You wouldn't believe what time we wake up."

"Albert and I will keep out of your way so you can . . . go pick eggs? What do farmers do at four in the morning?"

"From the sound of it, I'm worried you think eggs grow on trees."

"That's just my French getting in the way. Léon, how is composing going?"

"I make my stabs at it," Léon says. "Some moments might

actually be good. But I'll never be France's Mozart, not like they'd all once hoped."

Sargent pushes food around his plate. "Things didn't work out too well for that Mozart fellow, you know."

"Yes, I think about that sometimes," Léon says.

A voice rings out gaily from around front of the house. "Don't get up. We're coming right around back. Everyone get yourselves in order. We have dessert!"

Albert breaks off midstory. "Let me guess. That must be the Charlotte we heard about."

"And her family," Félix says. "Her husband's name is André. The child's name is Pascale." He stands up and cups his hands around his mouth. "Yes, come around back!"

Félix's mother startles awake. Léon, who is nearest, puts his hand on her arm. "Sorry, Maman. Are you ready for bed?"

She nods.

Léon offers her his arm and guides her into the house. As has happened a few times in his life, a moment has so much in it that it locks into his memory. Like he's had it painted. He knows he'll be returning to this in his mind until whenever he dies. Happiness isn't in the future; it is now, in this brief moment: fireflies over a freshly shorn field, plates empty of dinner, three men pushed back from the table, enjoying their conversation, his sister arriving with a box tied up in string, the hem of her simple dress wet from the evening dew, her husband with their wailing child on his hip, the setting sun lighting up the windowpanes of Félix's house, of their house, inside it a piano with a bitten-down pencil and a half-filled sheet of music.

Author's Note

THIS BOOK CAME TO ME ALONG AN UNEXPECTED PATH. In the summer of '07, my then-boyfriend and I had planned to live together while he worked a temporary gig in Denver. I sublet my New York City apartment for three months, packed my PlayStation 2 into my Samsonite, and we headed out on our big adventure.

We broke up on day three. I remember us crying into our breakfasts at some chain restaurant whose name was a pun on eggs. The Eggcellent Griddle Company maybe, or Eggspecially Breakfast. "I don't have anywhere to go live," I said. "I sublet my apartment, remember?"

"Oh crap," he said. "That's right."

While he was at work I piled my boxer briefs and PlayStation games into my suitcase and headed to the airport without a plane ticket.

"Where can you send me today for under two hundred dollars?" I asked at the airline counter. "Preferably under one hundred dollars."

"Oh!" the agent said from behind her computer screen. "Is this round-trip or one-way?"

"One-way."

She listed off cities, glancing at me nervously between each one. *Saint Louis, Tampa, Minneapolis, Seattle.*

Seattle. My best friend from college lived there. Things were looking up. We'd eat lots of donuts and watch '90s rom-coms. "How much does that cost?" I asked.

I texted my friend from the tarmac. "Um, how do I get to your house from the airport? Oh, and can I stay with you for a while?"

Once I was in Seattle, I started to feel better. My friend and I spent a weekend eating those donuts and watching Jennifer Aniston movies and going for long walks. On Monday morning I escorted my friend to work, hugged her goodbye, and wandered downtown in the rain.

I soon passed the Seattle art museum and went in. To fill my day and to keep my mind off the breakup, I decided to spend five minutes with each piece of art. With a pause for lunch, that would bring me to five p.m., when I could go find my friend outside her office and throw myself into her arms and ask where we were getting our takeout from and which movie we were watching next.

It was calming, spending time with little pieces of art that I would otherwise have walked right by. A Hopi comb, a folded revolutionary flag, little black-and-whites by Jasper Johns. As the afternoon was waning, I made it to the fourth floor, where I found, tucked near the men's room, a painting by John Singer Sargent.

It wouldn't have caught my attention normally, but I

dutifully spent my five minutes there. Once I stopped and looked, something in this young man's eyes pulled me. A sadness, a defiance, something ambitious and clear-seeing. I felt like I could see him, and—even though we were separated by over a hundred years—I felt seen by him. The audio guide told me his story as I dodged people coming and going from the men's room.

"Léon Delafosse." John Singer Sargent, 1895

[Warning to those who like to read the author's note early: spoilers follow!]

I learned that Léon Delafosse was born into poverty in rural France, where he showed a natural talent for the piano. He made it to Paris in the 1880s, where he was one of the youngest ever to enter the Paris Conservatory. At the age of thirteen, he won first prize in piano. In an era without mechanical means to listen to music, belle époque salons hired live performers for parties, and the young genius with the angelic face became highly sought after in society. Léon embraced the opportunity to meet patrons who could give him the financial freedom to write his own compositions. Marcel Proust, the same Proust who would go on to write one of the most influential novels of all time, *Remembrance of Things Past*, was at the time a young writer of society pieces. He latched on to Léon and used him as his calling card to even higher society, where he introduced the young man to the Count Robert de Montesquiou-Fézensac, who became Léon's patron.

Montesquiou was France's equivalent of Oscar Wilde, a larger-than-life writer and dandy. He was said to have had one of his own tears encased in a gold ring and an imported tortoise that had been encrusted with rubies wandering his home during parties. He brought Léon into higher and higher society, where he met John Singer Sargent (who painted the portrait I was seeing on that rainy day in Seattle), and eventually even the Queen of England.

This is where the historical record gets slender. We know that Léon and the count had a falling out. After their relationship soured, Montesquiou poisoned the connections he had made for the young musician. Once heralded as France's next great composer-pianist, Léon never lived up to that grand potential and largely disappeared from history— though Proust did wind up writing unkind portraits of him and Montesquiou in his *Remembrance of Things Past,* immortalizing them as the social-climbing violinist Morel and the odious Baron de Charlus.

I removed the headphones. The painting took on new dimensions to me. Léon's fingers were elegant, and vivid against the nondescript, dark background. A pianist would need those fingers. For navigating his relationships with Proust and Montesquiou, Léon might also have needed that face. I began to spin out his story in my mind, trying to fill in the gaps in the historical record, wondered what his life would have been like and what he might have gone through.

The question would come to haunt me: What had happened to Léon Delafosse?

I began writing this book that summer, getting much of my initial knowledge from the Seattle public library. My research took me to Paris, where Léon and Marcel's letters are in the National Library. (Proust is so beloved in France that most anything related to him is archived away.) The process of reading Léon's letters was all very French: I showed my credentials, then was seated in a somber, wood-paneled room, where I turned in an orange card to get a green one, which I then gave to a white-gloved attendant who came to my table with a velvet poof and a folio of letters. I put on my own protective gloves and leafed through.

The letters stretched my college French to the limit, and Léon's penmanship was nearly indecipherable, but holding the paper he'd used and the words he'd written in my hands was still thrilling. On one of the envelopes he'd addressed to Proust, he'd been sloppy sticking the stamp to the corner, and it hung over the edge. I slipped off my white glove and ran my fingertip along the underside of the stamp, where Léon, the real Léon, had licked it 117 years earlier.

I wrote a version of this book that year, a version that never satisfied me enough to send out. Finally, a decade later, I chucked that draft entirely and started over, and *Charming Young Man* is the result.

This book takes as its base what is known about the lives of Léon Delafosse, Marcel Proust, and Robert de Montesquiou, but it is not a historical record. I've taken plenty of liberties; what we know of Léon's life is too scant not to. I decided to place Léon in Vernon for his childhood, and I invented Félix and Charlotte entirely (we do know from the record that Léon's mother was a piano teacher). To tell the young-adult story I wanted, and because in my fictional tale I've postulated a romantic side to Léon's relationship with Robert, I also condensed age gaps, so the central figures would all be in or near their teenage years, which also meant altering the years that certain events occurred. The letters and reviews in this novel are written by me.

For those who lived outside of sexual and gender norms in 1890s Paris, it was a time both of great opening up and of great constraint. Those with social capital could flout convention, like the celebrated actress Sarah Bernhardt performing as a man and Robert de Montesquiou embracing his dandy side. But there were many articles bemoaning the decadence and corruption of this time, that by embracing "immorality," those who broke norms were risking their eternal souls and perhaps even bringing about the destruction of civilization itself.

Men with social standing, like Marcel Proust and Robert de Montesquiou, could be uncloseted and free in a drawing room, only to hide that side of them once they put their coats on and went back into the street, entering into marriages of convenience or weathering criticism and judgment or worse. Marcel never married, but in 1897 he fought a duel with a man who publicly questioned the propriety of his relationship with Lucien Daudet (who figures in this novel briefly, as Proust's friend at the Saussine salon; Proust is also widely acknowledged to have eventually entered into a romantic relationship with Reynaldo Hahn). Robert never married, and some historians believe that he never had sex with anyone either. The most common explanation is that he felt too much shame around homosexuality to act on it. It's hard to underestimate the effects internalized shame would have had on people who might have lived happier and more open lives had they been born in a different time. I wonder, however, if he might simply have been asexual, and that shame had less to do with it than historians assume. It's too late to ask Robert, so I try here to keep his characterization open to both interpretations.

Robert did have a lifelong union with his secretary, Gabriel Yturri, a man many assume to have also been his romantic partner. Yturri was known to be kind and gentle, a humanizing force to a count who could be capricious and cruel. They wound up buried next to each other in the Gonards cemetery in 1921, though the impropriety of two men lying in rest together meant that the grave is unmarked and officially anonymous. Above the grave, Montesquiou requested a certain statue be placed. He'd fallen in love with it at the Château de Vitry-sur-Seine and had it moved there to watch over them. It's known as the angel of silence. He stands guard over the anonymous grave of two men in love, a finger over his lips.

Acknowledgments

IT'S GOOD THE LITERARY WORLD HAS BEEN OBSESSED with Marcel Proust for decades, since it means I had many articles and books to turn to for information about Léon Delafosse's life. They're too numerous to start naming here, but the rich scholarly evocations of Proust's life were invaluable in my attempt to bring what had been a minor secondary character to the center of the narrative.

My editor, Ben Rosenthal, brought just what I most needed to this manuscript. He found the core of each character, and his questions helped me see each of them more clearly. This book owes much of its heart and humanity to him. Many thanks to Julia Johnson and the rest of the team at Katherine Tegen Books for their editorial help.

Richard Pine, my agent, has been reading this book in one form or another for fifteen years. You're a stalwart! Remember when it was all in the first-person-plural point of view?

Many thanks to the hardworking publicity and marketing teams at HarperCollins Children's Books, with particular shout-outs to John Sellers and Michael D'Angelo, and to the phenomenal school and library squad: Patty Rosati, Mimi Rankin, and Stephanie Macy. Gretchen Stelter was a wonderful copyeditor, and thanks as always to Laura Harshberger for shepherding this book so skillfully through the production process.

Thanks to David DeWitt and Amy Ryan, who designed the cover, and to Amber Day for her fresh and beautiful art.

Writing can be lonely, and I wouldn't find the fortitude to get through these many revisions without my friends and allies who read this manuscript and helped me find pathways through it: Elana K. Arnold, Nina LaCour, Marie Rutkoski, Daphne Benedis-Grab, Rebecca Chace, Jill Santopolo, Marianna Baer, Donna Freitas; thank you, all. My gratitude to my colleagues and students at the Fairleigh Dickinson and Hamline MFAs for the many conversations over many tables for the last few years. To my husband, Eric: Without the foundation of life with you, it would be so much harder to do something so ostentatious as write a book, and yet I can do so over and over because I have you by my side. Thank you.

Two moms helped me hugely with this book: as with every book I write, I upload a copy for the Clearwater, Florida, OfficeDepot to print, where my mom picks it up to do a complete line edit. My mother-in-law, Huguette Zahler, drove us around Paris and its outskirts, so we could see every known place Léon, Marcel, and Robert had lived. She got us tickets to every Proust exposition and play she could find. Merci, Maman!